"She's the queen of witty dialogue and sexy scenes!"
—*New York Times* bestselling author Rachel Van Dyken

PRAISE FOR THE WEDDING BELLES SERIES

To Love and to Cherish

"[N]ot only the fabulous culmination of a slow-burn love story, but the conclusion of a world I was delighted to visit for several books. These characters will stay with me for a while and I already miss them."

—*All About Romance*

"This was another fabulous addition to Layne's backlist and it's one that I'll reread again and again because Logan is full of yum! I definitely recommend this book."

—*Book Binge*

"*To Love and to Cherish* was my favorite tale in the Wedding Belles series . . . Go, grab the entire series, you won't regret it."

—*Caffeinated Reviewer*

For Better or Worse

"*From This Day Forward, To Have and to Hold*, and *For Better or Worse* are all enchanting and chock-full of all the witty repartee we have come to joyfully anticipate . . . an absolute delight."

—*Hypable*

"I highly recommend *For Better or Worse*. The second in a series, it can be read as a stand-alone, but I say start with the first because it's just as good. They've got the funny bickering that I love, and even as her stories have a light touch with cute flirty, they delve deep into the characters."

—*Harlequin Junkie* (Top Pick)

"I loved this book and can easily recommend you add it to your *#needtoread*. I am smiling like a lunatic while writing this and remembering Heather and Josh's journey. I laughed, cheered, cried, sighed, and almost swooned while reading *For Better or Worse*, and any book that can make me feel this wide spectrum of emotions is a book that qualifies as one of my favorite reads."

—*All About Romance*

"*For Better or Worse* is a love story that is carefree, real, and packed with emotion any reader can relate with!!! TRULY FANTASTIC!!"

—*Addicted To Romance*

To Have and to Hold

"Completely endearing characters . . . most definitely looking forward to the others in the Wedding Belles series. A great community of women I want to follow."

—*Harlequin Junkie* (Top Pick)

"A character-driven and sizzling romance!"

—*Fresh Fiction*

"Super entertaining, sweet, and sexy and it leaves you smiling big-time at the end."

—*About That Story*

From This Day Forward

"Layne packs as much into this sexually charged and emotionally intense novella as most authors do in a full novel . . . The heat between [Leah and Jason] is enough to melt steel, and the emotional connection and psychological struggles will keep readers engaged."

—*Publishers Weekly*

ALSO AVAILABLE FROM LAUREN LAYNE
AND GALLERY BOOKS

The Wedding Belles Series

*From This Day Forward**

To Have and to Hold

For Better or Worse

To Love and to Cherish

Passion on Park Avenue

LAUREN LAYNE

G

Gallery Books

New York   London   Toronto   Sydney   New Delhi

*ebook only

G

Gallery Books
An Imprint of Simon & Schuster, Inc.
1230 Avenue of the Americas
New York, NY 10020

First Gallery Books trade paperback edition May 2019

GALLERY BOOKS and colophon are registered trademarks of Simon & Schuster, Inc.

For information about special discounts for bulk purchases, please contact Simon & Schuster Special Sales at 1-866-506-1949 or business@simonandschuster.com.

The Simon & Schuster Speakers Bureau can bring authors to your live event. For more information or to book an event, contact the Simon & Schuster Speakers Bureau at 1-866-248-3049 or visit our website at www.simonspeakers.com.

Interior design by Davina Mock-Maniscalco

Manufactured in the United States of America

10   9   8   7   6

Library of Congress Cataloging-in-Publication Data

Names: Layne, Lauren, author.
Title: Passion on Park Avenue / Lauren Layne.
Description: New York : Gallery Books, 2019. | Series: The Central Park Pact ; 1
Identifiers: LCCN 2018045881 (print) | LCCN 2018050667 (ebook) | ISBN 9781501191589 (ebook) | ISBN 9781501191572 (paperback)
Subjects: | BISAC: FICTION / Contemporary Women.
Classification: LCC PS3612.A9597 (ebook) | LCC PS3612.A9597 P37 2019 (print) | DDC 813/.6—dc23
LC record available at https://lccn.loc.gov/2018045881

ISBN 978-1-5011-9157-2
ISBN 978-1-5011-9158-9 (ebook)

Passion on Park Avenue

Chapter One

*N*aomi Powell figured there was no good way to discover that the man you'd been dating for three months was married to someone else. But of all the possibilities, learning about the existence of a *Mrs.* Brayden Hayes via the cheating bastard's obituary?

Definitely the worst.

The taxi pulled to a stop outside Central Presbyterian, and Naomi nearly lost her nerve, her instincts screaming for her to tell the cabbie to take her back to the Lower East Side.

Instead, she handed the driver a twenty, shoved open the door, and stepped onto ritzy Park Avenue as though she belonged there. She pulled her Gucci sunglasses out of her bag and slid them onto her nose—the overcast July day didn't quite warrant the shades, but she was walking into a funeral. People would hopefully think the purpose of the sunglasses was to hide red, puffy eyes rather than what it really was:

A disguise.

Screw that, Naomi thought furiously, pushing the sunglasses back up into her dark red hair and marching with purpose toward the stately Gothic-style church. She didn't need a disguise. At twenty-nine, Naomi had spent most of her lifetime dealing with people trying to make her feel inferior, and she'd be damned if she let a turd of a playboy succeed from beyond the grave.

She had just as much right to be here as anyone else. It's not like she'd known he was married. She hadn't even known he lived in Manhattan. Naomi wasn't sure she knew a single damn thing about the *real* Brayden Hayes, but even around all her anger, she still wanted the chance to say goodbye.

The man had made her life better, for a while at least. Even if he was making it a hell of a lot worse now.

She sighed and slid the sunglasses back onto her face. Not to protect herself, but to protect Brayden's wife. Naomi had no idea if Claire knew of her existence, but on the off chance she did, Naomi didn't want to make this any harder on the woman than it already was.

Naomi walked up the steps to the church as Brayden's obituary rattled around in her brain, the way it had for days. *The victim of a tragic yachting accident, Brayden Hayes is survived by wife, Claire Hayes* . . .

A yachting accident. Really? *Really?*

Wasn't death by luxury boat just a *little* too good for a womanizer with the morals of a lump of coal?

The only saving grace of the situation, and Naomi had had to look *really* hard to find one, was that Claire and Brayden hadn't had any children. Thank God for that. It was the only thing that had kept Naomi from breaking completely when she'd learned of Brayden's double life. She knew all too well the havoc a philandering asshole could wreak on a child's life.

Naomi stepped into the dark, quiet church and walked

toward one of the back pews. Several people turned and looked her way, and her footsteps faltered.

On a rational level, Naomi knew they were merely turning instinctively at the sharp click of her Louboutin stilettos against the church floor. Some maybe even recognized her as *the* Naomi Powell from the latest 30-under-30 list, or from her interview on the *Today* show.

But everywhere she looked, Naomi saw only disdain. As though they could see beyond the conservative Chloé dress to her Bronx roots. As though they knew she was the *other woman*. The very identity that had destroyed her mother and that Naomi had sworn to avoid.

She sucked in a breath, trying to gather the defiance that had turned her from a nobody into one of the city's wealthiest women. She tried to gather the confidence that had earned her a spot on every "women to watch" list in the nation. But today, she didn't feel like a bright up-and-comer in the business world. Today she felt small. Worse, she felt *dirty*.

Naomi watched as a woman pursed her lips and turned away, as though unable to look any longer upon Brayden Hayes's whore. That's what he'd made her. A lifetime of trying to avoid her mother's footsteps, and one Upper East Side scumbag had turned her into her own worst nightmare.

Naomi didn't even realize she'd turned around and left the church until she felt the warm summer breeze whip at her hair. Didn't register what direction she was walking until she hit the eastern edge of Central Park.

Only then did she let herself truly breathe, sucking in big lungfuls of air. But she didn't cry. Naomi had promised herself a long time ago she'd never cry because of a man.

She was hardly dressed for a stroll, but the trees and winding path calmed her as she entered the park. A welcome respite from the nearby neighborhood and all its snobbery. In Central Park, it didn't matter what street you lived on, what borough you came from. Central Park belonged to all New Yorkers, one glorious shared backyard.

The park was mostly quiet. Most tourists entered at the south side, so she saw only a couple of joggers, a few elderly couples out for a walk, two moms on a stroller date, and . . .

Naomi did a double take at the blonde sitting alone on a park bench, and her stomach dropped out. *Are you* kidding *me with this right now, God?*

The first thing Naomi had done after the shock of reading that Brayden Hayes was freaking *married* was to google the crap out of his wife, desperate for an indication that the *Times* had been wrong about his marital status. That it was a misprint or he was divorced. The paper hadn't been wrong. There really was a Mrs. Brayden Hayes.

And she, too, had chosen Central Park over Brayden's funeral.

Nearly even with Claire Hayes now, and with the sunglasses still providing Naomi anonymity, she dared to sneak a look at the other woman out of the corner of her eye.

Brayden's widow looked pretty much like the picture Naomi had rummaged up online: a thirty-something Upper East Side WASP. Like Naomi, she wore oversize sunglasses, the Chanel logo glinting in a stray ray of sunshine. Naomi's trained eye pegged the basic black sheath as St. John, and the basic black pumps Louboutins—identical to Naomi's.

But *unlike* Naomi, Claire had a genteel poise about her. Like she'd never said *darn*, much less dropped an f-bomb. Naomi would bet serious money that Claire Hayes didn't eat Kraft Macaroni & Cheese straight out of the pan when she was stressed and that Claire had never been so poor that she'd actually once considered taking home a neighbor's discarded mattress, bedbugs be damned, simply because it was free.

Claire's placid expression betrayed nothing as Naomi passed her, the glasses too large to reveal any emotion on her face. For that matter, Naomi wondered if women like her experienced emotion at all. It didn't seem it. The woman was the picture of calm, except for . . .

Her hands.

Brayden's widow's hands were clenched tightly in her lap, the fingers of her right hand white-knuckled around the fist of her left hand. But it wasn't the subdued pink manicure that captured Naomi's attention. It was the bright red crescent moons *beneath* the nails.

Naomi had a lifelong bad habit of acting before thinking, and she did so now, crossing to the other woman and sitting beside her on the park bench.

"That's enough now," Naomi said, using her CEO voice, calm and commanding.

Claire didn't move. Naomi wasn't even sure the other woman heard her.

Naomi hesitated only for a moment before slowly reaching over and prying the nails of Claire's right hand away from her left hand. Little streaks of blood were left in the wake.

Claire looked down in confusion, as though just now registering the pain.

"Does that Givenchy have any Kleenex?" Naomi asked, nodding toward Claire's clutch on the bench.

Claire didn't move for a long moment, then taking a deep breath, she calmly reached for her purse, pulling out a travel-size package of tissue.

"We're wearing the same shoes. Same dress, too," Claire said, dabbing at the blood on the back of her hand with a tissue, using the same casual indifference of one dabbing up a drop of spilled water.

Naomi nodded in agreement, though Claire's St. John was a knee-length mock turtleneck, and Naomi's Chloé was a boatneck that hit at midthigh.

For a long moment, neither said anything.

"I'm supposed to be at a funeral," Claire said, balling up the tissue and dropping her hands back into her lap.

"Why aren't you?"

Naomi was genuinely curious. She knew why *she* wasn't at that funeral. But the widow being a no-show . . . that was some serious *Page Six*–worthy gossip right there.

Claire opened her mouth to respond but shut it when a pretty young woman with dark brown hair walked past them. Naomi waited for the other woman to pass and, when she gave the brunette a closer look, realized the other woman was walking a bit too slowly, as though tempted to approach. She looked vaguely familiar. Naomi was fairly sure they'd crossed paths at a couple of events, though Naomi couldn't put a name with the face.

Brayden's widow, however, could. Claire went rigid beside Naomi, even as she called out to the other woman, "Audrey."

Unlike Claire and Naomi, the brunette wasn't wearing sunglasses, and Naomi saw her round eyes go even wider. "You know who I am?"

"You're Audrey Tate. I did a little digging after you called the house that night," Claire said quietly. "I know you were sleeping with my husband."

Naomi's head whipped around in surprise, and then surprise escalated to shock as she realized Claire wasn't talking to her.

What the . . .

Audrey let out a hiccuping sob and walked to the bench, and Naomi almost laughed when she saw the other woman's shoes. Black Louboutin pumps identical to hers and Claire's.

"I didn't know," Audrey was saying in a rush as she sat beside Claire and stared at her with a pleading expression. "I didn't know until you picked up the phone that night that he was married. I swear to you, he told me his wife had left him, that he was separated . . . I *never* would have— You have to believe me. I didn't know—"

"Oh, honey," Naomi interrupted, half-sympathetic, half-horrified. "You've got to get it together."

Audrey stopped her sniffling and gave Naomi what she probably thought was an icy glare, but the impact was diminished by the red nose and puffy eyes. "Respectfully, you don't know the first thing about what's going on here."

"Well now, that's the thing," Naomi said, looking down at her manicure. "I sort of do."

Both women were studying her now.

"Who are you?" Claire asked.

Naomi studied the other woman for only a moment before acting on the same instinct that had taken her from Bronx high school dropout to entrepreneurial superstar; she sensed that Claire Hayes was the sort of woman who deserved the truth. The full truth.

Naomi pushed her sunglasses on top of her head and looked at Claire. "I'm Naomi Powell. The *other* other woman."

Audrey's mouth fell open, but Claire didn't react beyond a slightly too long blink. "What?"

Damn. She'd thought she'd been pretty clear.

"Your husband was putting his pickle into one too many

sandwiches," Naomi announced plainly. "Well, two too many if you count her." She jerked her chin toward Audrey.

"Did you just compare . . . pickle . . . oh my God, *sandwiches*," Audrey said, lifting a hand to her forehead.

Claire's head dropped forward, her chin resting on her chest, and Naomi winced. Perhaps she could have phrased it slightly differently . . . sticking his noodle in the wrong casserole? Cucumber into multiple salads?

But Claire Hayes surprised her. Her shoulders were shaking, not with tears but with silent amusement. Then she tossed her head back and looked at the sky, letting out an audible laugh.

"I hate to be the one to tell you this," Audrey told Claire, "but I don't think he's up there."

Now it was Naomi's turn to let out a surprised laugh as she realized she'd underestimated the brunette. She may look like a lanky Hepburn, but this Audrey had an edge beneath the sweet, doe-eyed appearance.

"Shouldn't we be at the funeral?" Claire asked. Probably more to herself, but Naomi answered anyway.

"Nah. I mostly showed up to tell God not to allow that one through the pearly gates, and as Audrey pointed out, I think He probably already figured that one out."

"I never thought I'd be here," Claire said tiredly, lifting her fingers to her temples and rubbing absently.

"You mean sitting on a park bench with your husband's mistresses while his funeral goes down just a couple blocks over?" Naomi asked.

Claire laughed. "Yes. That. I just keep thinking I know I should be sad, but instead all I can think about is how stupid I was, and that's *before* I knew there were two of you. How did I not see it?"

"We were just as stupid," Audrey said, setting a hand on

Claire's arm. "He was my boyfriend for a year. I just thought he traveled a lot."

"Three months," Naomi said, pointing at herself. "He told me most of his business dealings were in Hong Kong and that he had to work most nights. I totally bought it."

They all fell silent, lost in their own memories of the man, and Naomi was struck that despite the fact that this was perhaps one of the weirdest meetings in the history of female encounters, it didn't feel as odd as it should. Far from resenting the other women, she felt almost comforted by their presence. Claire's and Audrey's very existence was proof that Naomi wasn't the only clueless one. That she wasn't alone in being a victim of a heartless man's games.

Who would have thought that strength in numbers applied to a dead man's philandering?

Naomi straightened slightly and turned toward the others. "I have a confession."

Claire lifted her eyebrows. "Worse than the fact that you were having adult sleepovers with my husband?"

"Who I didn't know was your husband," Naomi clarified, waving her finger at Claire. "But no, my confession is that while I'm really mad at Brayden, I'm even angrier at myself. For letting him fool me."

Audrey nodded. "Same. I mean, it's a little more self-loathing than anger, I guess, but . . . I just can't stop thinking about how I didn't see it. And if I didn't see *him* being a snake, how will I ever spot another man being a snake?"

Claire looked down at her hands, running the pad of her finger along the small cuts caused by her own manicured fingers. "I'm not worried about it. After all this, I'm pretty dead set on turning into the old lonely lady with cats."

"*Nope*," Naomi said firmly. "We are not going to let him do that to us. I'm not really a long-term relationship girl, but I do like a male companion, and I have no intention of letting Brayden sour me on . . ."

"Pickles?" Audrey suggested.

"I was going to say sex, but yeah. That, too."

Audrey's smile was fleeting. "But I *am* the long-term relationship girl. I want the ring and the babies, and the—"

"Please don't say white picket fence."

"Oh God no." Audrey shuddered, then pointed to her shoes. "These red soles are meant for Fifth Ave, not the burbs. But I still want the fairy tale, and I just . . ." She swallowed. "It's harder to believe these days."

"So let me get this straight." Naomi turned to Claire. "You're going to turn into a cat lady, and you're giving up your Disney princess dreams," she said, turning toward Audrey. "All because of a *guy*."

Claire and Audrey exchanged a look, and Naomi pressed.

"Ladies, I know we just met, but let's face it, we have the same shoes and we were screwed over by the same guy, so as far as I'm concerned, we leapfrogged a few steps in the female-bonding process."

"Perfect, I'll invite you over for a slumber party," Claire said, starting to stand.

"Hold up." Naomi put a hand on her arm. "I'm not suggesting we get matching tattoos, just that we can help each other."

Claire stared at her but sat back down. "You want me to help my husband's mistresses—do *what*, exactly?"

"We watch each other's blind spots as it relates to men. Left to our own devices, obviously we're no good at seeing a guy for who—and what—he really is. But what if we combined forces? Help each other spot another Brayden."

Naomi knew it was spontaneous, a little bossy, a lot nuts, but it *felt* right. And Naomi had made a name for herself trusting her gut.

"Respectfully, I don't even know you," Audrey said, running a hand over her dark ponytail. "I get your point, but why would I have two strangers do a gut check on a guy I like instead of my friends?"

"Because who knows better how to spot another woman getting scammed than three women who just experienced it?" Naomi pointed out.

Audrey bit her lip and looked at Claire. "You know, I don't hate this plan?"

Claire fiddled with her watch, and Naomi's gaze tracked the motion. "Cartier."

Claire looked up. "Yes. How'd you know?"

"I know designers. I *also* know that I have the exact same watch at home."

Claire's eyes went wide. "Brayden . . . ?"

Naomi nodded.

"Me, too," Audrey said, almost inaudibly.

Claire stared down at the watch on her left wrist, and Naomi knew they had her.

Naomi extended her right hand. "Hands in, girls, we're making a pact, high school–style. May neither of you ever fall victim to a cheating bastard again. Not on my watch."

"*And* to helping each other find the right man. That's on my watch," Audrey said, placing her palm on top of Naomi's hand.

After a moment of hesitation, Claire set her hand atop Audrey's. "Oh, what the hell. I'm in. To no more assholes."

Naomi had never been a girl's girl, and she certainly wasn't the type to get all fluttery about fate. And though she'd been half-joking with the whole pact thing, something odd happened in the moment the three of their hands met. As though they were bound together now not by Brayden, but by something bigger. Something important.

And Naomi was suddenly certain that this moment with Claire Hayes and Audrey Tate was somehow going to change *everything*.

As they all let their hands fall away, Audrey let out a long sigh and looked eastward in the direction of the church. "I guess we should make an appearance, huh?"

Naomi stood and flicked her sunglasses back onto her face with one finger. "Screw it. Let's go shopping."

Chapter Two

TWO MONTHS LATER—MONDAY, SEPTEMBER 24

The moment Naomi Powell's Manolo Blahniks stepped off the elevator at Maxcessory headquarters, a pair of discount Nordstrom Rack pumps fell into step beside her. The synchronous click of their matched pace was as familiar—and dear—to Naomi as the woman wearing the other shoes.

"That better not be what I think it is," Deena Ferrari said, narrowing her eyes at the pink bakery box in Naomi's hands.

"Double chocolate birthday cake for my favorite assistant," Naomi said, making a smooching noise in Deena's direction.

"Reject," Deena said.

"You can't reject your birthday," Naomi argued as Deena opened the glass door to Naomi's corner office and followed her inside.

"Well, seeing as I've rejected it five years in a row now," Deena said, crossing her arms beneath her bosom and sending an impressive amount of cleavage heaving upward in her leopard-print wrap dress, "I've gotten *real* good at it."

"But wait, you haven't seen the best part yet," Naomi said,

setting the cake on the desk, tossing her Hermès purse in her chair, and opening the box with a flourish.

Deena's feet stayed firmly in place, her arms stubbornly crossed, and she craned her neck to see what it said.

Happy 35th!

Deena, who Naomi knew full well was not a day under forty-seven, grinned. "Birthday accepted."

"Thought so," Naomi said, flipping the lid closed so it could be taken to the break room for the employees to share.

"But no singing," Deena said, lifting a red-manicured fingernail tipped with gold glitter. "And *no* candles."

"Gifts?" Naomi asked.

"Gifts I will accept. But first, I have gifts for *you* . . ."

Naomi groaned as Deena held up a stack of sticky notes and gave them a little waggle.

"You've been dodging," Deena said as Naomi moved her purse from her chair and dropped into it.

"Not on purpose," Naomi said, putting her fingers to her temples. "Next time I decide to have my apartment lease and office lease end in the same month, slap me. Just right on the face. *Housewives*-style."

"Happy to," her assistant said, shuffling through her notes.

Deena probably meant it. The woman had always claimed that in a different life she'd have been a *Jersey Shore* cast member. And while it was true that Deena loved her drama, she was crazy efficient, though one wouldn't know it from looking at her. Four years ago, after Naomi's first assistant had left the corporate world to raise her two kids in Brooklyn, Deena had come into Maxcessory headquarters with no appointment, no resume, and way too much perfume.

Deena had never worked in an office and definitely hadn't known the first thing about typing—even if she had, her mile-long nails would have made it difficult. But the born-and-bred Jersey girl had something Naomi respected more than experience. She'd had *style*.

Deena Ferrari had strutted into the office, chin high, lip gloss glittery. Her black dress had been fitted and fabulous, the heels of her ankle boots sky-high. And though the woman was extra in just about every way, Naomi's eagle eye, always primed to assess someone's accessory game, had caught that Deena's wrist had the perfect amount of bangles. Noticed that she'd skipped the necklace in order to let her chandelier earrings have the attention they'd deserved.

And after a stream of recent college grads in their interview suits, stud earrings, mid-height pumps, and canned answers, Deena had been the breath of heavily perfumed air Naomi had needed. She'd hired Deena on the spot and never looked back.

"How's the team feeling about the move?" Naomi asked, spinning slowly in her chair.

Deena shrugged. "Excited. Much as they adore you and believe in Maxcessory, the desk sharing and fighting for the two conference rooms was wearing on everyone."

"I just feel bad we've got this weird monthlong hiatus in between leases," Naomi said.

Deena gave her an incredulous look. "Seriously? You think that your boss telling you you'll have to work from home isn't everyone's dream?"

"Really?" Naomi asked, startled.

"Absolutely. Conference calls in jammies, and no dealing with the F train at six on a Monday night? They're thrilled."

"Yeah, well, trust me, the luster wears off," Naomi muttered.

"Two years of working out of my tiny studio apartment trying to get this business off the ground nearly killed me."

"Sure, but you have to admit sometimes you wish you could work in yoga pants and no bra."

Naomi gave Deena a look. "When was the last time *you* forwent the bra?"

Deena shimmied her pushed-up 46DDs in Naomi's direction, but she knew one of Naomi's stalling tactics when she saw it.

"Be quiet and listen to your messages." Deena dove right in. "Movers are trying to push the relocation up by three days, wouldn't give me a good reason. I'm assuming I can tell them to stick to the contracted date or go straight to hell?"

"Rephrase, but yeah."

"Dry cleaner called. They couldn't get the wasabi off your white blouse with the bow."

"Damn," Naomi muttered. "I love that shirt."

"You've got your annual lady doctor appointment next Friday, massage on Tuesday, your hair girl needed to move your appointment from Wednesday to Friday . . . all that's on your calendar . . ."

Deena placed the sticky notes in front of Naomi as she read them, having learned by now that Naomi was more likely to absorb things when they were literally right in front of her face.

"Claire called," Deena continued. "Said to remind you that you're meeting at Audrey's at six tonight before the movie . . . ?"

There was a slight question in Deena's tone, and Naomi knew her assistant was wildly curious about the two women who had come into Naomi's life over the summer, seemingly out of nowhere, and become her fast friends in just a couple of months.

Naomi didn't answer the unasked question. She trusted Deena implicitly, considered her assistant a loyal friend. But there were some things you just couldn't explain to other people.

The fact that you'd become friends with the wife and girlfriend of your late lover was one of them.

Naomi, Claire, and Audrey might not have known of one another's existence until the day of Brayden's funeral, but they'd made up for lost time with frequent brunches and wine nights. Naomi liked to imagine that knowing the three women he'd betrayed had bonded was torturing Brayden Hayes from his front-row seat in hell.

Deena moved on to her next note. "Dylan Day called again, stupid name but—"

Naomi bumped her head against the back of her chair repeatedly in agitation. "That dude will *not* let up!"

"For what it's worth, I think you should go for it," Deena said.

"You'd think differently if it was *your* life they wanted to make into a TV series," Naomi muttered.

"Au contraire," Deena said, waggling her eyebrows. "I'm counting on them wanting to include your Italian diva of an assistant as an integral part of your success."

"You know that they won't let you play yourself, right? They're angling for one of those 'inspired by a true story' directions, not a documentary."

"Just wait until he meets me," Deena said confidently. Then she frowned. "Wait, he's not gay, is he? That'll hurt my chances."

"No idea."

"Well, what does your gaydar tell you? It's not as good as mine, but if he's one of the obvious ones . . ."

"I don't know because I haven't met him."

Deena's mouth dropped open. "But the network's been after you for weeks for this."

Naomi shrugged. "I've been dodging."

"But *why?* This is how legends are made, babe. You could be an actual Netflix binge-watch."

Maybe. But the Naomi Powell story was hardly the fairy tale they were hoping for. Or maybe it was. It was just that the early stages had been a hell of a lot grittier than *Cinderella.* And the later stages had no Prince Charming in sight.

"I'll call him back," Naomi said firmly, reaching for the sticky note and letting Deena know the conversation was closed. For now.

"Last message," Deena said, reading the final pink Post-it Note in her hand. "And it's a weird one. Some lady called saying you'd been approved for an interview with the co-op board. I thought you already found your new place?"

Naomi frowned. "I did. I signed the lease for that condo in Tribeca last week. Did Ann indicate that there'd been some sort of issue?"

"Wasn't Ann. This woman was Victoria, and the apartment she was talking about was Upper East Side, not Tribeca."

Naomi wrinkled her nose. "Upper East Side?"

After her experience with Brayden, she wanted nothing to do with the haughty, old-money part of Manhattan.

Deena's brown eyes scanned the note. "Yup. Building name is 517 Park Avenue?"

Naomi had been rotating slightly back and forth in her spinning chair, but she went still at the address. The *familiar* address. "What did you say?"

Naomi heard the sharp note in her tone, and Deena apparently did, too, because she gave Naomi a startled look. "You know it?"

Yeah, she knew it, all right.

And it was exactly that lurid part of her past that Dylan Day would just love to get his hands on.

And exactly the part that Naomi had spent a decade trying to forget.

Chapter Three

WEDNESDAY, SEPTEMBER 26

*N*aomi could have handled it over the phone, but in the end her curiosity got the best of her.

Which was stupid. She should have been packing up her office and her apartment, preparing for a double move. To say nothing of the fact that eventually she'd have to deal with the production company that wanted to turn her life into a prime-time special. And that wasn't counting all the other stuff that came along with running your own billion-dollar company.

Instead?

Instead, Naomi quietly slipped out of the office at noon on Wednesday, and rather than grabbing her usual sushi lunch or favorite Niçoise salad at her favorite Lower East Side bistro, she found herself heading uptown.

To an apartment building she hadn't thought about in years.

Well, that wasn't entirely true. She had *tried* not to think about it for years. She'd been mostly successful—except for the times when her mom's relentless bitterness had gotten under Naomi's skin, forcing her to remember.

Naomi paused outside the building and studied the facade of 517 Park Avenue. It looked . . . the same. Which was probably the point. Here on the Upper East Side, prewar architecture wasn't considered old; it was *dignified*. The highest praise in this part of town.

And just like that, as though a cloud had passed over her, Naomi felt herself change. It was as though the Stella McCartney dress, the shoes and purse that independently cost more than the rent on her first apartment, disappeared.

As though she were no longer Naomi Powell, the hotshot "girl boss" who had taken corporate America by storm.

Instead, she was Naomi Fields. The bony nine-year-old girl in hand-me-down clothes who didn't belong in this part of town and had been reminded of it every damn day.

Grinding her teeth against the memory, Naomi straightened her shoulders and marched up the steps, chin held high.

The foyer smelled familiar, but she ignored the familiarity as she announced herself to the doorman and was pointed toward the small office to the right that she'd always darted past as a girl. The gray-haired woman behind the old-fashioned secretary's desk was somewhere between middle-aged and senior citizen and probably had been for a very long time.

She peered at Naomi over her glasses. "May I help you?"

"I'm Naomi Powell. I have an appointment?"

"Yes, of course," the woman murmured, turning toward a pile of manila file folders to her right and handing the top one to Naomi.

"Your interview is scheduled at twelve thirty. Have a seat in the office to your left, and take a moment to review your file. We received it by mail, which is why it's a bit wrinkled."

The censure in the woman's tone was clear, but Naomi ignored it. What she *should* have asked was why she even had a file in the first place, by mail or otherwise.

Instead she nodded and took the file, going into the office indicated—a stuffy little sitting room with even stuffier furniture, and sat in a chintz chair opposite a large wooden desk. She opened the folder.

Her breath whooshed out. Not at the application itself—that was run-of-the-mill—but at the handwriting on the application. Her late mother's penmanship had always been the most dignified thing about her. Elegant, swooping script that belied Danica Fields's tattoos, chain-smoker's hack, and coarse accent.

"Oh, Mom," Naomi whispered quietly, running a finger over her name. "What did you do?"

A quick scan through the stack of papers confirmed Naomi's fears: her mother had applied on Naomi's behalf to live here, in the very building that her mother had mostly referred to as the Hellmouth.

Naomi's gaze found the signature at the bottom of the page. As expected, it was her own name but written in her mother's precise cursive. She looked at the date beside the signature: March 21.

Six months ago. And just two weeks before her mother's death.

Swallowing around the lump in her throat, Naomi closed the folder, clasped her hands in her lap, and waited.

And waited.

After five minutes, she began watching the old-fashioned clock on the wall that ticked tauntingly at her. After ten, she began *glaring* at the clock.

Whoever was "interviewing" her was late.

Naomi stood, intending to tell the woman at the front desk that she didn't have time for this. Heck, she didn't even want it in the first place. Naomi didn't need an apartment. Especially one that, given the date on her mother's application, had a six-month waiting list.

And even if she *did* need a place to live, she wouldn't have come to a stodgy place like this, which probably used the word *pedigree* when deciding whom to accept.

Although, if Naomi was honest with herself, the very thing she disdained about these people was the reason she was here in the first place. She had an almost-morbid curiosity to see if they'd accept her application.

Because although her pedigree was more mutt than pure breed, she was a mutt with a diamond collar. In the eight years since its launch, Maxcessory had gone from a tiny one-woman gig out of her East Village studio to a thriving business with seven-figure funding, hundreds of employees, and offices in New York and San Francisco and soon to open in Los Angeles.

If the co-op wanted to reject her application, she'd make them do it to her face, make them say out loud that her blood wasn't blue enough. Because God knew her money was certainly green enough.

But before she could go tell the receptionist to shove it, she heard voices. The first belonged to the receptionist, Victoria, but the second was the gravelly rumble of a man's voice. Her interviewer, perhaps?

Whoever it was, he was apparently unaware—or didn't care—that the door was open a crack and she could hear every word of their conversation.

"Find someone else to do it," the man demanded. "The co-op process is archaic."

Naomi raised her eyebrows. She didn't disagree, but it was hardly the attitude she'd been expecting.

"Don't be a child," the woman said in a bossy tone. "Get in there and interview the girl."

"Have Doreen do it. She loves this stuff."

"She's in Miami with her latest boy toy. The Italian."

Naomi's eyes lifted. *Well done, Doreen.*

There was a soft curse. "What about Janet? Or Ned? They both get off on asking candidates who their 'people' are."

"They've already done more than their fair share of interviews. We had hundreds of applicants, and more than fifty passed the initial screening. Everyone has to take a turn with the interviews, and they told me to give you this one."

"Why?" the man grunted.

"I don't have the faintest idea, but the poor thing's been in there close to twenty minutes. Here's her paperwork. Just pretend to consider her, and then we can all go on with our day."

Naomi's eyes narrowed. *Pretend* to consider her? How was she out of the running already?

Because you're trash. And they can sense it.

Naomi closed her eyes against the voice. She thought she'd stifled that sliver of her subconscious years ago, but something about this damn building . . .

Naomi had just a split second to whip her head around and feign ignorance before the door was shoved open. She waited with her hands folded as the man entered, slamming the door shut again with just enough force to make it clear he did not want to be here.

Naomi crossed her legs, staring demurely ahead as the man walked around to the other side of the desk. She watched as he dropped a briefcase by his feet and slapped the folder onto the desk before lowering himself to the leather chair opposite her.

He impatiently flipped the folder open, scanning until he apparently found her name, because he said it out loud with gruff irritability. "Naomi Powell."

Naomi inhaled ever so slightly and forced her expression into what she hoped was placid politeness and raised her eyes to his.

Her breath whooshed out again as her gaze collided with a searing one.

It wasn't that the man was good-looking, although he was— distractingly so. Thick brown hair, a face with no hint of five o'clock shadow to better show off the masculine edge of his jawline, broad shoulders . . .

And light blue eyes she'd know anywhere.

Mostly in her nightmares.

And memories.

Naomi thought she'd come today prepared for anything. *Anyone*.

But never had she let herself consider the possibility that her interview would be with Oliver Cunningham. Never had she imagined that the boy who'd tormented her mercilessly during their childhood would once again hold her fate in his hands.

Chapter Four

*O*liver stared in irritated puzzlement at the redhead currently glaring across the desk like she was trying to crush his windpipe Darth Vader–style.

Naomi . . . what was her last name again? He glanced once more at the paperwork. Powell. First impression? Slightly scary. Well, no. That was second impression. His first impression of the woman had been *hot*. Very, very hot.

Regardless, Naomi Powell was not what he'd expected when Vicky had strong-armed him into conducting this BS interview. For starters, the hair was all wrong. He'd been prepared for silver, not vibrant red. The rest of her was vibrant as well. The people in this building weren't exactly prone to outbursts of sentiment, but she seemed to crackle with emotion.

Most of the time, Oliver Cunningham didn't mind living in 517 Park Avenue. Sure, most of the people acted like their silver spoon had been shoved where the sun never shined. And yes, he was the youngest resident by a good thirty years.

But there were upsides. The board had agreed to let him tear down the wall between his kitchen and living room to create a rare, open-concept home on Park Avenue. The change made room for his top-of-the-line kitchen and seventy-inch flat-screen. And though he didn't particularly relish the "bragging rights" of living in the same building he'd grown up in, he appreciated that he could care for his father while still maintaining his own life. Sort of.

In other words, his place of residence was tolerable. Most of the time.

But then, there were times like now. Times when a rare vacancy occurred and the whole damn building turned more ridiculous than a sorority during rush. As Oliver saw it, the co-op process was little more than an opportunity for octogenarians of the Upper East Side to assert their flawless lineage, delighting in making those who didn't have some obscure connection to a Vanderbilt or Rockefeller feel inferior.

Oliver tried not to have any part of it, but he'd caved for Vicky's sake. It wasn't the longtime receptionist's fault that with Oliver's mother dead and his father out of commission, the Cunningham co-op duties fell to him. Like it or not, he had to step up. And to be clear, he did *not* like it. But since it would be Vicky's head on the chopping block if Oliver didn't obey orders and conduct the damn interview, here he was.

Still, Oliver hadn't been expecting *her*.

In addition to the red hair and strange animosity coming off her in waves, her face was . . . captivating. She was attractive in that intriguing "look again" kind of way. Her eyes were wide and blue and tilted at the corners, her mouth full and lush and a little bit sulky at the moment. Plenty of freckles that, as far as he could tell, she'd made no effort to cover with heavy makeup. Different from the perfectly symmetrical, made-up features he was used to seeing.

Still, none of this quite explained the death glare Naomi had locked on him. Generally speaking, Oliver didn't tend to elicit strong emotional reactions from women. Mostly he got a lot of exasperated sighs preceding long, calm dissertations about his inability to demonstrate emotion, followed by a bland parting of ways.

There was nothing bland about this woman.

Instinct took over, and years of following formal societal rules demanded Oliver extend his hand across the desk. "Ms. Powell. I'm Oliver Cunningham."

Her hesitation was plain, and for a baffling moment, he thought she might actually refuse his handshake.

Eventually she set her palm to his, and though the firm shake was routine, his reaction to it was anything but. His stomach tightened as her palm brushed his, and Oliver clenched his teeth.

Good Lord, had it been so long since he'd been with a woman that handshakes were doing it for him now?

He pulled his hand back and cleared his throat.

"All right, Ms. Powell," he said, his voice just a touch cool to counter the heat inside him. "I'm assuming if you've made it this far, your credit and background checks pass muster, so let's get right to it. Why do you want to live here?"

He heard her inhale as though trying to get a grip on her temper, although what he'd done to set her off, he didn't have the faintest clue.

"It's a lovely building. The prewar architecture is exquisite," she replied.

His stomach tightened even further. *That voice.* Low, husky, and seductive as hell.

Get yourself together, Cunningham.

He forced himself to focus on her words, which were as dull as the voice was compelling. Prewar architecture?

He knew plenty of people cared about that crap, but he wasn't one of them. And for some reason, he hadn't thought she would be either. *Damn.* Disappointing.

Oliver leaned back in his chair, picking up the folder and tapping it against his palm as he contemplated the best method for getting her out the door as quickly as possible. Later, a dry-aged rib eye, an ice-cold cocktail, and the Yankees game awaited. Not to mention the two-thousand-piece jigsaw puzzle he was dying to dig into. Not that he would ever mention the last around the office, or, well, ever. As his former fiancée had pointed out, there was something a little weird about a grown man who enjoyed puzzles.

Oliver disagreed. It's not as though he laminated and framed the finished puzzles for some sort of weird display. He just enjoyed solving things. Jigsaws. Sudoku. Crosswords . . . *People.*

"Where do you live now?" Oliver asked, realizing the silence had stretched too long.

"I'm sure it's in my file," she said with a wooden smile.

Oliver said nothing, and they had a silent staring—glaring?—contest that was as exhilarating as it was childish.

He won, only because her eyes rolled briefly in irritation. "Lower East Side."

Oliver nodded. He hadn't spent much time on the Lower East Side since his college days, but the neighborhood suited her. Vibrant, youthful, and just the slightest bit gritty.

It was also a long way from the Upper East Side, in vibe, if not distance.

Oliver lifted his eyebrows to be deliberately provoking and said as much. "Long trek."

"Yes, the two-mile cab ride was absolutely exhausting."

The folder paused just briefly in its tapping against his palm. Odd. Something about her expression and that dry sarcasm felt . . . familiar. He scanned his memory but came up blank. He didn't have a lot of gingers in his acquaintance. He'd have remembered her.

"Two miles is a lot in Manhattan," he said.

"Too true," she said with another of those "smiles" that wasn't even remotely friendly. "Two miles in this city can mean the difference between real people and pretension."

Oliver's jaw clenched. He did not lose his temper often, but this woman was seriously pushing his buttons.

"All right, I give up, Ms. Powell. What's your deal?"

"My deal?"

"You've been eyeing my jugular since I walked in the door."

He waited for her to deny it. Instead, she inspected her manicure. A deep navy, he noted, and not the demure pale pink or classic red he was used to seeing. And yet everything else, the expensive-looking dress, the brand-name handbag, the sleek hairstyle, was expected, just like every other woman he knew.

But there was something else there—something more interesting that he couldn't put his finger on. Almost like she was a blend of self-confidence and vulnerability all wound into one feisty, compelling package.

She was a contradiction.

Maybe Oliver didn't need to start that jigsaw puzzle tonight, after all. He had a hell of a puzzle right in front of him.

"You do realize that I'm the gatekeeper to the next round," he prodded again.

She craned her neck, pretending to look at his hands. "Oh, is there a ring I was supposed to kiss? I'm new to this whole process. Should I bow?"

There it was again. The flash of familiarity. Who *was* this woman?

"Have we met?" he asked, tossing the folder on the desk as he studied her.

She looked away, and Oliver's eyes narrowed. "We *have*. How do I know you?"

Naomi looked back, her eyes guarded. "You don't."

"You sure?"

Instead of replying, she rewarded him with her first genuine smile. And damn, what a smile it was. Seductive and lethal all at the same time.

He was still reeling from its impact when she startled him by standing.

"We're not done," he said, then hid a wince at how pompous he sounded. How much like his *father* he sounded.

"Oh, I think we are," she murmured. "I think we both know exactly what you're going to write on my application the second I leave."

"Yeah, we do," he snapped, standing up, too. *"Left interview early."*

She glared up at him, and Oliver was a little surprised to realize that they were both breathing hard.

Naomi Powell wasn't particularly short, but at six feet, he had the physical advantage. For the first time since he'd hit his growth spurt in high school, he relished his height. This perplexing woman got under his skin like nobody had in a long time, and he needed every defense he could get.

Just as he was gearing up for her retort—*anticipating* it—she turned away.

Oliver called after her. "You understand that I'm not going to recommend you for the next round of interviews, right?"

"No problem, Mr. Cunningham. And look on the bright side. With me gone, there'll be more room for your emperor complex up in here. I'll send your secretary in. You're looking a bit overdue for your daily hand-feeding of grapes."

Naomi sailed out the office door without so much as a backward glance.

Oliver stood staring at the doorway, feeling somewhere between dumbfounded and off balance. And most annoyingly of all . . .

Intrigued.

Who the hell *was* that woman?

Chapter Five

*N*aomi picked up her stapler, a fancy tortoiseshell one from Kate Spade, intending to put it in a moving box alongside the matching tape dispenser. Instead, she clicked it rapidly in agitation, looking around at the disaster zone that was her office.

So *this* was what one got for procrastinating on moving four years' worth of stuff until the last afternoon before the movers came. Chaos.

Not that Naomi minded the mess. She did some of her best work in the midst of mayhem. But she was rapidly regretting the fact that she hadn't taken Deena's advice and let the movers take care of the packing. Naomi'd had grand visions of using the office's relocation as an opportunity to sort through old inventory, maybe achieve that elusive dream of organization that was always *just* out of reach.

Instead she'd left it all to the last minute, ending up more disorganized than ever.

And, if she was perfectly honest with herself, her procrastination may have had an emotional component. Excited as she was by her company's growth, much as she knew her employees needed more space in order to do their best work, she would miss this place. Or at least what it represented. Maxcessory may have been born in her tiny studio apartment years ago, but it spent its formative years here.

Now the company was all grown up. Still her baby, but older now. Growing. A little less dependent on the one who'd birthed it.

"Don't make it weird, Naomi," she muttered to herself.

"How?"

Her head snapped up, and she blinked in surprise at the unfamiliar man standing in her doorway. "I'm sorry?"

"How were you making it weird?" the man asked with an easy smile. A *charming* smile, and deliberately so.

Red alert.

Naomi knew men like this. The ones who knew they had above-average good looks and used said looks to get whatever they wanted. Naomi didn't judge him for it. Hell, she was all for using every possible advantage to get what you wanted.

But she was smart enough to know a move when she saw one, and her guard went up. Her eyes flicked briefly through the glass walls toward Deena's desk, already knowing her assistant wasn't there. No way Deena would let anyone get to Naomi's desk without an appointment, no matter how great the smile.

And it was a *really* great smile, Naomi had to admit. Just a little too perfect for her tastes, but it nicely complemented the expensive cut of his dress shirt and slacks and the touch-too-much gel in his dark blond hair.

"May I help you?" she asked.

His smile never lost its confident edge as he came toward her, hand extended. "Dylan Day. Pleasure."

Naomi let out a startled laugh as she recognized the name of

the TV producer who'd been hounding her for weeks. "Congratulations, Mr. Day. You've reached a new level of pushy."

"Thought maybe all those voice mails and emails might have
gotten lost," he said with a wink. "Looks like I might not totally
have been wrong."

He glanced around at the mess. "Relocating?"

"Yup."

"When?"

"Tomorrow. Which is why I intentionally don't have any
meetings scheduled today," she added pointedly.

"Gotcha. And the past couple weeks that you've been dodging me, you've been . . . packing?" he said, glancing around at the
half-full boxes, piles of Bubble Wrap, and general clutter threatening to explode out of her office.

There was little doubt in anyone's mind that her packing had
started, oh . . . two hours ago.

But she wasn't about to explain herself to a man whose current mission was to turn her life into an exposé. She needed him
gone, sexy smile and all.

"Mr. Day. I appreciate your company's interest in my story—"

"So you *did* get my messages."

"Well, yes. You used every method but courier pigeons."

"Only because I heard they don't treat the birds well."

She smiled in spite of herself, and he saw it. Pressed his advantage. "Let me take you to dinner. Give me a chance to explain
what we're thinking. Why we think the world needs your story."

She rolled her eyes. "If the two dozen roses you sent didn't
work, the cliché lines definitely won't."

"Noted." He held out his business card. "Your terms. You pick
the time, the place, I pay the bill."

She told herself to ignore the card, that this man had trouble written all over him, his interest in her clearly personal as much as professional.

She took the card anyway. Ever since the uncomfortable confrontation with her past in the form of Oliver Cunningham, Naomi had been itching for a distraction.

In the same way some women turned to therapy or booze or pills when life got uncomfortable, Naomi sought diversions. And there was nothing more diverting than a flirtation. Even better if it turned toward sex. It was why she'd gotten involved with Brayden Hayes. He'd been the perfect antidote to the loss of her mother. Or at least he had been before she'd realized his playboy persona was actually a disguise for scum of the earth.

She looked up at Dylan. "You're not married, are you?"

He laughed. "Forward. I like that. I am not."

He looked around at the mess of boxes. "You know, I worked for a moving company during summers in college."

Naomi lifted her eyebrows. "That explains the brawn."

Dylan's eyebrows lifted right back. "Why, Ms. Powell. I'm flattered."

"What?" she teased. "You're seriously telling me you didn't buy your shirt one size too small on purpose?"

There was a clearing of throats. "Naomi?"

She looked toward her office door, and her smile froze.

Normally Naomi would be thrilled by a surprise visit from Claire Hayes and Audrey Tate. But if there was anyone she didn't want learning of her connection to these two women, it was the man who would love nothing more than to air her dirtiest laundry.

Chapter Six

*O*blivious to Naomi's turmoil, Dylan grinned at the sight of the two women hovering in the office doorway. "No meetings scheduled, huh? I'm wounded. Come on in, ladies, I was just leaving."

Audrey smiled. "No, it's our mistake. Claire and I thought it would be fun to surprise—"

"*You* thought," Claire muttered. "*I* thought we should call first."

Audrey waved this aside. "Champagne needs no appointment. We thought some bubbly might make packing go a little easier."

"And cupcakes," Claire said, holding up the box. "I was going to make muffins, but Audrey made me buy cupcakes."

"Noooo, I made you buy muffins with frosting on them," Audrey argued.

Dylan looked at Naomi. "Damn. Champagne and cupcakes. Two things no man will ever be able to compete with. I'll take off, but I'm holding you to that dinner date."

Naomi saw Claire and Audrey perk up, and her friends give

Dylan a closer look. Curious on Audrey's side, skeptical on Claire's.

She let out the slightest sigh at Dylan's use of the word *date*, but manners dictated that she give a perfunctory introduction. "Dylan Day, this is Audrey Tate and Claire Hayes. Ladies, Dylan."

"You're in the accessory business?" Claire asked politely.

Dylan shook his head. "Nope. I'm a TV producer, trying to woo your girl here into letting me take her from *semi*-famous to super-famous."

"Huh." Claire looked unimpressed.

"How do you two know Naomi?" Dylan asked. "Maybe there's room for *your* story in the movie. A guy can hope, anyway."

"Yeah, no. Big no. My friends are off-limits," Naomi said before Claire or Audrey could reply. She stepped forward and gestured pointedly toward the door.

He took his dismissal gracefully. "Until our date."

"Our business meeting," Naomi corrected.

"Sure," Dylan said with a wink.

"Ladies." He nodded farewell at Audrey and Claire.

Her friends managed to hold their tongues until she'd closed the office door. Audrey's brown eyes were wide with curiosity, Claire's hazel ones narrowed in suspicion.

"That was the big-time television producer you've been avoiding?" Audrey said.

"Yup." Naomi pulled her hair into a messy bun. "I thought he'd given up, but he's more persistent than I expected."

"He was super flirty," Audrey said.

"He was, wasn't he?" Naomi mused thoughtfully, glancing through the glass walls at Dylan's retreating back.

"You can't be serious," Claire said.

"Why not? He's cute," Naomi said, reaching out and pulling

the box of cupcakes from Claire's hands and taking it to the desk, where she rummaged through the mess and pulled out a stack of napkins.

"What. You don't think he was cute?" She paused in the process of peeling the wrapper off the cupcake."

"He was," Audrey said hesitantly. "But . . ." She looked at Claire for help.

Claire didn't mince her words. "He's a Brayden."

"Nope." Naomi shook her head and wiped frosting off her lip. "He's not married. I asked."

"Yeah, because guys like that always tell the truth."

"Guys like what?" Naomi asked with just the slightest edge in her voice. "You met him for seven seconds."

"And you met him for what, ten? And you've got a date set up."

Exasperated, Naomi looked toward Audrey for an ally. "Dylan did *not* give off Brayden vibes. Did he?"

Audrey hesitated. "It's hard to know. I mean, he seemed nice, but so did Brayden . . ."

"Why are we even talking about this?" Naomi said, shoving the rest of her cupcake in her mouth. "He's just some guy."

"Maybe," Claire said, her tone gentler than before. "But let's not forget how we first met—why we first became friends. I wouldn't be much of a friend if I didn't tell you that guy wants to jump your bones. Which I would have no problem with if he weren't also trying to get you to sign a contract to turn your life story into a TV show."

"She's right, sweetie," Audrey said with a sympathetic smile. "Maybe he's a super-nice guy, but we're just saying be careful, okay? Make sure he's not using all that yummy charm to get what he wants."

Naomi sighed. They weren't wrong. If there was a line between professional and smarmy, Dylan Day walked it.

"I'll be careful," she said dutifully.

"Good," Audrey said with a nod. "And now, I have to say, Naomi, your office is *exactly* how I imagined it."

"What, a hot mess?" Naomi asked, debating another cupcake but deciding against it.

"No, I mean it's *so* what a New York fashion entrepreneur's office should be," Audrey proclaimed. "You look like you belong here."

Naomi supposed she knew exactly what Audrey meant, because the moving clutter aside, it was exactly what Naomi herself had envisioned the space to be. It had gloriously beat-up wood floors and exterior brick walls that looked like they'd been around for centuries. The only modern thing about the place was the Wi-Fi and glass walls, which she'd selected mainly to ensure that those employees working in the bull pen at the center of the office could still enjoy the same natural light as the offices around the edges.

"You two fit right in," Naomi said.

"*She* does," Claire said, nodding at Audrey in a forest green turtleneck sweater, wide black belt, and over-the-knee boots.

"And you," Naomi insisted. Claire's wardrobe adhered more to classic than trendy, but the woman knew the basic rules of style and, even more important to Naomi's critical eye, knew her way around accessories.

Naomi was a big believer that the only crime worse than no accessories were too many, and Claire's gold necklace with a tiny diamond pendant and matching stud earrings were the perfect choices for her outfit. Anything more would have overwhelmed the white silk blouse and gray slacks.

"So I was going to come in here claiming that I *forgot* to put in earrings this morning," Audrey said, unabashedly poking through some of the merchandise on the table, "but I *may* have kind of, sort of forgotten on purpose on the off chance your selection was better than mine, which it so is."

"Help yourself," Naomi said, waving her hand. "Those are free samples. I haven't really had a chance to dig through them yet, so I'd love your thoughts."

"Oooh, rose gold," Audrey said with a delighted clap. "It's so *in*."

As Audrey browsed through the earrings, Naomi turned her attention to Claire, giving the woman a careful study. She'd known the woman only two months, but true to her premonition in the park that day, their friendship had been on the fast track. They'd already had countless brunches, happy hours, and most telling of all, that late-night, soul-sharing kind of texting that left you feeling like you *knew* the other person.

Maybe it was these texts, maybe it was their shared history with Brayden, or maybe theirs was just one of those friendships that was meant to be. Whatever the reason, Naomi knew she had a pretty good read on both Claire and Audrey despite their short acquaintance, and she knew that neither woman was doing quite as well as they wanted people to think.

Claire still had the same shadows under her eyes she'd had the day of the funeral, though she had decent skill with concealer and disguised the worst of it from a casual observer.

"So, when do you have to be packed?" Claire asked, looking around at the mess as though itching to help.

"Oh no," Naomi said, popping the cork. "You're not one of those neat freaks who actually *like* to clean, are you?"

"Clean? No. I'd skip scrubbing the toilets any day, but tidying up . . . I do like to organize things." She rubbed her hands together.

"That's disturbing," Audrey said, coming back to Naomi and

holding up two pairs of earrings, one a cluster of gray faux pearls, the other a dangling rose-gold flower charm. "Which?"

"Pearls," Naomi said automatically, digging through a box where she was pretty sure she had some plastic cups.

"You didn't even look."

"I saw the second you picked them up." Naomi found the cups and turned to face Audrey. "You've got big eyes, but the rest of your features are petite. The long earrings will overwhelm you."

Audrey looked at the earrings, then shrugged and began to put in the pearls.

"What about Claire?" Audrey chirped. "She needs something new and pretty, too."

Naomi glanced over at Claire as she poured the champagne. "Help yourself. I've got some new clutches and scarves around here if jewelry's not your thing."

"No, I'm good," Claire said, absently fiddling with her watch. The Cartier watch Brayden had given her. The same one he'd given Naomi and Audrey. To Naomi's thinking, that had been Brayden Hayes's worst crime—thinking that the same watch could possibly be the right choice for three very different women.

Claire seemed to realize what she was doing and glanced down at the gold band and froze.

Naomi and Audrey exchanged a look.

"You're still wearing it?" Naomi asked, trying to keep the incredulity out of her voice. She'd taken a hammer to hers. Wasteful? Yes. But necessary.

Claire was still looking at the watch, fiddling with the clasp once more. "I know. I know. It's just . . ." She looked up. "He was my husband. And he's *gone*. And . . ."

She pressed her hands to her lips and didn't finish the sentence.

Naomi racked her brain for the right thing to say and came up with nothing. She was good at a lot of things. Comforting and reassuring words weren't among them.

Luckily, Audrey was better at it. She took Claire's hands in hers. "What can we do?"

Claire sighed, then looked up. "Pour me some of that champagne?"

Naomi smiled, relieved to be of use. "On it."

She poured them three cups, then a fourth for Deena, who had reappeared at her desk and was barking into the phone. Naomi took a cup out to the main reception desk and handed it to her assistant, who gave her a grateful smile as she argued with who Naomi assumed were the movers on the phone.

Naomi went back into her office and noticed that though Claire was smiling at whatever Audrey was saying, her hand shook the slightest bit as she lifted the champagne to her lips.

Naomi's gaze caught once again on the glint of gold at Claire's left wrist.

That damn watch.

Inspiration struck. Naomi went to the cabinets that lined one side of her office. She'd had them custom built the same year she moved into the space and realized that conventional storage units weren't conducive to the accessory business. Accessories, by nature, were small, and Naomi had needed dozens of tiny spaces to store products, not a couple of big spaces. As a result, the wall was nearly covered in itty-bitty drawers, each labeled with a number that corresponded to a spreadsheet cataloging the vendor, the item, and whether or not Naomi wanted it ordered for the monthly accessory boxes.

After a few wrong guesses, she found the drawer she was looking for. She pulled out the blush-pink velvet pouch with the gold monogram logo. She'd gotten the sample last year, and she'd loved everything about the company, the packaging, their goal of designing watches with classic silhouettes and modern flair.

Naomi hadn't ordered from them—yet. The price was just a bit too high. But their product stuck out in her memory among hundreds, if not thousands, of pieces, and she kept them on her radar.

She handed the pouch to a confused-looking Claire.

"Open it," she urged.

Claire tugged at the ribbon and slid the watch into her palm.

"Oooh," Audrey breathed.

Naomi smiled at Audrey. "You're *really* a sucker for rose gold, huh?"

"Shiny and pink?" Audrey said reverently. "Somebody hold me back. But this . . . this one is all Claire."

"Oh, I don't know," Claire said. "Is it too . . . young for me?"

Naomi rolled her eyes. "I'd say we've got a few years before we need to start decorating your walker with rhinestones. But if you don't like it . . ."

"No, it's beautiful," Claire said quickly, holding up the watch for a closer look.

It *was* beautiful. The slim rose-gold links of the band were just the right amount of bling without being over-the-top.

"The slightly larger watch face is in right now," Naomi explained. "It used to be that women thought the smaller the better, since, you know, we're supposed to be dainty and all. But I actually think the slightly larger size *accentuates* women's smaller wrists."

But the band and the size of the watch face weren't the highlights. The tiny champagne flute at the five o'clock position was.

"The champagne really should be at noon," Audrey said, tilting her head to steady it. "That's *my* appropriate champagne hour."

"Cheers to that," Naomi said before shifting her attention back to Claire. "What do you think?"

Claire took a deep breath, and then opened the clasp of her current watch. "I think that I don't want to see *this* watch from Brayden for a while."

Naomi deliberately didn't glance at the piece as she tossed it on the desk. The watch deserved better treatment. But a gift from Brayden Hayes did not. She noted that Claire's eyes tracked the discarded watch, and realized the other woman wasn't ready to say goodbye entirely yet. But she put the new watch on. Progress.

"Oh, Claire," Audrey announced, looking at Claire's wrist. "It's perfect."

"It's not set to the right time," Claire pointed out.

"The actual minute's not important right now," Naomi insisted. "It's about the moment."

Audrey nodded. "Absolutely. It marks phase two of our fresh start."

"What was phase one?" Claire asked with a smile.

"Us figuring out if we could be friends," Audrey said as though this were obvious.

She had a point. After that day in Central Park with these ladies, Naomi had wondered if maybe it was a fluke. A strange little bubble of reality fueled by grief and anger and the need to best the man who'd bested them.

No, not bested. *Fooled.*

But in the past couple of months, Naomi had realized that as different as the three of them were, they had something in common other than having slept with Brayden. They were strong. Resilient. Most important of all, they *liked* one another. Naomi had never made much time for female friends. Sure, she counted

Deena as a friend. She was close with a bunch of her senior team. But for Naomi, work had always come first. Above romance, and above friendship. But these women gave her hope . . . gave her the sense that maybe she could be something more than a girl boss and ballbuster.

"So what's phase two?" Claire asked, still looking slightly skeptical.

"Moving on. Naomi's got a head start. Her office is moving. She's moving. She's got a date—"

"Business meeting," Naomi corrected with exasperation.

"Whatever. You're moving forward."

Am I?

Naomi's thoughts flicked back to 517 Park Avenue, to Oliver Cunningham's glacier-blue eyes. To people who didn't care how much money you had but how old it was. People who, even now, Naomi was letting make her feel inferior. *Less.*

And then, as though Fate was looking down on her and reading her very thoughts, Deena knocked on the door and popped her head in. "Sorry to interrupt. Ms. Gromwell from that Park Avenue building is on line one. Says it's a *pressing matter*. Her words."

Huh. Well, at least they wanted to give her the news over the phone instead of reject her over email. It was more than she was expecting.

"Give me one sec," she told her friends, leaning over her desk and picking up her phone. "Naomi Powell."

"Ms. Powell? This is Victoria Gromwell, from 517 Park Avenue. I'm calling to check on your availability next week. We know it's last-minute, but the board is hoping to make a decision by the following weekend."

It took Naomi a moment to register the woman's words, and when she did, her response wasn't exactly eloquent. "What?"

There was a long moment of silence, and Naomi heard it loud and clear as disapproval, but she didn't care.

"You were approved for the second round of interviews," Ms. Gromwell said stiffly, as though she herself couldn't imagine why. "There are only three remaining contenders for the apartment, and you're among them."

"Oh, well . . ." Naomi tried to sort this out in her head, but it didn't make sense. The only person to interview her in the first round had been Oliver Cunningham, and there was no way he'd have put her through to the final round, except . . . apparently, he had.

Naomi opened her mouth to explain the misunderstanding, that she already had a place to live.

But Audrey's words came back to her.

You're moving forward.

She was trying. She wanted to. But if her reaction to Oliver Cunningham this week had taught her anything, it was that maybe one couldn't fully move on until they'd faced the past.

For her mom's sake. And her own.

"I can make any time next week work," Naomi said without bothering to check her calendar. Whatever meetings she had could be rescheduled.

Because Naomi was on the cusp of achieving something her mom had spent her entire life wishing for:

An apology from Walter Cunningham—Oliver's womanizing, heartless father who made even Brayden Hayes look like one of the good ones.

Chapter Seven

*O*liver opened the door to his father's apartment and immediately ducked as an egg went flying over his head and into the hallway.

He winced and looked at Janice Reid, his father's caretaker. Janice gave him a reassuring smile. "Hard-boiled."

"Ah." Oliver had figured. His father had been on a kick with the hard-boiled egg requests lately. That, and celery and peanut butter. It was as though the sixty-one-year-old Walter was channeling his grade school self.

Oliver supposed that made sense. The nature of Alzheimer's meant that his father's memories were scattered, his place in time sometimes in the right decade, sometimes not. Why not go back to childhood? Lord knew Oliver wished he could these days.

Oliver retrieved the egg from the hall. The shell had cracked but luckily, having landed on the plush red carpet, hadn't made a mess. He reentered the apartment, setting his briefcase by the door, and dropped the egg into the garbage can. Oliver looked over to the table where Janice sat with his father, plucking an egg from his hand before that, too, was hurled against the door.

"Walter," she said in a calm, no-nonsense voice. "You said you wanted hard-boiled eggs. Have you changed your mind?"

Walter scooted down in his chair and crossed his arms, looking six years old instead of six decades.

From the first days of Walter's diagnosis, the doctors had warned Oliver that the disease affected everyone differently and that dramatic personality changes were not uncommon. Oliver thought he'd been prepared. Experiencing those changes, however, had turned out to be vastly different from hearing about them.

Oliver's father had been under the grips of Alzheimer's for nearly three years, and Oliver still struggled to reconcile the often surly, tantrum-inclined old man with the strong, rigid role model of his youth.

"Walter," Janice asked again, her voice patient. "Will you please take a bite of the egg you asked for?"

Walter reached out and picked up an already-peeled egg and ate half of it in a single bite. "I like to peel it myself."

"You asked me to peel this one for you, but I'll be sure to leave it for you next time."

She didn't add, *Don't you remember?* Both Janice and Oliver knew Walter didn't remember.

Walter glanced over, finally seeming to register Oliver's presence. "Son."

"Hey, Dad," Oliver said, pleased that despite egg-gate, it was one of those increasingly rare moments when his father recognized him. "How's it going?"

"She peeled my egg," Walter said, pointing accusingly at Janice.

"I know. Nice of her, wasn't it?" Oliver loosened his tie and shrugged out of his suit jacket. "You ready to watch the Yankees game with me?"

Not too long ago, they'd have added a jigsaw puzzle to the evening routine, maybe collaborated on a crossword puzzle. In the early stages, the doctors had encouraged anything to keep his brain focused on the task at hand, but as the disease had progressed, the puzzles had gone by the wayside. Jigsaw pieces inevitably were pushed to the ground in a fit of irritation, crossword puzzles a thing of the past.

Walter was already scraping back his chair. "They'd better do better than last night. Jeter's been in a slump."

Oliver nodded agreeably, despite the fact that Derek Jeter hadn't played in several seasons, much less last night. If Oliver had learned anything over the past couple of years, it was to pick his battles, and that correcting his father was pointless and frustrating for everyone.

"Rough day?" Oliver asked Janice quietly after his father had ambled over to the TV and settled into his easy chair. It was the type of leather recliner that Oliver's mother would never have allowed in her perfectly decorated home. But Margaret Cunningham had passed away four years earlier. Just in time to miss her husband's descent into dementia *and* the addition of the dreaded recliner.

"Not so bad," Janice said, clearing away Walter's plate and taking it to the sink. "The egg throwing was the first bad moment. We had a good walk. He's been into dogs lately, so we killed a good hour at the dog park, just watching."

Oliver smiled at the irony. Growing up, all Oliver had wanted was a dog. But despite the fact that he'd asked for one four Christmases in a row and every birthday during the same period, his mother had literally shuddered and ignored the request altogether. His father had impatiently declared dogs "a waste of valuable time." To this day, Oliver had never owned a dog.

It occurred to him that as an independent thirty-year-old with his own apartment and free will, he could certainly get one now, but caring for his dad was just about all he could manage at the moment. Thank God for Janice. Oliver didn't know what he would do without the dependable live-in caretaker.

Well, no. That wasn't true. He *did* know . . . he'd have to put his father in a home.

And eventually, it would probably come to that. So far his father hadn't been prone to the violent outbursts often associated with his disease—a particularly alarming development for male patients with Alzheimer's, given that they tended to be bigger and stronger than their female caretakers.

Janice had been easily able to manage the worst of Walter's tantrums, but if they progressed beyond throwing hard-boiled eggs, Oliver knew that even the sturdy Janice would be no match for the six-foot Walter.

For now, though, their system worked. Janet lived in the second bedroom of his father's apartment, and Oliver paid her *very* well to cook, clean, and keep an eye on Walter.

She took off two days a week, during which Oliver took over watching his dad, and whenever possible, Oliver stopped by after work to give Janice some time to herself.

"I was going to go over to my sister's for an hour or so," Janice said as she washed Walter's plate. "You want me to wait until you have a chance to grab dinner?"

"Nah, I'll order a pizza or something. Who knows, maybe it'll revive his pepperoni phase from last month."

She smiled. "I swear, every time, it was like he never had a piece of pizza before. His happiness was a joy to watch."

Oliver smiled at the recent memory, though he opted not to mention that pizza hadn't exactly been a common occurrence in the Cunningham household while Margaret was alive. His mother had been a staunch believer in the merits of a home-cooked, balanced meal. Although, Oliver secretly thought that by *balanced* his mother had actually meant *bland*.

A few minutes later, Janice let herself out, and Oliver had just placed the pizza order and settled on the couch to watch the game with his dad when there was a knock at the door.

Walter didn't even look away from the screen.

With an assessing glance to make sure his father wasn't on the verge of some tantrum or destructive fit, Oliver recognized that Walter was completely lost inside his head and seemed perfectly content to stay in his chair.

Oliver stood and opened the door to Ruth Butler, his long-time neighbor and the onetime best friend of his mother.

"Hi," he said, smiling at the petite woman as he bent to kiss her cheek. "Want to come in?"

"Oh, no, dear. You know I don't care for televised athletics," Ruth said, folding her hands in front of her as she glanced toward the TV. "How's Walter this evening?"

Oliver shrugged. "An okay night, all things considered."

"I stopped by earlier with some muffins, but he and Janice must have gone out. I'll bring them by later, now that I know that you're here. I didn't want to leave them by the door. You know how Chantzy gets."

"I do." Chantzy was the aging corgi who lived next door and had once devoured a plate of cookies Ruth left on the floor outside the Cunninghams' door.

"Now, Oliver," Ruth said, using the same tone she'd used when he was a boy and had gone sprinting through the living room, disturbing Ruth and Margaret's teatime. "I know that you've been very busy at work."

"No more than usual," he said, leaning on the door, knowing she didn't actually give a crap about his architectural firm. "What's up?"

"The board meeting this afternoon . . ."

Oliver groaned. "I missed it."

"Yes, dear."

"You know, anytime you guys want to kick me off that thing . . ."

He gave her his best grin, and she gave him a reproving look. "A Cunningham has been on the co-op board of 517 for three generations now. And with your father not able—"

"Yeah," he said, just a touch curtly. "I know. What'd I miss?"

"We took the final vote on 2B."

"Right. Who'd you decide on?"

"Well, nobody, yet. It was a tie."

He silently groaned, realizing now why she was here. Oliver, and his missing vote, was the tiebreaker.

"All right. Who am I voting for?" he asked, knowing Ruth had strong opinions about most everything, and the residents of her building were the top of her list.

Her lips thinned. "Well, I'm sure I can't tell you who to choose. And I'd have thought, with you living next door to the vacant apartment, you'd have a little more interest . . ."

"Who are my options?" he asked, suddenly envisioning a beer along with his pizza and puzzle downstairs in his apartment. Maybe a *couple* of beers.

"Well, there's that nice couple from Connecticut. The New-mans. And then that young girl. The redhead."

Oliver's gaze had been scanning over Ruth's head, hoping the delivery guy had made it in record time to give Oliver an out from the conversation, but his attention snapped back to the older woman. "The redhead? That Naomi chick?"

Gray eyebrows lifted in censure.

"Woman," he amended. "She was in the final running?"

"Yes, because *you* put her through," Ruth said.

"I guess I did," he murmured. The feisty redhead had passed through his thoughts quite a bit the past couple of days, in a sort of nagging, *what is with her* kind of way.

If he were being honest, he'd approved her to the next round mostly to mess with the elderly co-op board. As the youngest member by at least thirty years, he liked to do his part to push their boundaries a bit.

"I didn't think she'd make it to the last stage," he said. From what he'd seen, the woman had been far too volatile for the staid board, who preferred mild mannered, gray haired, and old moneyed.

Naomi Powell checked none of those boxes.

"Yes, well, one of the other candidates pulled out. A larger apartment on the Upper West Side opened up." She sniffed, to indicate her thoughts on the *other* side of the park. "Another had some questionable business partners. And though I can't say I understand the appeal of Ms. Powell's little jewelry business, there's no arguing that it's quite successful. But don't you think it's odd for someone so young to apply *here*?"

Oliver shrugged and glanced over his shoulder to make sure his father was still sitting peacefully in his chair. Ruth was astute enough to pick up on the gesture.

"I won't keep you. Just give me your vote, and I'll let you and Walter get back to your evening," Ruth said with a kind smile. Stuffy as the old woman could be, he knew that Ruth cared for him. Not Walter so much. Ruth had been too close with Oliver's mother to have any fond feelings toward the man who'd made Margaret's life hell.

Still, Oliver appreciated that for the most part Ruth hadn't held Walter's past sins—and there had been many—against him after he'd been diagnosed.

"Remind me one more time of my options. It's the redhead—Ms. Powell—or . . ."

"The Newmans," Ruth said with no small amount of exasperation that he didn't take this as seriously as the rest of the board. "They are a delightful older couple from Connecticut, empty nesters, looking to live out their golden years here in the heart of the city."

There was no mistaking the change in tone when Ruth spoke of the Newmans compared with Naomi. She may respect Naomi's right to apply, but clearly the Newmans were *the appropriate choice*.

"Ah, I guess . . ."

It was on the tip of Oliver's tongue to make the choice of least resistance. The Newmans would be just like everyone else here. They'd offer unsolicited but amusing dating advice, would enjoy the excruciatingly boring holiday party deemed mandatory for "community development," and would probably have strong opinions over the fact that he didn't get the paper version of the *Wall Street Journal* and the *New York Times* delivered to his front door like everyone else. Oliver also knew that no amount of explaining would ever convince someone over the age of fifty that the digital and paper version were the same thing.

On the *other* hand, they'd never play their music too loud, would never bring home obnoxious douche bags, and given their own advanced age, would likely be understanding when Walter slipped out into the hallways wearing only his underwear as he was prone to do if Oliver or Janice left him alone for even a moment.

"Wait, you said it was a tie," Oliver said, belatedly registering what that meant. It meant that *half* the board had voted for Naomi, which was a surprise. Oliver would have thought the Newmans would have been a shoo-in. He knew these people. They'd practically raised him. And the fact that half had been willing to let in someone as young and "un-pedigreed" as Naomi Powell surprised him.

"Yes, well." Ruth's lips pressed together. "I don't mean to be crude, but many of the male members of the board let themselves be persuaded by Ms. Powell's brash looks."

Brash. It wasn't a word he'd use to describe her. She'd been dressed conservatively; there'd been no tattoos or too-short skirts or unusual piercings. Then he pictured the fire in her eyes, every bit as bright as her hair. Yeah, she was . . . something.

Ruth looked pointedly at her watch. "Oliver, dear, I really need your answer. Whomever you choose will be fine."

He meant to say *the Newmans.* To give Ruth the answer he knew she wanted, knowing it would be easier for everyone, and yet . . .

"Ms. Powell."

She looked up, blue eyes wide and indignant. "I'm sorry?"

"Naomi Powell. She's my vote."

Ruth's mouth dropped open. "But, Ollie. Surely you can see—"

"What can I say, Ruth?" Oliver gave his best smile, ignoring her use of his hated childhood nickname. "I, too, am a male on the board."

"You cannot be serious," she said as he started to close the door. "You can't choose your neighbor simply because she's a dish."

He choked out a laugh. "A dish?"

"Or whatever the kids call it these days. A hottie."

"Good night, Ruth," Oliver said gently but firmly as he shut the door.

He heard the familiar crack of the remote hitting the wall behind the TV, followed by his father muttering obscenities at the second-base umpire.

Oliver let his forehead rest on the door just for a minute.

Despite what his mother's former best friend thought, he hadn't chosen Naomi because she was eye candy. He's chosen her because she was interesting. A puzzle he had every intention of solving.

Because what Oliver really needed more than anything?

A distraction from his own life.

Chapter Eight

I'm still confused. I thought you were moving downtown," Claire said, carefully handling a cheap glass vase that probably cost less than the packing material it was wrapped in.

"I thought so, too," Naomi said, opening yet another moving box and then sliding the box cutter back into the back pocket of her oldest jeans that were reserved for horrors like moving.

She didn't tell her friend that she actually had purchased this apartment *and* signed a lease on the Tribeca high-rise. Having more money than one knew what to do with was a cushy problem to have. Most of the time.

Apparently, it also enabled her to make really, really stupid decisions. Like moving into an old building, with even older neighbors, in a snobby part of town just so she could come face-to-face with the man who'd all but destroyed her mother. To make Walter Cunningham see that he'd knocked her down, but not out.

And maybe to finish what she'd started with Oliver Cunningham. Whatever that had been.

"You guys really didn't have to come over," Naomi said for the third time as she half-heartedly began unpacking some plates.

"Are you kidding?" Claire said, diving into the box she was unpacking. "This is sort of my fantasy."

"What, packing peanuts?" Audrey asked, taking a sip of white wine and wrinkling her nose at the box of knickknacks she'd been unpacking at record-slow speed.

"No, I just love new places."

"I don't quite know that *new* is the word I'd use to describe 517 Park," Naomi said, beginning to place her assortment of mugs with motivation girl-boss-esque notes in one of the cabinets. "We could add up all three of our ages, and I think the building still has us beat."

"You know what I mean," Claire said. "New to *you*. It's a fresh start. A brand-new place to live."

"Why this building?" Audrey asked curiously. "I mean, don't get me wrong, it's gorgeous in a stately, prewar kind of way, but you seem too hip for the Upper East Side. And as someone born and raised on Madison, I know what I'm talking about."

"I'll echo that sentiment," Claire said, grabbing Audrey's wine out of her hand and taking a sip. "I'm a Connecticut girl by birth, but I've lived on the Upper East for six years now, and you're way too cool for us."

"Trust me, I'm really not cool," Naomi said. "I can name just about every *Star Trek* character, ever, and that includes the much-maligned *Enterprise* series."

"Okay, I don't really know what that means," Audrey said, going to the fridge to retrieve the bottle of chardonnay. "But even *that's* cool. Your confidence about it. And look at what you're wearing."

Naomi glanced down at her ripped black jeans and fitted

black T-shirt with *Slay* written across the front. "Seriously? This?"

"*Cool*," Audrey repeated, pointing the wine bottle at her. "Now, where are your wineglasses?"

"I only seem to have unpacked the one," Naomi said, looking around at the mass of boxes and tissue paper. "And I gave it to you."

Audrey pulled down two mugs and filled them liberally with wine, handing one to Naomi and taking the other to Claire before refilling her own stemmed glass.

"So?" Claire asked as Audrey put the bottle back in the fridge.

"So what?" Naomi took a sip from the mug and smiled, remembering her early twenties when wine from a coffee mug was pretty much the status quo because her kitchenware contained about three glasses, *total*, and a wineglass wasn't one of them.

"Why here?" Claire repeated Audrey's question, which Naomi had yet to answer.

Naomi set the mug aside and reached into the box to pull out a small carafe she usually used for juice. "I used to live here."

Both Audrey and Claire looked up from their respective boxes. "What?"

"*Here?*" Audrey said, using her glass to gesture at the messy space.

"Well, not this particular apartment." Naomi set the carafe on a shelf more carefully than she needed to. Buying time and wondering if she was ready for this story. Or if her friends were.

"You don't have to talk about it if you don't want to," Claire said, apparently noting Naomi's apprehension.

Audrey nodded in agreement.

"Eh. I might as well get it over with," Naomi said with a shrug. "Better you guys know what you're dealing with now rather than later."

She picked up her wine mug and gestured at the small kitchen table by the window. Much of her furniture was still covered in the protective plastic wrap it had been moved in, but the kitchen chairs were accessible.

Naomi shoved off a couple of boxes and sat in one of the chairs, curling her right leg beneath her.

Audrey and Claire joined her, wineglass and mug in hand.

"Wait, do we need cheese for this?" Audrey asked as she plopped into the chair. "Because I can have some ordered, like, ASAP."

"You mean you just order cheese?" Claire asked, giving her an incredulous look. "Like, a block of cheddar?"

"No, like . . ." Audrey gestured at the table with her hands. "A plate. A cheese plate. A fancy one. My favorite place is right around the corner, and they deliver."

"God, I love Manhattan. Make it so," Naomi said. "I've got lots more wine . . . somewhere."

Audrey busily started tapping something on her phone. "*Aaand* . . . done." She set her phone on the table, screen down. "Cheese will be here in thirty minutes or so. Now. Speak."

"I don't even know where to start with this," Naomi said, plunging her fingers into her hair and tugging just slightly in agitation, trying to quiet her thoughts.

"All right," Claire said quietly. "You said you used to live here. How old were you?"

"Nine when I moved in," Naomi said without hesitation.

"Which apartment?"

"Five E. There are only five units on each floor, A through E. E's the largest, with four bedrooms, three bathrooms plus a powder room, separate dining area . . ."

"So, *fancy* New York," Audrey said with a comprehending nod.

"Very. Unfortunately, my family wasn't the fancy one."

"But if you lived here . . ." Audrey trailed off in confusion.

"One of those four bedrooms I mentioned? I shared it with my mother. Who was the housekeeper of the family that lived there."

"Naomi," Claire said softy. "Please tell me you're not ashamed of that. It's perfectly respectable."

"I'm not," Naomi said, using her finger to flip the handle of her wine mug one way, then the other. Back and forth.

"But"—she looked up—"that's also not the ugly part. I mean, don't get me wrong, a stubborn, high-energy third grader having to share a tiny room with her equally stubborn and high-energy mother wasn't exactly a pretty picture. But sometimes I like to imagine that she and I could have gone down the *Gilmore Girls* path. BFFs, or whatever."

"You didn't?" Claire asked.

"Definitely not." She blew out a breath and took another sip of wine. "Okay, short version? My mom was a wildly mediocre housekeeper, and I'm sure if the woman who had hired her had been around, her job wouldn't have lasted a week. But. The *lady of the house*, as she called herself, no joke, was gone most of the time caring for her sick mother in Newport, or some other fancy place."

"Uh-oh," Audrey said softly.

"Right?" Naomi said, her smile brittle. "It has all the elements of a thoroughly unimaginative movie."

"Wait, what am I missing?" Claire asked.

"I'm guessing Naomi's going to tell us next that while her female employer was gone all the time, her male employer was *very* much around."

"Oh. *Ohhhh*," Claire said, hazel eyes widening in comprehension.

"Yeah. In the cliché of all clichés, he was banging the help. And the help was a very willing participant."

"Did you know? I mean, while it was going on?"

Naomi's shoulders lifted. "I mean, sort of? I was nine and didn't care enough about sex and relationships to really register that my mom often put me to bed and then wouldn't come back to our room until much later in the evening. If she came back at all. I think maybe I told myself that she was sleeping on the couch or something to give me some space. I don't know if it was self-protection or what . . ."

Naomi trailed off and gathered her thoughts before forging ahead.

"Anyway. Whether my ignorance was intentional or not, I lost all ability to pretend it wasn't happening when I caught them together."

"Oooof," Audrey said with a wince.

"Yeah. Just, you know, banging in the kitchen like it was no big deal."

"While you were *there*? In the apartment?"

"To be kind of fair, they thought I'd gone to the park to play. Rather, they'd *sent* me to the park to play."

"Alone?" Claire's nose wrinkled. "And you were nine?"

"No. Though I wish I'd been alone. Instead they sent me with my mom's employer's son. He was a year older, and we got along *never*. He was the spoiled rich brat who was both older and taller than the housekeeper's dorky daughter. I was also a brat, except the mouthy, defensive kind who was all too aware of her secondhand clothes and crooked teeth and donated schoolbooks. Plus, let's be honest. Even in the best of circumstances, boys and girls don't get along at that age, and these were not good circumstances. I mean, he called me Carrots."

"Oh, how very *Anne of Green Gables!*" Claire said.

"No," Naomi said, lifting a finger, knowing exactly to whom Claire was referring. All redheaded girls were familiar with their soul sister Anne Shirley. Pippi Longstocking, too. "I assure you, this is no Gilbert Blythe scenario."

"Wait, huh?" Audrey asked, looking between them. "Who's Gilbert Blythe?"

"Movie night, my house," Claire said. "You'll just die from the romance of it. But sorry, Naomi. Continue. You and the non-Gilbert tormenter were at the park . . ."

"Right," Naomi said, lost in thought as she went back to that long-ago day. "I don't think either of us realized that they were just trying to get us out of the house, so when our instructions to 'go kick the soccer ball around' only got as far as me throwing it at his head and him throwing it right back and breaking my glasses, I went home in tears that I'd tried desperately to hide. He followed me, because even after all of that, he couldn't let me have my dignity."

"Or maybe he felt guilty," Claire supplied.

Naomi gave her a glare.

"Or not," Claire muttered into her mug.

"And you guys walked in on your parents doing it," Audrey said in a slightly awed tone.

"Bingo," Naomi said, shooting her temple with a finger pistol. "Scarred for life."

"What'd they do?" Claire asked. "Your mom and his dad?"

"There was a lot of profanity from him. I vaguely remember screaming, while my mom hurriedly tucked her tits back into her shirt and dragged me into the bedroom begging me not to tell anyone."

"Did you?"

"No! I was too embarrassed. I'd seen my mom's boobs *and* her boss's *thing*. That was about as far as my thoughts on it went. Doesn't matter though. His wife somehow figured it out anyway a few days after that."

"Oh, sweetie."

"That's not even the worst part," Naomi said, gripping the mug so hard she was surprised it didn't shatter. "This woman, his wife, was *screaming* her suspicions at her husband and my mother, which, you know, I guess that was to be expected. But instead of handling it like a man and telling his wife what really happened, the asshole denied the whole thing."

"No," Audrey said, wide-eyed.

Naomi nodded. "Yup. He claimed that my mother was a whore—that was his precise word—who'd tried her hardest to seduce him, but that he'd never touch trash."

"The liar!" Audrey breathed in outrage. "That jerk!"

"Yeah," Naomi replied, voice flat. "That's what I said. But I was the only one in the room who spoke the truth. Even my mom didn't say a single word in her defense. She just stood there, staring at him, and it was like . . . it was like she'd *died* inside at that very moment. I think she loved the guy." Naomi shuddered. "I begged the son to tell his mom what we'd seen, but he just stood there and said he didn't know what I was talking about."

Naomi shrugged. "Needless to say, we were out on the street the next day."

"That's appalling. Why would you want to come back?" Claire said.

Naomi let out a laugh. "I don't know that I did. But my mom never let it go. Those people blacklisted her, which meant she could never get another housekeeping job. Not that she was that good at it to begin with, but after that she just sort of quit trying at *everything*."

She took a sip of her wine and continued. "I knew she held on to her bitterness, but I didn't realize how much until the building called me about my application to live here."

"Which I'm guessing you didn't fill out," Audrey said.

Naomi shook her head. "My mom did before she died. She always said she wanted them to see what I'd become. I never intended to see the application through, but next thing I know, I made it through interviews, and then I was signing the paperwork . . ."

She wasn't sure which was more of a mystery: that Oliver Cunningham had passed her on to the next round after their disastrous meeting, or that she'd pursued the process.

"You wanted closure," Claire said softly. "It's understandable."

Naomi met her friend's eyes and saw what Claire wasn't saying. That she understood because she too wanted closure. Though judging from the still-present shadows under her friend's pretty hazel eyes, Claire was a long way off from making peace with Brayden's betrayal and death.

"I guess so." Naomi shrugged in agreement. "I know it's stupid to be hung up on something that happened twenty years ago, but it's always haunted me. Not as much as my mom, but people shouldn't get to act like that."

There was a long moment of silence, interrupted by a knock at the door that had all three women jumping slightly. Audrey hopped up. "Ooh. There's our cheese!"

Audrey went to the door, Louboutins clicking on the hardwood as she opened the front door. You had to admire a woman who wore four-inch heels on moving day and got a composed cheese plate delivered.

"Oh. Hello there! You're not cheese."

A masculine chuckle came from the other side of the door, then a low voice irritatingly familiar. "No, ma'am. And if that's what you were expecting, this champagne might be a disappointment."

"It's Dom," Audrey told the man cheerfully, with a quick look at the bottle. "That's never a disappointment. You must be here to see Naomi?"

Naomi stood up as Oliver Cunningham stepped into her living room, looking obscenely expensive in a sleek gray suit, a two-hundred-dollar bottle of champagne in hand.

She swallowed, suddenly very aware of her ratty jeans and T-shirt. It was annoying as heck that this man could make her feel like a nine-year-old again, wanting desperately to belong in his world.

"I didn't mean to interrupt," he said with a slight smile. "Just wanted to say welcome to the neighborhood. We could use some fresh blood around here."

So *that* was how it was going to be. He was playing nice, as though they hadn't been like oil and water at her interview for this apartment. As though he hadn't made her childhood completely miserable.

Naomi didn't smile back.

And it took all of her self-control not to retort that she wasn't fresh blood at 517 Park Avenue, and if anyone should know that, it should be Oliver Cunningham. After all, it had been his casual lie that had damned Naomi and her mother all those years ago.

But judging from his bland smile? He still didn't have a clue that he was standing face-to-face with the childhood nemesis who'd once thrown a soccer ball at his face.

Chapter Nine

*O*liver didn't have sisters, but he'd had enough girlfriends over the course of his life to know when to tread carefully. Stumbling unwittingly into a girls' night was one of those times.

The pretty brunette who'd answered the door seemed friendly enough. Tall and slim, she had a refined prettiness that reminded him of the girls he'd gone to prep school with. Thankfully though, her smile was genuine and refreshingly free of the snobbishness he so often saw among what he thought of as the "headband set": girls whose primary goal had been shiny hair, Ivy League, and marrying money.

But while the brunette was friendly, the redhead he'd come to see in the first place looked . . . well, ready to shank him.

If Naomi Powell had seemed surprised and irritated by his very existence when he'd met her last week, she looked as though she'd had some time to think on it and had come up disliking him even more.

The thought was intriguing. And a little puzzling. Truth be told, Oliver wasn't really accustomed to people not liking him.

He'd heard his mother telling Ruth once that she was almost grateful he'd been such a menace as a kid, because he'd worked out all the bad parts of his personality early on. He supposed it was probably true. He had been a bit of a jerk as a boy, but by high school he'd sort of figured out who he was, or who he wanted to be, and had quit being the nightmare on the playground, so to speak. Now he thought of himself as perfectly affable, if perhaps a bit reserved and sarcastic.

Naomi Powell didn't seem to agree. Her blue eyes were narrowed, arms crossed, as though he'd brought her a rat from the subway instead of some rather expensive champagne.

"Oliver?"

He dragged his gaze away from the irrationally irate redhead as he finally registered the third woman in the room. He blinked in recognition, quickly filed through his mental Rolodex, and came up with a name. "Claire. How are you?"

Then he winced, as his brain caught up to what he knew about Claire Hayes. What a crap question to ask to a recent widow.

"I was sorry to hear about Brayden," he said, going to her, and, setting the champagne on the table, took both her hands in his.

She squeezed and gave a brief, forced smile. "Thank you."

"You two know each other?" Naomi asked, sounding severely displeased about the fact.

"Loosely," Claire explained. "Oliver and I . . ." She looked at him. "Well, how *do* we know each other?"

Oliver scratched his cheek and thought it over. Claire and her husband, Brayden, weren't friends of his, per se, but they'd been friendly enough when they saw each other at the same fund-raisers and holiday gatherings. The New York elite set could be a little incestuous in its connections—everyone knew everyone, but you rarely knew *how* you knew someone.

"Rob Eagel?" Oliver said, taking his best guess.

Claire snapped her fingers in confirmation. "*Yes*. He used to work with Brayden."

Oliver pointed at himself. "Rob's my poker buddy."

He didn't add the fact that Brayden had joined them a few times for poker night as well. He doubted a recent widow wanted to hear that her late husband had generally lost large sums of money before drunkenly announcing he was headed over to his mistress's.

"How do you all know each other?" he asked politely but also curiously. He and Claire had never gotten much beyond small talk in their various run-ins, but he had a hard time imagining the calm, mild-mannered Claire being close with Naomi. One was friendly and socially appropriate, the other snarly and volatile, from what he'd seen so far.

There was a long moment of silence, and Oliver was astute enough to notice that the look the three women exchanged was loaded. He couldn't quite decipher their silent communication, but apparently Claire did, because she nodded slightly at Naomi, who gave him the sweetest smile he'd ever seen.

Oliver immediately was on edge. A sweet smile from this woman somehow felt like a weapon.

"Audrey and I were sleeping with Claire's husband."

As Oliver blinked, trying to absorb that, Naomi's smile grew even more sugary. And more dangerous. She nodded at the champagne, fluttering her eyelashes. "Is that for me?"

He looked down at the Dom Pérignon, still too stunned by her bombshell to do anything other than wordlessly hold out the bottle.

"How does the high society set play this?" Naomi said with an affected air in her tone, taking the bottle and holding it up slightly. "Am I supposed to open it now so we can all enjoy, or is it a faux pas not to save it for a special occasion?"

"Open it," Oliver commanded a little gruffly. Rudely, actually. But, hell, he needed a drink.

Brayden Hayes and Naomi had been having an affair? *And* the woman who'd answered the door?

And all three women were . . . *friends*?

Surely Naomi had been messing with him. But a quick glance at Claire and the brunette showed that she hadn't. The brunette took pity on him and stepped forward, hand extended. "Hi, I'm Audrey Tate. Brayden and I had been dating nearly a year before he died. I thought he was the love of my life—turns out he was the scourge of the earth."

Oliver let out an involuntary laugh as Naomi popped the cork on the champagne. "I only have coffee mugs to serve it in. That a problem?"

It was more of a challenge than a question, and Oliver was irritated that she obviously expected snobbery from him. So he gave it to her.

"Dom Pérignon in a mug? I think not. I'm happy to run next door to get the proper stemware."

Wordlessly she held his gaze as she slowly, deliberately upturned the bottle and unceremoniously glugged a liberal amount of champagne into the porcelain mug. Her auburn brows lifted in challenge, daring him to comment.

Instead, he ignored her completely and turned back to Audrey. "I'm Oliver Cunningham. I live next door and was *not* having sex with Brayden Hayes."

She laughed. "Well, that makes you the only one in the room."

Unintentionally, Oliver looked at Naomi, who was rummaging through a box, coming up with more mugs, but no wine-glasses. He suspected even if there were wine flutes around, she'd have ignored them to spite him.

"Yup," she said without looking up. "I was Brayden's whore."

Claire exhaled. "Naomi."

"Well, wasn't I?" Naomi asked, looking up. "I mean, you were married to him. He at least took Audrey on *dates*. But me?" She shrugged, and though Oliver knew it wasn't his business, he was more intrigued than he should have been by how she would finish that sentence.

The thought of Naomi Powell and Brayden Hayes hooking up was— *Nope*. He didn't want to go there.

And the thought of Naomi Powell naked . . .

No, he didn't want to go there, either. She was the exact opposite of his type. And while he'd voted her into the building with the hopes of her being a distraction, he hadn't intended it to be of the naked, hookup variety.

Though if she kept wearing those tight-fitting jeans, he may have to reconsider.

"Well, now that that's out of the way," Audrey said, clapping her hands and coming to retrieve the mugs of champagne Naomi had just finished pouring. "Shall we toast? To Naomi's new home and her handsome new neighbor? How long have you lived here, Mr. Cunningham?"

"Oliver," he said with a smile, accepting the bulky white mug and realizing it was the first time he'd ever drunk champagne out of anything other than crystal. Suddenly he felt very much like the uppity snob Naomi seemed to think he was. And his next words all but confirmed it. "And I've actually lived here most of my life."

The realization was a little jarring. Oliver had never really thought of himself as a snob, but seeing himself through Naomi Powell's hate-filled eyes, he had to admit that he was a little . . . fuddy-duddy.

"Really!" Audrey said. "Naomi was just telling us that she—"

Audrey broke off midsentence, and it didn't take a psychic to see why. And refreshing as it was to see Naomi's death glare directed at someone other than himself, he was curious to know what Audrey had been going to say.

Claire stepped in and covered the awkward moment. "Thank you so much for the flowers you sent after Brayden's passing."

Oliver tugged lightly at his tie. "Honestly, had I known how he treated you, I might have sent something a little less lavish. And I— Well hell, this is awkward, isn't it?"

Claire laughed. "It is, although selfishly it's also refreshing. Other than Naomi and Audrey, I haven't been able to discuss Brayden's true nature with anyone. I'm sure plenty of people have their suspicions, but nobody will speak of anything other than tragedy to me. Not that I'd speak ill of the dead, but . . ."

"Oh, go for it," Naomi said. "I do."

"Well now, there's a surprise," Oliver muttered.

She ignored him. "Seriously though, Claire, you don't have to let people speak to you like you're a victim. You have your life back."

"Yes, but at the cost of his," Claire said softly.

Naomi sighed and then walked to Claire, putting her arm around her shoulders. "You're right. I'm being a bitch."

"No," Claire said, just as Oliver thought *yup*. "You're just, well, let's say I'm jealous. You've got your business to keep you busy, a new apartment to distract you . . ."

Claire glanced at Oliver. "I'm so sorry. This probably isn't what you were expecting when you came over to welcome your new neighbor."

"Definitely not," he admitted. "But I'm grateful you're here. I'm afraid without witnesses, Ms. Powell would be putting that box cutter in her pocket to lethal use."

Audrey laughed. "Naomi wouldn't hurt a fly."

"A fly, no," Naomi said, flicking a gaze his way to let him know that he wasn't *nearly* as safe as said fly.

"All right, I give up," he said, spreading his hands to the side. "What did I do, Ms. Powell? What about me put me on your list before I even knew your name?"

He saw Audrey and Claire exchange a look, and then Claire tapped her watch. "Oh my goodness. Is that the time? Audrey, we've got to go if we're going to make that movie."

"Really?" Naomi said, her tone making it clear what she thought of her friends' flimsy excuse to get out of the apartment. "What movie?"

Claire and Audrey named two different movies at the exact same time, and Naomi rolled her eyes. "I thought you guys were going to help me unpack."

Audrey slid her purse over her shoulder and held up her fingers. "I tried, I did, but I've reached the max on what I can do without chipping a nail."

Claire now looked slightly less sure about leaving Oliver and Naomi alone, but Audrey was dragging her toward the door.

"What about your champagne!" Naomi said. "I'm pretty sure it's an *actual* crime to leave Dom behind in this neighborhood. You could be arrested. Oliver here probably has the etiquette police on speed dial."

"You two can finish it. Maybe the fancy bubbles will remind you of your manners," Audrey said with a pointed look at Naomi.

"Oh, do you have those?" he asked, turning to Naomi.

"Well, it's not like you were an invited guest," she snapped, turning toward him. "You just came in here with your fancy booze and your stick-up-the-butt—"

The door clicked closed as Audrey and Claire left.

Naomi pointed at the door accusingly. "Look what you did."

"Me?" He set his mug on top of a stack of boxes and, hands on his hips, turned to face her fully. "You've acted like an irrational child since the moment I met you. Tell me exactly what it is I've done that so offended you."

She opened her mouth, but he wasn't done and charged ahead.

"Was it the champagne gift? The fact that I tried to welcome a new neighbor? That without my vote, you wouldn't be living here? Which of these many crimes am I being punished for?"

She chugged a large swallow of Dom Pérignon as though it were a Bud Light at the local pub and, setting her mug aside, reached behind her and pulled out the orange box cutter.

Her thumb flicked the blade open, and he gave her a look. "Really? Is that supposed to be threatening?"

Instead of responding, she turned toward the nearest box and dragged the blade across the tape with more force than necessary. "If you'll excuse me, I need to get settled in."

Retracting the box cutter's sharp edge, she shoved it back into her jeans pocket and turned her back to him. His dismissal was clear. And it pissed him off. Acting on instinct, Oliver stomped toward her and pulled the box cutter out of her pocket, sorry-not-sorry that the backs of his fingers brushed her denim-clad rear as he did so.

Naomi whirled back toward him, eyes disbelieving and angry, but this time it was he who flicked open the blade. It represented a shift in power, and they both knew it.

He took a sip of his champagne, set it on the small kitchen

table beside Audrey's and Claire's discarded mugs, and then slowly, taking his sweet time, opened one of the boxes labeled KITCHEN.

"What are you doing?"

"You said you needed to get settled in. What are neighbors for?"

"Collecting your newspapers when you're out of town and not playing loud music after ten p.m.," she said, snatching the box cutter back.

"I can do those things, too," he said, lifting out a heavy bundle of tissue paper and unwrapping it to find a bunch of forks. "Where are you putting your silverware?"

"Leave," she said through gritted teeth.

"Not until you tell me why you hate me," he said, stepping around her into the kitchen, opening drawers until he found one that held what appeared to be a brand-new silverware organizer. He put the forks into one of the slots and returned to the box, pulling out a similarly shaped bundle.

"This is the most juvenile conversation I've had in decades," Naomi said, running a hand over her hair and glaring at him as he placed her tablespoons next to her forks.

Oliver shrugged. No argument there. Though, ridiculous as the whole situation was, he was a little surprised to realize he was enjoying himself. He'd voted Naomi Powell into the building in hopes of a distraction, and so far the woman was delivering marvelously.

"You know, I've never been in this unit?" he said, looking around.

"I'm not surprised. It's the smallest floor plan in the building, right?"

"Yes, and the walls aren't made of gold in this one," he said, wandering in the direction of the other rooms. "And no money tree, either. Shame."

Unabashedly he stepped into one of the rooms, the connected bathroom telling him it was intended to be the master bedroom. She followed him, standing in the doorway, and he lifted his eyebrows. "King mattress. Lot of bed for a single woman," he said, just to provoke her.

She gave a smile that reminded him of a satisfied cat. "Who said I'm single?"

The mention of her love life reminded him of the bombshell Claire had dropped earlier. "So. Brayden Hayes, huh?"

Her smile dropped. "Not open for discussion."

"You're the one who brought it up," he pointed out.

She gave him an icy glare and turned away, but he grabbed her arm, a little surprised by his own action. Still, he didn't let her go. "I'm not a bad guy, Naomi."

Naomi remained stubbornly silent before letting her gaze drop deliberately to where he held her arm.

Oliver sighed and gave up, releasing her. "Fine. It's been a few years since I've had an immature nemesis, but I can get on board. Just so I know the rules, is this a cold war, prank war, noise war . . . do I just launch spitballs at you in the mail room?"

Something flickered in her gaze, but before he could identify it, she turned away.

Oliver followed her back into the living room, but instead of resuming his unpacking of her silverware, he headed toward the door.

"Enjoy your solitude, Ms. Powell."

He stepped into the hallway and shut the door before she could reply—though he was fairly certain she had zero intention of replying.

Oliver stormed back to his own apartment, feeling more irritated and also more alive than he had in months. What the hell was the woman's problem, he wondered, yanking open his fridge only to slam it shut again when he realized it was empty.

He'd encountered his fair share of man haters, but this seemed personal somehow.

Oliver pulled out his phone and was debating ordering something for delivery when there was a sharp, businesslike knock at his door. He checked the peephole and, seeing nobody, opened the door.

Just in time to hear his neighbor's door close.

Oliver glanced down. At his feet was a white coffee mug of champagne—she must have topped it off because it was fuller than when he'd left it—as well as a plate piled high with an assortment of fancy cheeses.

He glanced to his right down the deserted hall, then smiled a little as he bent and picked up the items. He set the mug and plate on his kitchen island and flipped up the folded index card she'd used as a note.

I didn't spit in the champagne. Probably.
—N.

Oliver grinned at the begrudging peace offering, and took both the cheese plate and champagne to his coffee table, where he turned on the TV. For a split second, he considered putting the Dom Pérignon into one of the Waterford champagne glasses his mother had given him as a housewarming gift when he'd moved into his apartment.

He decided against it. Turned out, it tasted better from the mug.

Chapter Ten

If there was an award for settling into a new apartment in record time, Naomi would like to think she'd be a contender. She'd worked her butt off for three straight days to unpack and break down every box, hang up every item of clothing, and find a new home for every last knickknack and handbag.

She'd even hung curtains.

Not that anyone had come around to see her handiwork, and . . . well, that was all on her, now wasn't it?

Somehow, Naomi had managed to cause two friends and a new neighbor to go running out of her apartment in the span of thirty minutes.

None of them had been back since.

Not one of Naomi's finer moments to be sure. And though she'd apologized profusely to Claire and Audrey for her churlish mode, she hadn't *quite* gotten around to facing Oliver Cunningham again.

On one hand, she probably owed him an apology. His gesture had been neighborly—friendly, even. And she'd been nothing but rude. On the *other* hand, she was having a hell of a time separating out her memories of *young* Oliver Cunningham. The version whose manners hadn't been nearly as pretty.

Was it fair to punish a man for a boy's mistakes? Perhaps not.

But they didn't just have name-calling in their history. They also had a boy's careless lie that had *literally* ruined lives.

She wasn't quite ready to forgive him for that, no matter how charming the man was. Or how handsome.

If she were honest with herself, her irritation at his presence had been just as much directed at herself, for *noticing* the man. When she'd first come face-to-face with him at her co-op interview, she'd been too frazzled by his presence to properly register just how good-looking he was.

But the other day, she'd *noticed*. She'd noticed the way he'd lost the soft edges of his boyish features. Noticed the way the nose that had been just slightly too long as a kid was now perfectly balanced by a strong jaw and a piercing gaze.

Even his *eyebrows* were sexy. Straight and thick and dark, especially in contrast to the light blue eyes.

Handsome though he was, she was a little surprised by just how reserved Oliver had become. The boy she remembered had been boisterous and rowdy, loving worms and sports and dirt.

Adult Oliver looked like he wouldn't be able to identify dirt if it hit him in the face (now, *there* was a tempting thought), and there was a coolness about him that she didn't remember.

Irritated with herself for dwelling on Oliver—again—Naomi stood and, putting her hands over her head, began stretching as she looked out at the rainy afternoon.

Her new apartment had two bedrooms, and since she had no use for a guest room, she had plans to turn the second one into a home office. But the new furniture she'd ordered wouldn't arrive until tomorrow, which meant she was working at her kitchen table.

Deena had been right about the team loving the temporary "work from home" arrangement. During their usual Monday-morning conference call, Naomi had noted less makeup and more messy buns, and though everyone had put on business-appropriate attire on top, she wouldn't be surprised to learn that below the camera's view, everyone was in yoga pants.

Or maybe that was just her.

Still, luxurious as it was to not have to leave her home and commute to an office for the next few weeks, she was learning the hard way that her kitchen chair was not cut out for an almost-thirty butt and back to sit in for long amounts of time.

Naomi pressed her fingers into her lower back, arching backward as she mentally began composing an email to a potential advertiser whose pushy tactics were starting to piss her off. She had just settled on her phrasing when she heard a commotion outside her front door.

She ignored it at first. One of her neighbors had a bichon that delighted in getting out of the apartment and engaging in a five-minute battle of wills with its owner as it decided whether "a yummy, yummy doggy cookie" was incentive enough to go back home.

But the sound kept on, and finally she registered that this was different. There was no quick little patter of tiny-dog feet or cajoling voice of the elderly owner promising chicken.

This was more of a slow shuffle and occasional muttered oath.

Naomi went to the door and checked the peephole. Nothing. Slowly she opened it and stepped into the hall, her eyes going wide in surprise at the source of the noise.

An older man was wearing an expensive-looking sweater over what seemed to be a perfectly starched collared shirt.

And on the bottom? Light blue boxers and argyle dress socks.

Pants? Not present.

She watched for a moment as he shuffled a few feet, paused. Pounded the wall lightly with his fist, then put his ear to the wall as though listening for something. He muttered something, then repeated the process.

"Sir?" Naomi asked tentatively.

He went still, then slowly turned on slightly unsteady feet to face her.

Naomi gasped.

She'd envisioned this moment dozens of times. Maybe hundreds of times. She'd pictured, in very vivid detail, the moment she'd come face-to-face with Walter Cunningham, the man who'd had an affair with her mother and then thrown her and her mother out on the streets like they were trash. Hell, he'd *called* them trash.

She'd pictured entering his cushy downtown office, chin held high. She'd envisioned knocking on his door and him angrily asking who the hell she was, only to pass out in shock when she told him.

She'd envisioned seeing him in a bar, buying him the most expensive Scotch on the menu, and then observing his surprise when he realized who'd just paid for his drink.

There'd been a handful of more vindictive scenarios as well, but not *one* had come close to the reality of *this*.

Naomi hadn't expected him to recognize her on sight. He'd barely paid attention to her twenty years ago, and she was a far cry from her nine-year-old self. Her hair was several shades darker than the neon orange of her childhood. Her first "big" purchase once Maxcessory began to take off was braces, so her horribly crooked teeth were a thing of the past. She still wore glasses, but only at night and first thing in the morning. And even without all of that, she'd simply grown up.

But while she hadn't expected him to recognize her as his ex-lover's daughter, Naomi hadn't been prepared for the possibility that he perhaps didn't recognize *anyone*.

His gaze was vacant and confused, and though she wanted desperately to hate him—still *did* hate him on some level—her heart twisted a little in sympathy.

The fog in his eyes cleared slightly, replaced with irritation. His hands went to his hips, thick brows drawn into a glower. It was a move that she remembered as being extremely intimidating when she'd accidentally knocked over a water glass as a girl. The effect was diminished now by the lack of pants.

"May I help you, young lady?"

Oh boy. Naomi was thoroughly out of her depth here. She hadn't spent much time with senior citizens and certainly not with someone who she suspected was affected by dementia.

Did she act like nothing was wrong? Did she take charge of the situation?

She glanced at Oliver's door, wondering if the man was home, though she suspected at one p.m. on a Monday, he was likely at work.

"Are you looking for Oliver?" she asked tentatively.

Walter Cunningham's frown deepened, looking lost in thought. "Oliver . . ." His expression cleared slightly. "Oliver's my son."

"Yes, and he lives right there," she said tentatively as she stepped further into the hallway, pointing at Oliver's door. "You were looking for him?"

"No, I don't think so," Walter mused, glancing at the wall opposite Oliver's door. "I thought I heard something. A person."

"In the walls?" Naomi asked, keeping her voice light.

"Yes."

"It's an old building. Perhaps the pipes?" she said, stepping even closer.

"Perhaps, perhaps." He knocked again, then seemed to lose interest in the walls altogether, turning toward her. "Who are you?"

"My name's Naomi. I just moved in," she said, pointing to her open door.

Walter frowned. "That's Harriet's place."

"Yes," Naomi said, relieved that he was mentally present enough to know that much. The woman who'd just vacated Naomi's apartment had indeed been named Harriet. "She moved to Pennsylvania to be closer to her daughter."

"Shame. Everyone's leaving." He looked at her sharply. "Have you seen my Margaret?"

Margaret. His wife. His *dead* wife. There it was again. That twist of sympathy for a man she'd spent her entire life despising. She pursed her lips, now officially panicked. Did she tell him his wife had passed away? Or would that only confuse him further?

"Do you live upstairs?"

She'd kept tabs on the Cunninghams over the years, and was pretty sure they'd never moved, but she wasn't positive.

"Upstairs?" He frowned. He started to push past her. Not toward the stairs, but toward Naomi's own apartment.

"Would you like to come in?" she asked needlessly, since he was already entering her apartment. "I could make us some coffee? Or tea?"

She hoped he wouldn't say tea. She didn't drink the stuff and didn't have any.

"I'd take a whisky," he was already saying, charging into her living room on steadier steps than before.

A whisky? Oh dear.

She followed him into her apartment, smiling a little as she saw him already settling on her couch, pulling one of her throw blankets over his lap and reaching for the remote. "Got any Scotch?"

"Um, I'll check," she said, stalling for time.

What now? Surely someone stayed with him during the day, but she didn't want to leave him alone while she went up to his apartment to check. She didn't have Oliver Cunningham's phone number. She did have the number of Ms. Gromwell, the woman who'd facilitated the move-in process, but it didn't feel right to call her about the Cunninghams' personal business just yet.

Wait! Didn't the elderly sometimes wear those bracelets? The medical emergency kind, with a contact number?

Walter's thumb pressed the remote with deliberation, obviously looking for a specific channel. "Wish there was a day game today," he muttered before stopping on the History Channel.

"You like baseball?" Naomi asked casually, sitting beside him on the couch, her gaze scanning his wrists. She closed her eyes in relief when she saw the silver bracelet on his left wrist. It was stylish, compared to the flimsy one in her imagination, but she was pretty sure the red symbol was a medical indicator of some sort.

"May I see your bracelet?" she asked with what she hoped was a calm, friendly smile.

Not friendly enough, apparently. Walter snatched his hand away from her reach, giving her a suspicious look. "Who are you?"

Naomi kept her smile in place as she repeated her introduction. "I'm Naomi, Mr. Cunningham."

He narrowed his eyes and studied her. "I know you?"

In ways you can't even imagine.

"We're friends," she lied smoothly, because he was starting to look a little bit scared beneath his defiance. "I was hoping to look at your bracelet."

He pulled his arm even further out of reach, his agitation increasing along with his suspicion.

Inspiration struck.

"Did you know I run an accessory business?" she asked, pretending to lose interest in seeing his bracelet and pulling her legs beneath her on the couch.

"A business?" His gaze sharpened with alertness, and she saw a flash of the cutthroat Walter Cunningham of her memories.

She nodded. "I started it myself. It's called Maxcessory, and it's a subscription model. Members pay an annual fee to receive a box of accessories selected for them every month. Earrings, bracelets, necklaces. Sometimes a scarf or sunglasses."

"Feminine trinkets."

Naomi couldn't help the quick laugh at the description. It was such an old-fashioned male thing to say, and yet his tone hadn't been disparaging so much as trying to understand.

"Most of our members are women," she admitted. "But last year we introduced an option for men as well. Cuff links, belts, pocket squares. We've seen some tremendous growth."

He seemed to think this over. "You should put some suspenders into the mix. I can't find any good ones these days."

"I'll mention it to the team," Naomi assured him. And she would, because she kept promises, though she was fairly sure suspenders were too niche a market for Maxcessory's average customer.

She continued, keeping her voice casual and calm. "I don't know if I have any of my male accessories here in my home office, but would you like to see what we're sending out to the women?"

Walter looked unconvinced. "You make a profit from this?"

Naomi named Maxcessory's astronomically high revenue from the previous year, and Walter's bushy eyebrows went up. "All right. I'd like to take a look. I used to invest in businesses, you know."

She did know, but his investment money, whether real or imagined given his current state, wasn't her goal.

Naomi went into her office. She didn't have her desk furniture yet, but she had organized her inventory as best she could in boxes along the wall. She picked an assortment of items with emphasis on one type of jewelry in particular.

Returning to the living room, she laid out the pieces on the coffee table, and Walter scooted forward on the couch to take a look. He patted his right breast pocket where she imagined he often kept readers. "Damn," he muttered. "Forgot my glasses."

He made do by bringing the pieces extremely close to his face, studying each item with more interest than she'd have expected, given they were all "feminine trinkets."

"Quality seems pretty good," he admitted.

"Yes, I'm keeping an eye out for high-quality products that can easily be scaled, since we need thousands of each piece. It's why I was so interested in your bracelet," she said offhandedly. "It's a bad habit of mine, studying just about any piece of jewelry I can get my hands on."

He stared at his wrist for a moment, as though surprised to see the bracelet there. Then he shrugged. "It's better than the last one they gave me. Nicer. Good metal, see?"

She closed her eyes in relief when she saw him reach for the clasp.

"You need any help?" she asked. "Bracelets are always hard to get on and off yourself with one hand."

Wordlessly, he extended his wrist to her, and Naomi's fingers quickly found the fastener and removed it before he could change his mind again.

In the blink of an eye, Walter's attention had shifted away from her and the jewelry, and back to the TV, where the monotone narrator was describing the gruesome details of a World War I battle.

Naomi looked down at the bracelet.

Walter had been correct—the bracelet itself was nice. Lovely for a men's piece, with thick metal and excellent craftsmanship on the links.

The placard though . . .

Even though she'd had a good sense of what she'd see there, the top two lines of inscription still caused a pang of sadness.

Walter Cunningham. Alzheimer's.

She exhaled.

Below that was a name and phone number.

With a quick glance to see that Walter wouldn't freak out on her, she stood and went to the counter where she'd plugged in her cell phone.

"You got any Scotch?" Walter asked again, without turning around.

"I'll look in a minute," she said as she punched in the phone number on Walter's bracelet, and with one eye on the back of Walter's gray head, she lifted the phone to her ear as it began to ring.

Chapter Eleven

*I*t wasn't the first time that Janice had called him to calmly and apologetically inform him that his father had gotten out of the house, but those bad-news phone calls never got any easier to hear.

Oliver bit the inside of his cheek to keep from shouting at the cab driver to go faster. It wasn't the driver's fault that Manhattan traffic generally sucked. It wasn't the driver's fault that his father had wandered out of the house.

It wasn't even Janice's fault. She'd apologized profusely, but he knew all too well it was a risk of having one person alone caring for this father. The woman had to use the restroom at some point, and she couldn't very well lock his father up while she did so. And considering Walter often went from happily eating his hard-boiled eggs to deciding to take himself for a walk within five seconds . . .

Oliver only hoped his father hadn't wandered far. Most often he went to one of the neighbors' on their floor, or to Oliver's apartment. Janice had checked all the usual places, and then went to look at the more alarming option: Central Park.

Ironically, his father had always refused Oliver's childhood begging to go to the park to throw a ball around, but in his current state, he *loved* the park. Trouble was, Central Park was several hundred acres. Walter didn't move very fast, but it was a hell of a lot of space when trying to locate one man.

Oliver was stopped at a traffic light two blocks from his apartment, debating whether it would be faster to get out and walk the remainder, when his cell rang.

It was an unfamiliar number, but Oliver answered without hesitation, even as he braced for bad news.

His tone was curt. "Oliver Cunningham."

"Oliver, hi."

He frowned. The voice was female and husky. Distinctly so. "Naomi?"

"Yeah. Hi. Um, well, okay, no *non*-awkward way to say this . . . I have your father here?"

His hand fell away from the door handle of the cab, his body slumping back in relief. "Here? As in, he's at your apartment?"

"Yep. I found him wandering the hall outside your door. He's okay," she said softly, anticipating his next question. "He's watching TV and demanding Scotch?"

Oliver smiled slightly. Counterintuitively, Scotch days were *good* days in Walter Cunningham's world. A connection to his old self who had an affinity for Macallan.

"Don't judge me for asking," Naomi said slowly, "but can he?"

"Can he what?" Oliver asked, fishing a few bills out of his wallet and handing them to the cab driver. He exited the taxi without waiting for change.

"I have some Scotch . . ." She trailed off.

His relief at knowing his father was safe and warm instead of lost in the city was settling in now, and Oliver grinned as he stepped out onto the sidewalk. "Ms. Powell. Are you suggesting giving my sick father alcohol in the middle of the afternoon?"

"Right," she said quickly. "Forget it. I don't know what—"

"A finger with ice with a splash of water. A *big* splash. He'll fuss, but if you tell him it's that or nothing, he'll settle down."

There was a moment of hesitation. "Really?"

"Really," Oliver assured her. "Listen, his caretaker's still out looking for him. I need to give her a call. But I'll be there in just a couple minutes. You okay until then?"

"We're fine."

"Good. Thank you. See you in a few."

He hung up the phone and immediately called Janice, who picked up on the first ring, a little breathless. "You find him?"

"The neighbor did. He was outside my apartment."

Her breath whooshed out in relief. "Thank God. Which neighbor? Why didn't she call me?"

"The new neighbor," Oliver clarified as he walked up Park Avenue. "She doesn't have your phone number, but I'll make sure she gets it."

"I'm so sorry, Mr. Cunningham, it won't happen again—"

"Yeah, it will," Oliver said gently. "We both do our best, but we're human, Janice. And for the hundredth time, call me Oliver."

"Yes. Oliver," she said stiffly, clearly uncomfortable. "But I really am sorry. I just went to the restroom, he wasn't out of my sight for more than a minute."

"I know," he said, feeling a wave of regret. Not because of Janice—he'd meant what he said. Even a full-time caretaker couldn't be with Walter every second of every day. But regret over the disease. Because while these scary moments were rare now, it's possible they wouldn't always be.

"The new neighbor's in 2B, right?" she said, her tone returning to its normal no-nonsense mode. "I can be there in less than ten minutes to retrieve Mr. Cunningham."

"Don't worry about it. I'm closer."

She huffed in dismay. "You left work."

"I did. Not a big deal, I didn't have any meetings that couldn't be rescheduled. Why don't you take the afternoon off?"

"Oh, I couldn't."

"That's an order, Janice," he said as he let himself into the main door of the building. "Dad and I will see you later tonight."

She apparently knew him well enough to know that arguing at this point was pointless. "All right. Thank you, Mr. Cunningham."

He rolled his eyes. He didn't know why he ever bothered with the *call me Oliver* bit. Oliver took the stairs two at a time until he was standing outside Naomi Powell's apartment.

He heard the unmistakable sound of the History Channel playing softly on the other side of the door, and he gave in to a moment of weakness, resting his forehead lightly on the wall outside her apartment, acknowledging his relief that his father had been found by someone kind.

He pulled his head back at that. *Kind* was not a word he'd ever thought could be applied to the prickly Ms. Powell, but there'd been no mistaking the gentleness in her tone on the phone. It had given the low rasp of her voice a whole new level of intrigue.

He lifted his hand and knocked.

Naomi opened the door, and Oliver's mouth went dry, his tongue sticking to the top of his mouth for a long, humiliating moment. She didn't look glamorous. Far from it. Her hair was straight and tucked behind her ears, her face free of makeup, or at least any that he could notice.

It was the attire that got him.

Black pants snug enough for him to know the exact shape of her thighs, cut to midcalf, and until this moment he hadn't understood why it had been scandalous for women to show their ankles back in the day.

It was because bare ankles and feet could be *hot*.

Thank God she wore a baggy sweater, because he didn't think he could handle anything formfitting above the waist. Though the sweater did hang off one shoulder just a bit, revealing the slim strap of a bra or tank top and . . .

Naomi gave him an irritated look. "What's with you?"

He shook his head. Right. "Sorry," he said, running a hand through his hair. "It's always a little unnerving when my dad gets out. Guess I'm still off balance."

Oliver's conscience was shaking its head disapprovingly. Had he really just used his sick father to avoid admitting he'd been checking out Naomi?

"Understandable," she said, hesitating for just the briefest moment before stepping aside. "Come on in."

Oliver's gaze went straight to the TV, where his father sat on Naomi's white sofa. His conscience was *slightly* mollified by the fact that Oliver really was relieved to see his dad sitting peacefully. Safe and warm.

"Hey, Dad," he said, keeping his voice breezy and casual as he walked over to the living room.

Walter's eyes reluctantly dragged away from the television screen to Oliver. Walter lifted the glass in his hand. "The girl gave me Scotch. Pretty good stuff, but she watered it down too much."

"Hmm, I'll talk to her about that," he said, noting Naomi's eye-roll out of the corner of his eye, though she didn't call him out on how she'd only been following his instructions.

"Say, Dad, what do you say we go finish this show upstairs so we can let Ms. Powell get back to her day?"

His dad's attention was already back on the TV. "Not done with my drink."

"I bet she'd let us take it with us and return the glass later," Oliver said. Then he glanced over at Naomi for confirmation.

"You Cunningham men do like to keep my glassware."

"Missing that mug, are ya?" he asked, referring to the coffee cup full of champagne she'd left over the weekend.

"It was a favorite."

"What did it look like?"

She pursed her lips. She didn't have a damn clue what it looked like, and they both knew it. "It was one of my only ones."

Oliver walked into her kitchen, opened the cupboard to the right of the sink—guessing correctly the first time—and turned to face her, eyebrows lifted.

Her lips pursed even more. There were close to a dozen mugs in the cupboard, which he'd known, since he'd seen her unpacking them on move-in day.

"But by all means," he said coolly, closing the cupboard once more. "I'll *definitely* rush to return the one you lent me."

Instead of replying, she rounded the kitchen counter toward him, opening the cupboard he had just shut. Their fingers brushed, just for a moment, and she went perfectly still before shoving his hand away and pulling two mugs out of the cupboard.

She set both on the counter and, in silent question, lifted the bottle of Scotch she'd poured his father's drink from.

He nodded in silent response. Generally speaking, he wasn't prone to day drinking, but then he also wasn't accustomed to verbal battles with attractive women who lived next door.

"Ice?"

"Please," he said as she opened the freezer. "One cube."

She dropped one ice cube into his, two into her own, and handed him a mug.

Hers said *Work, Play, Slay* in hot-pink letters, his had a dumb cartoon kitten. Ten bucks said the selection was no accident.

"Cheers," he said before she could take a sip.

Naomi looked at his mug skeptically. "To what?"

"Well, I'm not dead yet," Oliver said wryly. "More than I expected based on our encounter on Saturday. And at your interview."

He meant it in jest, but she winced slightly, and too late he remembered: Brayden Hayes. She may not have been married to the man, but presumably she'd cared about him if they were sleeping together.

"Shit," he muttered. "I wasn't thinking—"

"Forget it," she said. "Also, before I forget . . ." She picked up Walter's medical bracelet off the counter and handed it to Oliver.

He accepted the heavy weight of the masculine bracelet. He'd purchased it for his father after about a dozen fights over the old one being "too prissy." When his father was in a lucid state, he was with it enough to know that in Walter Cunningham's reality, men didn't wear jewelry.

"I'm surprised you got it off him," Oliver said, juggling the bracelet in his hand.

"Oh, we had a little you show me yours, I'll show you mine."

Oliver choked on his Scotch. "Excuse me?"

She gestured at the coffee table, where an assortment of jewelry pieces lay scattered about. "The perks of running an accessory business. I've got plenty of pieces on hand."

"Maxcessory," Oliver said distractedly.

Naomi gave him a curious look.

"It was on your application," he explained.

"Speaking of that day, why did you put me through to the next round?"

"You mean after you stormed out of the office for no reason?"

"Oh, I had reasons," she said into her drink.

"Mind telling me what they were?"

She set down her mug with a heavy thunk. "You're just very . . ."

Naomi waved her hand over him, wrinkling her nose as she tried to think of the right word.

"Polite? Professional?" he prompted, recalling the interview from his perspective.

"Arrogant. Supercilious. You made it clear that I didn't belong."

"*Supercilious?* And you think *I'm* snobby."

"I didn't say *snobby*," she said, taking a sip of Scotch. "I said *supercilious*."

"You're impossible," Oliver muttered, tossing back the rest of his drink, relishing the burn. "Dad, let's go."

Walter didn't respond.

"Dad." Oliver's voice was just a bit sharper than he usually used with his father, but he needed to get out of here before he did something absurd. Like kiss the woman who he wasn't even sure he liked. And who definitely didn't like him.

Walter gave him a baleful look over his shoulder. "What?"

"Let's go."

His dad got a mutinous look on his face, and Oliver softened his tone. "Janice said she recorded yesterday's Yankees game. I haven't seen it yet."

Walter shrugged and turned back to the History Channel. "You go watch it, then. I already saw it. Five–four, Angels."

Sure, *that* he remembers. Oliver immediately regretted the frustrated thought and dropped his chin to his chest, defeated. Tired.

He'd nearly forgotten Naomi was there, until her low voice came, quieter than usual. Softer. "When was he diagnosed?"

"A few years ago."

"I'm sure it was a shock."

Oliver lifted a shoulder. "There'd been some warning signs, so a part of me was braced for it, but . . . yeah. It still came as a shock, especially so soon after my mom's death."

"I'm sorry," she said genuinely, if a bit stiffly. "That must have been difficult."

He exhaled. "Up until then, I thought *cancer* was the worst diagnosis one could get. It was in the case of my mom. She was gone eleven months after the doctor told us the news. But this . . ." Oliver tilted his head toward his father. "It's a whole other level of hard. It's slow, it's inconsistent. Some days it's almost like I have my dad back, other days he's lost to me completely."

Naomi glanced back at the back of Walter's head, rolling her mug between her small hands. "Who watches him while you work?"

"A full-time caretaker. She's great, but Alzheimer's patients are unpredictable. One second they're watching TV and you think you're fine to take a quick bathroom break, the next moment . . ."

"Does it happen a lot?"

"No. Thankfully. But if it increases, I'll have to consider a home for him. I'm just grateful he's not violent."

Her eyes went wide. "Was he . . . before . . ."

"No," Oliver said quickly. "I mean, he could be a cold son of a bitch before the disease, but he never lifted a hand to me or my mother. Mostly he was just . . . indifferent. But Alzheimer's patients can get frustrated easily and lash out. Not as big a deal when it's a frail five-two woman, but a sixty-something male with a lifetime of regular squash games behind him . . ."

Oliver exhaled and loosened his tie. "I don't know why I'm telling you all of this. But again, thank you."

"Anyone would have done the same."

He shook his head. "Invited a strange man into the home of a single woman? I don't think so."

Her dark red eyebrows winged up. "Not sure the *single* differentiator was necessary there."

"A woman living alone," he amended.

"Better, I guess," she said begrudgingly. "Though why do you keep assuming I'm single? Brayden passed a few months ago, and I didn't date him for that long. Time enough to move on."

For some reason the thought of her being not single made his bad mood even worse. "Sorry to be presumptuous. Who's the lucky man?"

He put just the slightest sarcastic emphasis on *lucky* to needle her.

She dodged the question. "What about you? Any little lady dying for the role of Mrs. Cunningham?"

Was there a note of interest beneath her snide tone? Or just wishful thinking on his part? And then, appalled at what he was about to do, even as he hoped his father would keep his mouth shut, Oliver nodded. "There's someone."

"Oh yeah? What's her name? No, let me guess—"

"Lilah," he blurted out. It was the first name he thought of, courtesy of his receptionist always trying to set him up with her cousin of the same name.

"Mmm. And what do you and Lilah do for fun? Opera? Caviar tastings?"

"Naturally. When we're not at our thrice-weekly Met visit or discussing Tolstoy over tea. Unless it's our Friday-night glass of sherry and poetry."

Her lips twitched in a giveaway smile that she pulled back just in time. "Nice."

"And you and . . . Bob?" he said, supplying the first name that popped into his head.

"Not your kinda guy. Lots of NASCAR. PBR. Spitting contests."

"Spitting contests."

"When he's not adding to his ink."

"How do you know *I* don't have a tattoo?"

He meant the question teasingly, but the way her gaze quickly roamed over him felt teasing in an entirely different way.

Her blue eyes came back to his. "Skull?"

"Clown."

"Of the crazy Stephen King variety?"

"Naturally. Is there any other?"

For a split second, they smiled at each other, amusement replacing animosity. But before it could blossom into something more, Walter decided he'd had enough History Channel, coming into the kitchen and making a beeline for the Scotch bottle.

Oliver swiped it out of reach, and his father gave him an exasperated look. "Give me that."

"It's not ours, Dad. It's Ms. Powell's."

She opened her mouth, likely about to offer more to be hospitable, but she shut it before saying anything. He was grateful that she saw his comment for what it was: less manners, more limiting his father's alcohol consumption.

Oliver let his dad drink sometimes. The doctors frowned on it, but the man had already lost so much. Oliver couldn't bear to take away this one simple pleasure as well.

But he was careful about it. And he wanted to see how the drink Walter had already had would mingle with his current mood.

Walter glared at Naomi. "Who's she?"

"I'm Naomi, Mr. Cunningham," she said, probably not for the first time that day.

He gave her a hard look, up and down in a degrading way that was very much Walter before his illness, but there was no relief at this glimpse of the old Walter. The old Walter, plainly put, had been a womanizing ass.

Walter smirked at Naomi. "You look just like your mother."

Oliver inhaled for patience, knowing it was pointless to tell his father that Walter didn't know Naomi's mother.

"All right, Dad, time to go," Oliver said firmly, picking up his briefcase.

His father didn't move. Neither did Naomi—they stood, locked in a strange staring contest. He expected Naomi to look unnerved, and she did a little, but she also looked angry, and that wasn't fair. It wasn't Walter's fault he was sick.

"He doesn't know what he's saying," Oliver told her stiffly. He hated having to explain his dad's condition in front of his father, but he had to say something to get that look off her face.

She swallowed and gave Oliver a fleeting look, but the earlier flirtation was gone.

Instead she nodded stiffly, and a moment later he and his father had been ushered out into the hallway like unwanted garbage.

Walter looked down his body and frowned. "Where are my pants?"

"Hell of a question," Oliver muttered.

He put his hand on his father's shoulder. "Come on. Let's go get you some pants."

"I could go for some eggs," Walter was muttering. "And maybe some Scotch. Where's my bracelet?"

Oliver dutifully answered his father's questions, handed over the bracelet, then started to follow his father to the elevator.

But not before he cast one last thoughtful glance toward Naomi Powell's closed door, more certain than ever that he was missing a crucial piece to the puzzle.

And more determined than ever to solve it.

Chapter Twelve

*O*kay, you can't expect me to listen to all that and not beg you to sign a contract."

Naomi gave a noncommittal smile and took a sip of her cabernet. It was mediocre, but the producer had insisted on picking the wine, and she wasn't enough of a connoisseur to care.

"Seriously, Naomi." Dylan Day leaned forward and gave her a smile a good deal more earnest than her own. "You've got a hell of a life story."

That was one way to put it.

"Now, which part was *most* enthralling," Naomi said, putting her elbows on the table and resting her chin on locked fingers as she looked at him. "The part where there was no father figure? The fact that my mom was a hot mess whose primary talents were getting fired and getting evicted? Or that my idea of high living was being able to buy name-brand peanut butter to go along with my rice cake dinners?"

"Gold. All of it," Dylan said without hesitation. "You're a

fighter. An underdog. People love that shit. Your story's got almost everything."

"Almost?" Naomi couldn't keep from asking.

Dylan lifted the wine bottle and topped off her wineglass, then his own. "Romance, babe. Your story's decidedly lacking men."

"Maybe because I've been focused on building an empire," she said with just a bit of edge. Honestly, were there still people who thought a woman's life wasn't complete without a man?

"Sure, sure," Dylan agreed readily. "And Maxcessory will be the heart of the story. I'm just saying there's a gap there. Nobody's going to believe that someone who looks like you hasn't left behind a string of broken hearts."

There was a compliment in there, but there was also a question. Where was the Prince Charming of this story? The Mr. Big? Why was there no Ross to her Rachel, no Jim to her Pam?

It wasn't a question she particularly wanted to answer. It had been weird enough sharing the inner workings of her professional life. The only reason she was even considering signing over her story to the network was the hope that maybe her story could inspire someone.

If even one girl, somewhere, would know that it was possible to overcome a seriously crappy childhood, then the invasion of privacy would be worth it. If Naomi empowered another woman to know that she didn't need the picket fence or cookie-baking mother or Ivy League education to make something of herself, then Naomi could stomach the idea of "selling out."

Her personal life, though . . . that was different. For starters, there was *no* inspiration to be found there. Any little girl dreaming of having it all—the doting husband *and* the thriving career—would have to find another role model than Naomi Powell.

The problem wasn't that she didn't have men in her past. It was that she had more than she cared to count. Men who came into her life and left, without either party scathed, or even affected, by the encounter. The exception, perhaps, being Brayden Hayes, whose departure was of the more tragic variety.

This sort of revolving romantic door had been exactly as Naomi wanted it, and yet there was something distinctly uncomfortable about having to say, out loud, that she'd never been in love. That she wasn't sure she was even capable of it. It felt vaguely tawdry to confess that she treated romance more as a diversion, especially to someone she was fairly certain wouldn't mind being one of those diversions.

"Come on," Dylan said with a cajoling smile. "Just give me a hint. Something to work with. A childhood sweetheart. A mysterious stranger you keep crossing paths with. An illicit affair?"

Naomi's hand froze just slightly at the last in his list. How would he—

She looked closely at him, looking for any signs that he knew about Brayden, that his list of possible dalliances had been more than his imagination at work.

He waggled his eyebrows. "Or if you told me you'd been holding out for a very handsome, charming TV producer to come your way and sweep you off your feet, I wouldn't be upset."

She relaxed slightly. Naomi wasn't ashamed of her relationship with Brayden—it's not as though she'd known he was married. But she cared enough about Claire to want to keep her affair as far from Dylan Day as possible.

"Are you asking on behalf of StarZone?" She asked, referring to the production company looking to produce the show. "Or as Dylan Day?"

He grinned, quick and unapologetic, his eyes smiling and open. "Can I ask as both?"

Naomi laughed even as she scanned the dining room, wanting to hurry along the bill. "You're persistent."

"I want what I want," he said, lifting a finger to flag down the server. Dylan paid for dinner on his corporate Amex and, a few minutes later, helped her into her coat as they stepped out into the fall evening.

"There's a great cocktail bar just around the corner. Nightcap?" His fingers brushed her neck under the guise of freeing a straud of hair caught on her earring as he asked it, and Naomi waited for the tingle. Hoped for it.

Nothing.

She was both relieved and disappointed. "Actually, I should be heading home," she said, pointing in the direction of her apartment.

To his credit, he knew when to back off. "I'll get you a cab."

"I'm just a few blocks over. I can walk."

"Did I mention I'm from Alabama?" Dylan asked, adding a bit of Southern drawl to his voice.

"And?"

"And I was raised to see a woman home, walking or otherwise," he said, gesturing for her to lead the way.

Naomi shrugged, rapidly learning that the best way to handle Dylan Day was to pick her battles. A half block later, she was regretting her decision. What she'd hoped would be a semi-quiet, relish-the-first-nip-of-fall kind of walk quickly turned into his hard sell.

"I don't mean to push you," Dylan said for the third time. "It's just that we really want to get this in for the fall season, and to ensure we get the right cast, the right team . . ."

He droned on for two more blocks about the opportunity, how the exposure was exactly what could bump her business to the next level, how it was the chance of a lifetime . . .

Finally her building came into view, and she could say without hesitation that she had never been so glad to see 517 Park Avenue. They came to a stop outside her building and she faced him. "How much say do I get?"

"Sorry?"

"If I agree to this show, do I get to review the script? A say in casting? The stories you tell?"

He hesitated. "Well, you'd work with our team upfront to get the details of *Max* right—"

"*Max?*"

"That's what we're hoping to call the show. A catchy shortening of your company name, easy to remember."

Naomi nodded. She didn't hate it.

"I want to do this," she told him honestly. "But there are parts of my life that are off-limits."

"Which parts?"

She smiled slowly. "The ones I haven't told you."

"The men?"

She laughed at his persistence. "Among other things."

He rocked back on his heels, hands in his pockets. "What about one guy? There's got to be one we can talk about. Sexy investor in your business, maybe a little off-limits?"

Naomi shook her head again. "I specifically targeted female investors who'd get the vision."

"What about a charming TV producer?"

Naomi rolled her eyes. "Good night, Dylan."

He caught her arm. "Look, Naomi. There's a conflict of interest here, I get that. What if I hand off the proposal for your show to my boss? I'm just the acquiring producer, anyway. That way you won't technically be mixing business and pleasure by going out with me."

"I didn't realize we were going out."

"I was getting to that," he said, his smile cocky and reminding her uncomfortably of the night she'd met Brayden at a West Village wine bar. Brayden's smile had been equally as cocky, his confidence level through the roof, and she'd bought it. Every bit of it. And maybe it wasn't fair comparing Dylan to Brayden just because they were quick with a smile and a line, but all she could think was that it didn't feel like *enough*.

For the first time in her life, she had the sense that maybe she wanted more, *deserved* more, than a fling with a good-looking guy. The realization was . . . annoying. She'd never overanalyzed flings with guys before. Usually she picked the ones who were uncomplicated, made her laugh, and didn't make her feel anything too deep.

In other words, Dylan Day was exactly her type. And yet . . .

"Dylan, I'm flattered, but—"

Her rejection froze on her lips when another couple approached from her right. She glanced their way, then back to Dylan, then her gaze swung back to the couple again. To the male half of it, anyway.

Oliver Cunningham met her gaze steadily before looking at Dylan, his expression unreadable.

Well, crap.

The woman with Oliver was chattering away, unaware of Oliver's attention on Naomi. Unaware of Naomi and Dylan altogether. Oliver said something that made the woman laugh, and she reached out for his hand.

Naomi's stomach clenched, and that was the exact moment she realized:

There it was.

The feeling she'd been missing all night with Dylan Day had just occurred with Oliver Cunningham of all people. That awareness, that *want.* Surely her reasoning for suddenly wanting more in her relationship with a man wasn't due to her childhood nemesis.

But then it got so much worse, because as she watched Oliver smile at the other woman, another emotion took over. *Jealousy.*

Her eyes slammed shut. This was not happening. She was not actually jealous of . . . what had Oliver said his girlfriend's name was? Layla? Lana?

"Naomi?" Dylan's voice was bemused.

She opened her eyes. "Sorry. I must have had too much wine."

Oliver's girlfriend giggled, but Naomi kept her gaze purposefully on Dylan, ignoring the other couple.

"We should go out again. Definitely," she said.

Dylan blinked in surprise, smart enough to have realized that just a few moments ago she'd been gearing up to reject him.

He recovered quickly. "Sure. Friday?"

"Done," she said before she could change her mind. "I'll text you?"

"Okay—"

"Great. Looking forward to it." Naomi stepped forward and gave him a quick peck on the cheek to end the conversation.

She kept her pace deliberately slow as she walked toward the front door, casually digging in her bag for her keys, even as her heart pounded, far more aware of Oliver and his date than she was of Dylan Day.

Still, she didn't look back, and once inside, she leaned against the wall, just for a second.

Had that just happened?

Had she just agreed to a date with Dylan simply because she couldn't bear the thought that she might actually want to date *him* . . . The front door opened, and she opened her eyes to see Oliver Cunningham, pairing his usual conservative navy suit with an impervious glare.

Chapter Thirteen

*F*rom the way Naomi had all but run into the building, Oliver had assumed she'd be in the safety of her apartment before he got to the main door.

Instead he stopped short, surprised to find her still standing there.

For a long moment, neither said a word as they gave each other a wary look.

"So," she said, standing up straight from where she'd been leaning against the wall with the same ugly wallpaper that'd been there since he was a boy. "That was . . . ?"

"Lilah," he supplied.

Yeah. *The* Lilah. After he'd stupidly told Naomi that he was dating her, his conscience had kicked his ass until he'd finally dialed the number that had been languishing on a Post-it Note on his desk for weeks. He'd thought to schedule something for sometime next week. Next month, even.

Instead, Lilah had dropped a half-dozen hints about some wine tasting this week, obvious enough that he couldn't figure out how to say no without sounding like an ass.

It had been . . . fine.

Lilah was kind. Sweet. Laughed a lot. As in, *a lot*.

And while he liked a decent glass of wine as much as the next guy, spending all night discussing whether he was getting more red fruits or dark fruit in the finish of the '03 Barolo was not exactly how he'd envisioned a rare night away from work and Walter.

"So," Naomi said as they both began climbing the stairs. "She seemed nice."

"Quite," he said, trying not to notice the way her hips moved from side to side as she walked up the steps in front of him. "And your date. Very . . ."

She gave him a dark look over her shoulder. "Yes?"

"Let me guess," Oliver said, as they stepped onto the landing of the second floor. "His name has a *Y*."

"What?" she snapped.

"His name," Oliver said, leaning a shoulder against the wall next to her door as she palmed her keys as though debating whether to open her apartment or stab his jugular. "Does it have a Y? Ryan. Myron. Bryson."

"Says the guy named *Oliver*."

"What's wrong with my name?"

"Nothing, if you're a nineteenth-century orphan."

"So what's his name?" Oliver pushed, leaning toward her slightly.

She huffed. "Dylan."

Oliver smiled. "Now, is that spelled . . . ?"

"With a Y, yes, and now tell me, how *is* Dickens these days? Do you call him Chuck, or . . ."

"Invite me in for a drink," he interrupted.

Naomi blinked. "You're inviting yourself into my apartment?"

"You can serve the drink in a mug. I'm starting to like it that way."

"What about *Lilah*?" she said, singsonging the word while crossing her arms, keys jingling in her left hand.

"Well, get this. Every now and then, she allows me to consume a beverage without having to get permission first. What about Dylan with a *Y*? You guys serious?"

"Actually," she said, sticking her key into the lock and shoving open the door, "he's trying to make a show about me."

"Like porn?" Oliver asked, following her in, even though he hadn't been specifically invited.

Naomi laughed, a genuine laugh, and tossed her purse on the couch. "No. God no. A TV series about my life."

"That interesting, are you?" Oliver asked. His voice was joking, but secretly he thought it wasn't a half-bad idea. The woman fascinated him, though it grated to know he wasn't the only one captivated. He'd seen the way Dylan with a *Y* looked at Naomi, and the man wanted a hell of a lot more than a television show from her.

Naomi shrugged and opened the cabinet above the fridge, which apparently served as her liquor cabinet. He watched as she pulled down a tiny bottle of something he'd seen bartenders use, then went to her toes, reaching for a bottle of Woodford Reserve.

Even in the black stilettos, the bourbon was just out of reach. Oliver went to her side, reaching above her to grab the bottle. He didn't mean to—not consciously—but the gesture had him pressing against her side, just for a moment.

They both froze. Damn. This was what had been missing with Lilah tonight. That elusive *something*. For that matter, he'd been missing it a hell of a lot longer than that. He cleared his throat and handed her the whisky bottle, which she accepted with a nod of thanks. Still, instead of moving away, her eyes crept from his tie up to his face, giving him a suspicious look.

Oliver smiled ruefully. "Why do you do that?"

"Do what?"

"Look like you're always bracing for the other shoe to drop and me to do something wretched."

She laughed softly and looked down at the bourbon in her hand, tracing the label with a red fingernail. "Let's just say I've been sort of conditioned."

Oliver felt a sharp flash of anger at whoever had treated her badly, even as he felt relief that he was making progress, that she was finally showing her cards just a little.

"Ah," he said softly, not wanting to scare her off. "Corner piece."

Her head snapped up. "What?"

"You're like a puzzle," he said with a smile. "And I've just found one of the corner pieces."

"The corner piece?" She looked genuinely, adorably nonplussed.

"Have you never done a jigsaw puzzle before?" he asked, reaching out slowly. His fingers brushed her neck, and she lurched back.

Oliver held up a hand in an easy motion, the way he would to a skittish animal, a little alarmed at her reaction. "Sorry. You're just still wearing your coat. Your collar was . . ." He made a motion to indicate it was flipped, and that he'd been trying to fix it.

Her hand flew up to her neck, and she blinked rapidly before letting out a forced laugh, as though her reaction to his touch had been no big deal. She set the bourbon on the counter and shrugged out of her coat.

"Here," she said, shoving it at him.

He glanced down at the woman's trench coat he was now holding. So she was still putting barriers between them. Literally. Still, she wasn't kicking him out, and that bourbon looked hopeful. Even more so when she pulled out two glasses.

She looked at him and paused a moment. His heart sank when she turned to put the glasses away. Then lifted again when she pulled out two mugs instead.

"Ah," he said with a smile. "Our thing."

"We don't have a thing," she muttered irritably, pulling a box of sugar cubes out of a cupboard.

"Sure we do," Oliver countered, walking across the room and opening the door of her coat closet. He hung her trench and turned back. "Booze out of a mug."

"How do you know this drink is for you?" she asked, measuring ingredients into the mugs without looking at him.

"Because you left Dylan with a *Y* out there on the sidewalk looking pissed."

Her head snapped up. "He was not."

"Pissed? Sure he was. I know a dude with blue balls when I see one. He thought he was getting lucky."

"It wasn't like that. He just wants me to agree to his show."

"Do you want to do it?"

Her attention was back on the drinks. "Hmm?"

"The TV series," Oliver said, coming back to the counter. "Do you want to do it?"

A small crease appeared between her eyebrows, and she tucked a strand of dark red hair behind her ear. "Nobody's really asked me that."

"Well, they should," he said, loosening his tie before he realized he was at her apartment, not his. Strange, that he should feel so at home in the lion's den. He decided to chalk it up to the fact that their apartments were next door to each other, and not that this prickly woman could feel . . . comforting.

Like *she* was home.

He pushed the thought aside. "So, do you want to do it?"

"I don't know," she said, resuming her drink-making by dropping a handful of ice cubes into each mug. "It's weird."

It *was* weird. He couldn't imagine having his life translated on the big screen, small screen . . . any screen. But then he wasn't a billionaire entrepreneur with a scrappy background. Yeah, he'd done his Wikipedia stalking, though there hadn't been much about her pre-Maxcessory days beyond her being from the Bronx.

"I'm thinking about it," she said by way of answer, shoving the mug across the counter toward him. "I like the idea of encouraging girls and young women to build their own thing, chase their dreams and all that."

"Hell of a thing you've built," he said, meaning it.

She nodded in thanks. "What do you do?"

"I'm an architect," Oliver said, lifting the mug.

Naomi looked surprised. "Really?"

He laughed. "Yeah, really. Do I not look it?"

"Not at all," she said honestly. "You're more of a take-over-the-family-business type."

Her words caused a pang, and Oliver looked quickly down at his drink to hide it, but either he wasn't fast enough or she was more perceptive than he'd anticipated.

"I'm sorry," she said quietly. "I guess with your father . . ."

"I'm almost glad he doesn't remember," Oliver said quietly, not meaning to say the words until they were out there. "It was our biggest fight, me telling him I wanted to go to architecture school rather than take the reins of his company. He told me it was a phase. Then we had an even *bigger* fight when I told him I wanted to start my own firm and he realized it wasn't a phase, that I'd truly dared to defy him. And I don't know why I'm telling you this," he muttered, a little embarrassed.

"I'm sure he was proud," Naomi said, her tone gentler than usual.

"I'm sure he wasn't." His and his father's relationship, always rocky, had never truly recovered after that. And then Walter had gotten sick, and everything had been redefined. Not that Oliver was glad that his father had lost a part of himself. Alzheimer's was a true shit disease. But selfishly, Oliver had been relieved to lay some of their old fights to rest, to be able to watch a baseball game, father and son.

He took the first sip of his drink and looked down in surprise. "This is good. Very good."

"I know," she said, smiling immodestly. "I make an excellent old-fashioned. Cooking eludes me, but cocktailing? I'm not bad."

He nodded in agreement, taking another sip. "Why here?"

"Why here what?" she asked, sipping her own cocktail and watching him.

"Why this building? You're thirty years old and not to be crass, but your financial success is no secret. You could afford to live anywhere."

"Ah yes, but this is *the* Park Avenue," she said.

Oliver sighed. "And just like that, the pieces are all over the floor again."

"What?" she asked with a laugh.

"The puzzle pieces. *Your* puzzle pieces. You might as well have scattered them all over the floor."

"How's that?"

"Because, Naomi," he said, her eyes sharpening as he said her name. "You don't care about the prestige of Park Avenue. You lied."

"I'm allowed."

"To lie?"

"To not share every detail of my life and motivations with a man I barely know."

"And yet here we are, having a nightcap together instead of with our respective dates," he pointed out.

She opened her mouth, then closed it, frowning in confusion. "You're right."

Her grumpy tone should have bothered him, but instead he found himself grinning, relieved that he wasn't the only one trying to solve a puzzle and finding it difficult.

He lifted his drink. "Can I borrow this? The mug?"

"Why not, might as well add to your collection," she said, referring to the coffee mug he still had from move-in day. "You're leaving?"

He carefully hid his smile at the puzzled, almost petulant note in her voice.

"I want to check on Dad. Janice is there, but he was having a rough night before I left. I want to make sure everything's okay."

"Sure, of course," she said.

Oliver nodded goodbye and stepped into the hallway, feeling only a little bad about his partial truth after accusing her of lying. He *did* want to check on his father, but Janice had already texted him to say that Walter had gone to bed without issue. But it wasn't the real reason he'd left.

The woman had disliked him from their first meeting. He still didn't know why, but he did know that in order to redefine her opinion of him, he had to throw her off balance. To surprise her.

And if her assessing look as he'd walked away had been any indication, she'd be thinking about him tonight.

Much in the same way he'd be thinking about her.

Chapter Fourteen

*D*espite her poorer-than-poor upbringing, in the wake of Maxcessory's success, Naomi had seen her fair share of Manhattan wealth, from black-tie fund-raisers to fancy museum cocktail parties to overpriced dinners with potential investors. She'd thought she'd finally wrapped her head around what life was like for the 1 percent.

But walking into Audrey's apartment? She realized there was a whole other level.

She'd been invited to Audrey's once before for a *Sex and the City* night, but she'd had to bow out at the last minute to deal with an inventory crisis in the San Francisco office. So she was *fully* not prepared for the fact that she was about to attend a dinner party in what was surely *the* most expensive building in New York City.

The lobby, with its soaring ceilings, marble floors, and floor-to-ceiling fish tank that looked bigger than Naomi's apartment, should have prepared her. The fact that the formal, suit-wearing concierge at the reception desk directed her to a private elevator to the penthouse *really* should have prepared her.

And yet somehow, she still let out a gasp of shock when she stepped off the elevator into the private entryway of Audrey's apartment, complete with gold damask wallpaper and an enormous chandelier.

This is where her friend *lived*? To say it was a far cry from the string of one-room apartments and motel rooms Naomi had grown up in was an understatement. Naomi shook her head in disbelief that *this* was her life now. That she was friends with people who lived like this.

Dylan Day seemed equally impressed by his surroundings. He was openly gawking as Naomi rang the discreet doorbell beside the front door. Audrey greeted them in a black halter dress, strappy sandals, and a wide, welcoming smile.

"You came!"

"Of course we did," Naomi said with a laugh. "Though you might have mentioned that you live in a high-rise palace."

"I know, right? Family money, lots of it. My parents bought this apartment, then decided to move to Hollywood to be near my sister and her producer boyfriend a month later. They gave the place to me, and if I had any sort of pride, I'd have said no, but—"

"If you had any sort of brains, you'd say yes," Naomi finished for her. "Audrey, you remember Dylan?"

"Sure, of course, we met that day in your office," Audrey said. Her tone was welcoming, but Naomi caught the way her friend's smile turned just a little bit fake when she turned it toward Dylan.

"Thanks for having me," he said politely as Audrey motioned for them to hand over both their coats.

"Of course," Audrey said brightly. "Manhattan social groups can get so small so fast, I'm always trying to bring new people into the fold."

Dylan laughed. "Well then, I'm glad you thought of me."

Naomi looked away, not wanting to tell him that he'd been the *second* man she'd thought of, and only because they'd already committed to plans on Friday. She didn't want to admit even to herself that the *first* person she'd thought of had been her stuffy, unexpectedly charming neighbor.

"Dylan, the kitchen's right through there. Help yourself to a drink. Can I steal Naomi here for a second? Girl talk."

"Sure thing," he said, heading in the direction she'd indicated.

Audrey waited until Dylan was out of earshot before turning an accusing look on Naomi.

"Him?"

"Don't start," Naomi said, lifting her finger. "You said bring a date. He's a date."

"He's a guy trying to get in your pants so you'll agree to do his TV show."

"Which wouldn't be the end of the world," Naomi pointed out. "The TV show's a great opportunity, and as far as him getting in my pants, let's just say I have needs that haven't been taken care of in . . . a while."

"No pickles in your sandwich since Brayden?" Audrey asked.

"Nope. You?"

"Not even close, but to be honest I haven't really thought about it. Having my boyfriend of over a year die messed with my heart. Knowing he was married messed with my head. Sex has been the last thing on my mind lately."

"Huh." Naomi couldn't say the same. In the past few days alone it had been on her mind more than she cared to admit. For reasons she was worried had nothing to do with Dylan Day.

"Okay, well, if you like him . . ."

"Like who?"

Audrey rolled her eyes. "Dylan? Your date?"

Right. *Right.*

"Okay, so can I have a glass of wine, or . . . ?"

Audrey gestured toward the sound of voices, and Naomi had taken only a few steps when she skidded to a halt at a familiar masculine chuckle. *What the . . . ?*

Wordlessly, Naomi grabbed Audrey's hand and pulled her friend none too gently through a door to their right, which turned out to be a powder room.

"Seriously?" Naomi hissed, shutting the door. "You invited Oliver?"

"Not explicitly. Claire brought him as her date!"

Naomi's head snapped back slightly at that. The thought of Claire and Oliver was . . . well, *right*, on an intellectual level. They both had that sort of old-world classiness to them. Claire had gone to Smith, so they both looked like the alumni section of a prep school brochure. And though she wanted desperately to think of Oliver as a real pain in the ass, she couldn't deny that maybe, just maybe, a little sliver of him was a good guy who brought expensive champagne to new neighbors and took care of his sick father.

And as for Claire, nobody deserved a nice guy more than she did, and yet . . . and yet . . . Her brain sputtered, trying to wrangle the almost stifling jealousy. While some part of Naomi knew Oliver and Claire were perfect together, another part of her felt decidedly panicked at the thought that there could be romantic interest there.

"Is Claire interested in him?" *Is he interested in her?*

Audrey shrugged. "I guess so. I mean, she wasn't like wearing his ring or anything, but if she brought him to a casual get-together, she must be carrying his baby—"

"Audrey!"

"What is the big deal? Why do you hate him so much?"

She took a deep breath. "Remember my story about my mom and the affair with her employer that ended up with her fired?"

"Of course."

"Okay, remember the little boy who lied to protect his father?"

"Yeah . . ." Audrey's eyes went wide in realization. "*No.*"

"Yup."

"Oliver was that boy?" she hissed.

"Yup."

"Are you sure?"

"Yes, Audrey, I'm pretty sure. Also, he has a girlfriend and yet he still came tonight with Claire," Naomi said, still preoccupied with the thought of Claire and Oliver together.

Audrey's nose wrinkled. "He doesn't seem like the two-timing type."

"Right, because we're all so good at spotting those," Naomi said.

"Shoot. You're right. Still, he seems so nice . . ."

"He is *not* nice."

"Well, maybe he wasn't when he was ten," Audrey said in exasperation. "But he's a perfectly polite adult. And I'm glad she brought him. When we met him that first day, he seemed a little . . . lonely."

Naomi tugged gently on her gold hoop earring, hating the little twist in her stomach at the thought of Oliver Cunningham being lonely. Hated, almost as much, that Audrey had taken enough interest to notice.

"I'm truly sorry, Naomi," Audrey said, her tone contrite. "If I could get him out of here without being unbearably rude, I would."

"No, don't do that," Naomi said, letting her hands drop and giving her arms a quick shake, trying to gather herself. "I'm a grown-up. I can do this."

"Yes, you can," Audrey said emphatically, reaching out and smoothing a flyaway on Naomi's hair like a calming mother. At least Naomi assumed that's what a soothing mother would do. She didn't have much experience with that sort of maternal figure.

"Let's do this," Naomi said, opening the bathroom door.

Naomi followed Audrey into the kitchen area, her attention no longer on her friend's stunning apartment but on the nemesis she knew awaited her.

"So sorry, everyone," Audrey said as they joined the small group gathered around her kitchen counter. "This is Naomi Powell, the entrepreneur superstar I was telling you about. It was her first time over here. I just had to give her the grand tour."

Naomi's gaze sought and immediately found Oliver. She'd only ever seen him in suits, and tonight was no different, though he'd forgone the tie and left his light blue shirt open at the collar. She was annoyed to realize he pulled off the slightly more casual look every bit as well as he did the full formal attire.

Naomi waited for his shock of surprise at seeing her, but he merely raised his eyebrows slightly in acknowledgment of her presence. Her gaze flicked to Dylan, standing next to Oliver, but her date seemed more interested in checking out Audrey's apartment, a vaguely assessing look on his face. Irritably, she wondered if Dylan was ever present in the moment, or if he was always looking for this next win, whether it be a woman or a new production idea.

Naomi glanced distractedly at the other man in the room, then did an immediate double take. He was *absurdly* good-looking. Like George Clooney, Hugh Jackman level of *wow*. Dark hair, golden-brown eyes, and twin dimples on either side of a rather fantastic smile.

"Dree must not have given you the full tour," said the World's Hottest Man. "In this mausoleum, that's a two-hour venture."

"Dree?" Naomi repeated, her brain finally catching up to his words, even as she gaped at his perfect face.

"Audrey. She loves the nickname," he explained with a grin. Naomi's ovaries fainted dead away.

"*Really?*" Audrey said dryly as she poured a glass of champagne and handed it to Naomi. "Because I could have sworn I've spent the past twenty-something years begging you to quit using it."

"Twenty-something years," Naomi said in surprise. Audrey was only twenty-seven. "You're a . . . brother?"

"Might as well be," the man replied, extending his hand. "Clarke West. Dree's oldest and favorite friend."

"I'll give you the first one," Audrey said. "But the persistent use of the nickname puts you on thin ice on the latter."

Naomi's gaze flicked between them, searching for any sign that the just-friends routine was a euphemism for *complicated*, but to her surprise, they both seemed completely easy around each other and, well, friends.

Clarke gave her a quick wink as though reading her thoughts, and Naomi was appalled to feel herself blushing.

"Ugh, Clarke, put that away," Audrey said with a dismissive wave.

"Put what away?"

"You know exactly what. My friends are off-limits for your dubious charms."

"I'll try to keep my appeal under lock and key."

Good luck with that.

Naomi gave Audrey's friend another smile before looking over at Claire and smiling in greeting.

Claire's purple sweater should have perfectly complemented her hazel eyes, but Naomi was dismayed to realize that the shadows under the gorgeous eyes were even darker than the last time she'd seen her.

"I guess you know everyone else," Audrey said to Naomi. "Not quite the meet-new-people dinner party I expected, but at least we can skip some of the small talk."

Dylan's attention finally snapped back to the conversation, and he looked at Naomi in surprise. "You've met Owen?"

"Oliver," Audrey corrected quickly.

Oliver, for his part, ignored Dylan completely, still watching Naomi.

"Hello," he said softly when she met his eyes.

"Hi." She tore her gaze away to look at Dylan. "Oliver and I are neighbors."

Dylan snapped his fingers. "That's why you look familiar. Didn't we see you the other night? You were with another . . ."

He looked at Claire, then back at Oliver, and though he stopped short of pointing out that Oliver had been with a different woman that night, his silence was just as damning. At least, it would have been, had Claire seemed to care even a little bit that Oliver had been on a date with someone else. Instead, she seemed far more interested in the bubbles in her champagne flute.

Still, Naomi inwardly cringed that her date didn't seem embarrassed, much less regretful about the awkward moment he'd caused. In fact, a little part of her wondered if he'd done it on purpose to make Oliver look bad.

"Oh dear," Audrey muttered just quietly enough for Naomi's ears but nobody else's. Then she slipped right back into hostess mode, moving toward the refrigerator. "You guys must be *starving*. I've got a lovely bruschetta that I'll just pop together real fast. Clarke, be useful for once and come give me a hand?"

Audrey handed a baguette to her friend, who took it and used it to point at the small TV mounted discreetly onto one of the kitchen cabinets. No, it had been built *into* the cabinet, Naomi realized. A whole other level of fancy.

"I'll cut this if I can turn that on," Clarke said, waving the baguette like a weapon.

"Nope. No TV. It's a dinner party."

"It's the Yankees," Clarke countered.

"Clarke."

"Audrey."

Audrey's eyes narrowed in warning, and Clarke gave her a smile that Naomi suspected would have made most women weak in the knees. Audrey merely raised the large kitchen knife in her hand in warning.

Clarke turned back toward the group. "Let's take a vote. Yankees game in the background? On mute," he added, when Audrey made a low growling noise.

Dylan's hand immediately went up. "Sorry, Audrey. Yanks playing Atlanta, and as a Braves fan I've got a good feeling about their win . . ."

"Well, *that's* not going to happen," Clarke said before pointing his baguette at Oliver. "Can I count on your vote?"

"You can't say it like that," Audrey protested. "He'll feel like he'll have to turn in his man card if he says no."

"Perfect. Peer pressure for the win. What's it to be, Cunningham, man card or Yankees?" Clarke asked.

Naomi already knew what Oliver was going to do. Even without the man card threat, as a kid, he'd been obsessed with all things Yankees. Apparently the man was, too, because he raised his hand in a vote for the game, though he gave Audrey an apologetic wink as he did so that did something unpleasant to Naomi's stomach.

He was here as Claire's date, was flirting with Audrey . . . it was like freaking fertilizer on the seed of jealousy that had been planted last weekend when she'd seen him with Lilah.

Naomi frowned. Where *was* Lilah?

"That's three for the game," Clarke said, turning his baguette to Naomi and Claire. "Ladies?"

Audrey gasped in outrage as Claire reluctantly raised her hand in favor of the Yankees. "Claire Hayes!"

"Sorry," Claire said, not sounding sorry at all. "I'm kind of a baseball nut."

Audrey shot Naomi a pleading look. "You're on my side, right?"

"I don't think it matters, babe," Naomi said with a smile. "It's already four to two." Plus, Clarke had already gone straight for the drawer that held the TV remote and turned it on.

"Fiiiiine," Audrey said with an exasperated sigh as she glared at Clarke. "But I want that baguette sliced on the bias."

"Yeah, I'm not doing that," Clarke said, one eye on the game as he unceremoniously plopped the baguette on the cutting board and began making rough cuts at the bread.

Audrey accepted her defeat graciously as she pulled an apron over her head and began slicing tomatoes alongside her friend. Even losing the TV battle, she looked suspiciously happy, and Naomi's eyes narrowed slightly on her friend's back. The little sneak. She'd set up a couples' dinner party but had ensured that she had the plastic safety of her BFF, while she and Claire had put themselves out there and brought an *actual* date.

Except that wasn't exactly going to plan, either. Dylan had joined Claire in front of the TV, and though Claire still looked a little skeptical of the guy, she really *was* a baseball nut, from the way they were talking RBIs and Golden Gloves and a bunch of other crap Naomi didn't really care about.

Which left her with . . . Oliver.

Naomi glanced over, found him watching her. She picked up her champagne flute, moving closer to stand beside him.

"Out of curiosity, what would your vote have been?" he asked, nodding toward the TV.

She lifted a shoulder. "I don't have a strong preference either way, but I will say it serves Audrey right."

"For?"

Naomi pointed the base of her flute toward Clarke and Audrey. "She made me and Claire bring a date. Part of our whole move-on-from-Brayden thing, and she goes and brings her oldest friend. Chicken."

"So, you and Dylan with a Y. Still a thing?" He kept his voice low to match hers.

Naomi shrugged, not about to tell him that her agreement to going out with Dylan in the first place had only been a knee-jerk reaction to seeing *him* with Lilah. And she definitely wasn't about to tell him that she'd specifically used tonight to fulfill that date obligation because a dinner party felt preferable to spending one-on-one time with Dylan.

"TBD," she answered noncommittally. "What about you and Claire?"

His eyes dragged to the blonde. "She got my number through a friend. Said she needed a no-strings companion to get a matchmaking friend off her back. I didn't realize she meant Audrey until we got here."

"How'd Lilah feel about that?" Naomi asked casually, reaching forward and picking up a carrot off Audrey's elaborate crudités platter.

He said nothing until she forced herself to meet his gaze.

"Lilah and I didn't work out."

Naomi's heart did something stupid, and she mentally shut down the idiotic organ. *Remember who he is. Remember that he made your life miserable. Remember that he lied to save his dad and ruined your mom's life.*

But it was getting harder to reconcile this man who seemed to reel her in with every encounter with the little boy who'd been a jerk. Plus, hadn't Naomi known for years that her mother had made it her life's mission to blame other people for her situation? If it hadn't been the Cunninghams, it would have been someone else.

"Did Audrey know you were bringing Dylan?"

"Yeah, of course. Why?"

He nodded back at the dining table behind them. She saw immediately what he meant. "Oh, Audrey."

He laughed. "Yeah."

Audrey had placed herself and Clarke at either end of the table—Naomi would bet that it wasn't the first time Clarke had played her platonic plus-one in a game of setup. The name cards facing Naomi and Oliver read *Claire* and *Dylan*, which meant that Naomi and Oliver were seated on the opposite side of the table.

Side by side.

Naomi was going to kill Audrey.

"We could switch them," he said, looking at Naomi out of the corner of his eye. "Really mess with her plan."

"Tempting, but I'd never hear the end of it."

"True, and my mother would roll over in her grave. The woman used to spend *hours* planning her dinner table."

Naomi flinched at the mention of Margaret Cunningham, but Oliver was sipping his champagne and missed it.

"Did Claire mention me in the invite?" Naomi asked curiously.

He glanced down at her, his blue eyes landing on her mouth for a second too long before meeting her eyes. "She did."

"And you still came?"

"Sure," he said with a shrug. "What dude doesn't want to spend Saturday night sitting next to a woman who hates his guts?"

Oliver glanced down with a wry smile when she didn't reply. "No denial, I see."

"Sorry." She looked away from where she'd been staring absently at the table. "Was just wondering how we're going to manage the wine with dinner. No mugs."

"Ah, now see?" Oliver said lightly. "We *do* have a thing."

"Quit making it weird."

"It's hard for you, huh?" he said with faux sympathy.

"What?"

"Dealing with your attraction to me."

"Yes. Yes, very much. Which is why when Audrey asked me to bring a date tonight, I called Dylan instead of you."

"Yes, you seem very into him," Oliver said with a deliberate look toward Dylan on the other side of the room.

"And you into Claire."

"I never said I was into Claire."

Naomi's heart tumbled in her chest, but just when she hoped he'd say more, Audrey came toward them. "Okay, here we are!"

she announced proudly, bringing a platter of bruschetta to the counter. "I present my gorgeous tomatoes, as well as Clarke's hack-job bread."

"It's bread. It's supposed to taste good, not look pretty," Clarke protested.

"It can do both."

Clarke shook his head and picked up a piece of the bread, taking an enormous bite and facing the group. "This is my bad, guys. I got her a cooking class for Christmas, and she's been insufferable ever since."

Conversation turned briefly back to the Yankees, then some exhibit at the Met that Naomi could not have cared less about, and then, as the group began to loosen up with the wine flowing a bit more freely, onto more interesting topics. Most embarrassing TSA story (Claire had won, with an anecdote of her fourteen-year-old self enduring a male TSA agent rifling through her backpack stuffed mostly with maxi pads), and then back to the topic of museums, at which point everyone confessed they didn't give a rat's ass about the new exhibit.

By the time Audrey pulled a butternut squash lasagna out of the oven and put Claire and Dylan to work taking food to the table, Naomi was just the tiniest bit tipsy, a little bit relaxed, and having the best time she could remember in ages.

She jumped at the brush of fingers against the nape of her neck, snapping her head up to give Oliver a startled look.

"Easy," he murmured. "I was just going to fix your dress. The tag's sticking out."

"Great. Very classy, Naomi," she muttered to herself. Honestly, this was the second time in a week this man had had to fix her clothes.

She started to lift her hand, but his hand was already there, slipping beneath her hair once again, his fingers lightly brushing the sensitive skin at the nape of her neck as he gently adjusted the tag. And lingered.

Naomi's breath caught at the contact, just as it had the other night. When Dylan's touch had done zilch, and when Oliver's touch had kept her up half the night.

She'd convinced herself it'd been a fluke.

It wasn't.

She looked around to see if anyone had noticed, but Dylan and Claire had paused to watch a full-count pitch on the TV, and Clarke and Audrey were bantering about whether or not squash counted as a vegetable.

The only person paying any attention to Naomi was . . . Oliver. And she saw that he *knew*. He knew exactly what his touch did to her. And yet there was no gloating in his gaze, no triumph, just awareness. Of her. Of them.

He slowly pulled his hand out from under her hair. "There," he said quietly. "All better."

No. No, it was not *all* better. Her pulse was all jumpy, her breath was a little staccato, and she didn't even recognize herself.

Naomi was always the seductress, never the seduced, and yet here she was, feeling distinctly fluttery about the one man she was determined to despise.

"Okay," Audrey said, "Dinnertime. TV off. My house, my rules."

"Yes, Mom," Claire said, dutifully turning off the television.

The group took their places at the table, and Naomi realized maybe she'd been wrong about Audrey's placement of the name tags. Maybe she hadn't been placed next to Oliver, so much as across from Dylan, making it easier to talk to her date.

She knew this, not because she was actually talking to her

date, but because Oliver was talking to his. Regardless of why Claire had asked Oliver tonight, or why he'd agreed, it was hard not to see that they got along marvelously. *Apparently*, they'd both gone to the same leadership camp back in the day, and Claire, a couple of years older, had been his group leader. *Apparently*, they had a mutual friend who'd recently been arrested for growing pot at her Hamptons home. *Apparently*, they both loved spy movies.

The rest of the group laughed at the trip down memory lane. And just as Naomi was pep-talking herself that she wasn't jealous, that she didn't care that he didn't even seem to be aware of her, Oliver glanced over and caught her eye. And winked.

And she knew, with that one should-have-been-cheesy-but-was-unbearably-sexy wink, that he was right.

She was attracted. They did have a thing.

And she didn't have a clue what to do about it.

Chapter Fifteen

*Y*ou didn't have to walk me home," Naomi said, pulling the collar of her jacket up around her ears and shoving her hands into her pockets.

"Probably not," Oliver said, tilting his head up slightly to look at the night sky.

She let out a startled laugh. "I guess we're past the point of nice platitudes?"

"Naomi, you haven't given me anything *close* to a nice platitude in the time I've known you."

"Well, that's true." Her shoulders hunched slightly. "So why did you?"

"Why did I what?"

"Offer to walk with me."

"Did I offer?" he mused. "Or did your friends point out eight hundred times that we were headed the same direction?"

Naomi laughed. "Yeah, sorry about that. I thought it was just Audrey, but Claire seems to have joined her in the matchmaking efforts."

"They care about you."

"Yeah. Well, that and we sort of made a pact."

"A pact?" He glanced down at her.

"So, you know that we were all . . . involved with Brayden?"

He nodded.

"We didn't know it. Obviously. Not until the day of the funeral."

Jesus. Oliver winced. "You met at his funeral?"

"Sort of. We all *meant* to go to the funeral, but instead we found ourselves in Central Park. We had the same shoes, and, well, whatever, that doesn't matter. We were all a little adrift after realizing how thoroughly Brayden had used us, and we agreed to help each other avoid falling into the same trap."

"That seems like an anti-matchmaking scheme. Claire and Audrey all but linked our hands before shoving us out the door."

"Don't flatter yourself—I suspect that's more steering me away from Dylan than it is steering me toward you."

That bugged him more than he cared to admit, but her friends were right. Dylan was no good for her. Oliver nearly told her as much, but she spoke first.

"Who's with your father tonight?" Naomi asked.

Oliver inhaled as reality settled back down around him. As he realized he was in no position to enter a relationship. Not with Lilah. Not with Claire. Definitely not with Naomi.

He'd tried, once, to balance a woman and his father. It had worked for a while. His ex had been sweet, mild mannered . . . and completely uninterested in being with a man who had a sick father.

"Janice," he replied, answering her question. "She usually takes weekends off, but every now and then I'll pay her extra for a weekend night."

"How often does that happen?"

He looked down at her as they walked, surprised at the question. "Why do you ask?"

Her shoulders lifted. "Just seems like it must be hard. Giving up all your nights and weekends."

They were close to their building, and though not quite ready for the night to end, he was equally confident that she'd dart away from him the second she got close to the safety of her apartment, so Oliver slowed to a stop on the quiet sidewalk.

She stopped as well, giving him a questioning look.

Oliver shoved his hands into his pockets, matching her posture in a protective stance against the brisk fall wind.

"It's not always easy," he admitted. "I never pictured that my weekend nights at thirty would be spent picking up hard-boiled eggs from the floor and answering my father's repeated questions as to whether or not his son—me—is home from soccer practice yet. But . . ."

He looked over her shoulder for a moment, gathering his thoughts. "What can you do, you know? He's my dad."

"Do you miss him? I mean, how he was before?"

Oliver blew out a breath at the question, and she quickly brushed aside the question. "I'm sorry. We don't have to—"

"He was an asshole," Oliver blurted out.

He'd gotten plenty of platitudes since Walter's diagnosis, but even the Cunninghams' closest friends hadn't dared speak of the real truth.

That maybe it wasn't the worst thing in the world that the old Walter Cunningham was mostly lost to the world.

"He was difficult," Oliver amended slightly. "Cold. Demanding. Selfish."

Naomi blinked. "Wow. That's—"

"Honest?" he said with a quick laugh.

"Unusual," she said softly. "Most people I know idolize their parents, at least a little."

"I used to. When I was a kid, I wanted to *be* him."

"What happened?"

Oliver's shoulders lifted and fell. "I grew up. Started to develop as my own person and realized who I wanted to be."

And it sure as hell hadn't been a womanizing workaholic who'd carried on more affairs than Oliver could even remember, often right under his wife's nose.

"And yet, you're still taking care of him," Naomi said, a note of question in her voice.

"Yeah, well. The person I decided to be wasn't one who'd walk away from a family member who needed him."

"Noble."

He smiled and stepped toward her. "That almost sounded like a compliment."

"Did it?" she asked, pursing her lips. "You must have heard it wrong."

He stepped even closer, wanting to pump his fist in victory when she didn't step back. "Why?" he asked.

"Why what?"

"Why are you so determined to remind yourself that you don't like me?" He searched her face, struck again by the fact that it seemed familiar, though he knew he didn't know her. Men didn't forget women with faces like this one.

Naomi met his gaze steadily. "I have reasons. I'm working on them."

He let out a surprised laugh at her honesty. "May I know the reasons?"

She lifted her chin and answered his question with a question. "Why did you push me through to the next round? Of the co-op board. I was rude to you, and you pushed for me to live in the building anyway. Why?"

Oliver smiled and stepped even closer, just inches separating them now. "I have reasons." His gaze dropped to her full mouth. "I'm working on them."

Naomi's face tilted to his, and for a moment Oliver's breath caught with an unfamiliar sensation. Want, yes. Desire, sure. But this moment was different. Fuller somehow, as though this woman belonged to him not just for right now, not just for a night, but for always.

She felt it, too. He knew she did, because for a moment her eyes widened in surprise and then narrowed slightly in wariness.

Don't, he thought in frustration. *Don't turn away from this.*

"He's no good for you," Oliver blurted out, because it was either speak his mind or kiss her, and though the latter was a hell of a lot more appealing, instinct told him this wasn't the moment.

"Who?"

He gave her a look. She pulled to a stop and glared at him. "You don't even know Dylan."

"Neither do you."

"I—"

"He spent half the evening pumping your friends for information about you. And then when he didn't get what he wanted, he left for the airport instead of seeing you home," Oliver pointed out.

"He has a shoot in Dallas tomorrow afternoon."

"So he could have flown out tomorrow morning."

"I'd never ask a man to change flight plans for me."

You shouldn't have to ask. Still, her admission was another piece of the puzzle. Not a corner piece, but an important one. It told him that she wasn't accustomed to men making her a priority.

"Why'd you ask him to come with you tonight?"

Her shoulders lifted. "Audrey told me to bring a date."

Damn it, Naomi, open your eyes. I've been right here.

"He still trying to get you to sign on for the TV series?"

"Yeah."

"You thinking about it?"

She nodded, but the moment of hesitation spoke volumes.

Normally, Oliver would have bit his tongue, but she just . . . pissed him off. And it's not like he had anything to lose—even when he was the perfect gentleman, he hadn't won her over.

"You're scared," he said.

She stiffened. "What?"

Oliver didn't back off. "You're a chicken. It's why you're even entertaining the idea of dating someone like Dylan Day, while at the same time hesitating on the TV show."

"What are you talking about?" She started to walk away, but he reached out and grabbed her arm, pulling her gently around.

"That guy won't demand anything from you. Not your brain, not your heart. He's *easy*, and it's what you think you want. Conversely, the TV show the guy is pushing for is the very opposite of easy. It's a risk. It's putting yourself all the way out there. Not just your work. *You*. It terrifies you."

Naomi had gone very still, watching him through wide, unreadable blue eyes. Then she shook her head. "You don't know what you're talking about. You don't even know me."

"And he does?"

"You don't know me," she repeated, enunciating each word clearly as she jerked her arm free of his grip. "So stay the hell out of my business."

Naomi started to storm away but turned back with one last parting shot. "I will do that TV series. And in case there was any doubt, you'll have *no* part in my life story."

Chapter Sixteen

*T*hough she sometimes had a hard time believing it herself, somehow over the past couple of years Naomi had become one of those women who enjoyed running.

On her twenty-fifth birthday a few years earlier, she'd had a frank conversation with herself that an able-bodied woman had no good reason for not paying attention to the countless recommendations that movement was a crucial part of good health. Particularly for an entrepreneur whose long working hours meant a lot of time sitting behind a desk, on the phone, and in cabs. At the gym? Not so much.

As with most new habits, exercise had started out rough. She'd tried it all. Yoga. Hot yoga. Pilates. Hip-hop dance classes. CrossFit. Cycling classes. In the end, Naomi's lone-wolf tendencies hadn't liked anything that required a schedule or, well, social interaction. Her need for exercise became as much about the desire to clear her head as it did the health benefits, and running had been a natural fit.

She ran a few days a week, outside if weather permitted, the treadmill at her gym if not. Today's cool and crisp morning had demanded an outdoor run, but instead of pacing herself with her usual steady, sustained long run, her rhythm had been almost frantic in its relentless speed.

After she'd sprinted through Central Park at an almost punishing pace to burn off the extra pent-up energy from working from home, she finally allowed herself to drop into a cool-down walk, gasping for air as she forced herself to acknowledge the truth:

She'd been running from demons.

Naomi had spent the past couple of days reliving her almost-kiss with Oliver.

Had spent her past couple of nights dreaming about it. *Wanting* it.

And hating herself for it.

She'd had her fair share of boyfriends, lovers, whatever you wanted to call them. She'd even liked most of them, including Brayden, though that obviously didn't exactly speak to her judgment of character.

But never before had she felt *that*. That pull toward another person, not just at the physical level, but on an emotional, almost soul level. And then he'd picked a fight.

Damn it.

Naomi picked up her speed again, as though a grueling pace would help put Oliver Cunningham out of her mind.

Wanting him was not part of the plan. Not even close. The plan was simple, nonemotional.

Step one: move into the building to honor her mother's wishes.

Step two: confront the Cunninghams, letting them know the girl they'd once treated as disposable was now their equal.

Step three . . .

Well, step two was really as far as she'd gotten. If she were being honest with herself, her plan had been more about a nagging need for closure than anything else. Not only for her mother's sake, but so that Naomi would *finally* feel like she'd put Naomi Fields behind her.

She didn't want revenge, just acknowledgment. She wanted the Cunninghams to come face-to-face with the actions of their past, to be reminded of what their carelessness had done. To apologize.

But Margaret Cunningham, that cold woman who'd so heartlessly ignored Naomi's mother's pleas for *just one more night* so she could make alternate arrangements for her daughter, was dead.

Walter Cunningham, was, well . . . even if Naomi wanted to confront him about his past actions, she wasn't sure she could be that cruel or that he would remember the incident, much less feel remorse.

And as far as Oliver Cunningham . . .

Naomi groaned aloud on the mostly deserted sidewalk and, putting her hands on her hips, stopped in her tracks and tilted her head back to the sky.

Why? Why did she have to want him?

New plan, Naomi told herself, as she resumed walking the final blocks back to her apartment. *Avoid the Cunningham men*.

Clearly they messed with her head, and Naomi did not do well with feeling out of control. She needed to get back to where she'd been just a few months ago.

Three months ago, she'd felt like the most in-control woman on the planet. Her work life has been perfectly structured. She'd had a lover whose company she enjoyed, and with whom she could see herself potentially getting serious. And she'd had a solid plan for moving on from her nasty past once and for all.

Fast-forward to the present, and her lover was dead and an asshole, and the ghosts from her past were complicated. And she didn't even have an office to escape to for another few weeks.

It was as though the universe was telling her she could run as fast as she wanted but sooner or later she'd have to sort out her jumble of emotions. And much as it pained her to admit, even to herself, her emotions were involved as far as the Cunninghams were concerned.

To undo that, she needed some distance. To regain perspective.

And don't even get her started on Oliver's harebrained assertion that she was avoiding the TV series because she was scared. Screw that. She'd woken up this morning so determined to prove him wrong she'd emailed Dylan to say she was in.

The contract was on its way to her lawyer, and Naomi felt . . . well, she'd deny it to her dying breath if Oliver ever asked, but she was nervous. Excited. Confident that it was the right decision, and yet she was vulnerable as all heck. Somehow she had to figure out how to maneuver the story to reveal the inspirational truth about starting a billion-dollar company from a tiny studio apartment while also protecting the people she cared about.

Naomi's personal life could be an open book, but she'd go to her grave protecting her mother's memory. Claire's and Audrey's privacy as well.

Naomi was nearly back to her apartment, but her footsteps slowed when she spotted a man several feet ahead of her shuffling down Park Avenue wearing only a white T-shirt and blue boxers. At least he was wearing shoes this time.

His familiar gray hair ruffled against the cold autumn breeze, and Naomi winced. The cool air had been perfect for her morning run, but she was wearing gloves, running leggings, two top layers, and a headband to keep her ears warm.

Walter was in no way dressed for the thirty-something temps. Naomi glanced hopefully at the front door of their apartment building, wishing that Oliver or Janice would come bursting out to retrieve him.

Nothing.

Naomi blew out a breath. All right then.

"Hey, Walter!" she called out. So much for steering clear of the Cunningham men.

He didn't turn around, so she broke into a slow trot to catch up to him, which wasn't hard, considering his slow gait.

"Hey there," she said, tapping his arm.

Walter gave her a startled glance. "Hello."

"It's Naomi," she said with what she hoped was a reassuring smile, since he didn't seem to recognize her. "I live in your building. We're friends."

He smiled. "I like pretty friends."

I bet you do, you old geezer.

The thought was without any real animosity, and . . . damn it. Was she starting to feel a bit of affection toward the man?

"Where are you going?" she asked casually as he started walking once more.

"Going?" The wind picked up again, and Walter shivered, then looked around, seeming heartbreakingly confused. Wherever he'd planned to go when he'd started out, he'd clearly forgotten.

She maneuvered so she was in front of him, blocking his path. "I'm in the mood for some breakfast. You want to eat with me?"

"What are you eating?" he asked skeptically.

"Pancakes?"

He made a look of disgust.

"Or eggs?" she said, grasping at straws. She was pretty sure she was out of eggs, but hopefully Oliver had some. If not, she'd order them from one of New York's dozen food-delivery services. Anything to get the man safely back inside.

He shrugged. "Okay."

"Perfect," Naomi said in relief, hooking her arm in his.

He let her lead him back toward their building. She kept her pace slow to match his so he wouldn't think he was being maneuvered and balk at her.

Walter glanced at her attire. "You've been exercising. My wife likes Jazzercise."

"Oh yeah?" Naomi asked. "What about you, any exercise?"

"Pretty good at squash. You play?"

"Definitely not. I barely even know what squash is," she said, pressing the button in the elevator for Walter's floor instead of her own. She'd kill for a hot shower, both to warm up and get rid of the dried sweat, but she needed to get Walter back to his apartment before Oliver and Janice freaked out.

Heck, Oliver probably was *already* freaking out.

Walter had switched topics from squash and was rambling something about the Dow dropping two hundred points, and she had no idea whether he was talking about today, yesterday, or twenty years ago, so she just made *mm-hmm* noises as she led him to his apartment.

"Do you have a key?" she asked him.

"Key?"

"Never mind." She lifted her hand and knocked.

The door jerked open midknock, her hand suspended in the air as she came face-to-face with Oliver.

A *nearly naked* Oliver.

Naomi's mouth was suddenly very dry, her pulse a little . . . jumpy.

And she was definitely no longer cold.

"Dad," Oliver said, his eyes closing in relief. "Dad, you can't do that!"

"Can't do what?" Walter said, going inside. "Why are you wearing a towel?"

"Because I was in the shower," Oliver said in exasperation. "You were still asleep, and— Never mind." He broke off on a deflated sigh, running his hand through his wet hair.

He still hadn't acknowledged Naomi, which was probably a good thing, considering she seemed to be having a heck of a time remembering how to breathe. And an even harder time looking away from his bare chest.

He was . . . well, nicely shaped. She'd suspected as much from the way he filled out his suit, but the reality was even better than expected. She found herself wondering what he did for exercise, because she suspected it wasn't Jazzercise or squash, and the cut of his biceps told her he did more than run.

There seemed to be no fat on the man—his torso was narrow as it tapered down into the navy towel knotted around his waist, and—

Oliver cut his eyes over to her without moving his head, and their gazes collided.

Whoops.

She'd definitely been caught ogling the man she'd all but ordered out of her life.

"Thank you," he said, his voice rough and a little hesitant. "I was in the shower for less than five minutes, I thought—then he was just gone—"

"It's okay," she said quietly, reassuring him. "Walter's fine. I caught up to him before he got more than a block away."

His eyes closed. "I was just calling the neighbors. Usually he sticks within the building, but if he's starting to go outside . . ."

Her heart went out to him at the genuine anguish on his face. Not only because of the magnitude of terror he must feel at the thought of his father wandering alone in New York City, but because he knew the days of his father living at home were perhaps limited.

And even with their antagonistic moment from Friday fresh on her mind, even with the memories of their childhood always lurking, she realized she wanted to help. She couldn't slow the progression of Alzheimer's, but maybe she could help in a small way.

"Do you want me to stay with him while you finish getting dressed?" she asked, even as she realized that watching Walter would mean entering the apartment—the same apartment where her mother's life had completely gone off the rails.

Closure. Remember? That's what you're after.

Oliver gave her a startled look, then glanced down at his body and groaned, obviously just now realizing his state of undress. "God."

She gave a small, hesitant smile. "If it makes you feel better, I've got a few miles' worth of sweat on me."

Naomi immediately regretted the careless admission, because his gaze raked over her, and she *felt* it. Sure, she was more clothed than him, but her blood was still pumping from the run, her emotions still simmering from the other night, and there was a rawness in the air.

No, that was too vague. There was a rawness between *them*. A heat that she didn't want, and sure as heck didn't know what to do with.

A loud thump from inside the apartment ruined the moment, as did Walter's muttered cursing. Oliver closed his eyes, as though for patience. "It's been one of those mornings. If you could just keep an eye on him for five minutes. Two minutes . . ."

"Absolutely," she said, already stepping inside, her eyes going to Walter, who was near the coffee table. The thump they'd heard was a pile of books, and Naomi went immediately to pick them up.

"You don't have to do that," Oliver said, closing the door to the apartment.

"Better me than you in a towel," she said with a sly grin over her shoulder.

He winced. "Right. I'll be back."

"I've got this, Walter," she said to the other man. "You can go ahead and sit down."

"Who are you?" he asked irritably, doing as she suggested and lowering himself to the recliner.

"I'm Naomi."

"Are you here to see him?" he asked, pointing in the direction of the room Oliver had disappeared into.

"Nope, here to see you." She stacked the books on the coffee table, noting that while most were generic coffee-table books with fancy colors and pretty photographs, there was also a Stephen King novel that, while seemingly brand-new, didn't at all look like it went with the others.

"This yours, Walter?" she asked, holding up the book.

He looked at it blankly. If it was his, he obviously didn't remember. Though it could have just as easily been Janice's. Or Oliver's.

She ran a finger down the spine. It was one of his newer titles that she hadn't read yet.

"I used to love Stephen King," she told Walter, even as he

reached for the remote and turned on the TV, ignoring her completely.

"What happened?"

Naomi whipped her head around to where Oliver was coming out of the bathroom. His hair was still damp, but he'd shaved and was dressed in a black sweater and jeans. The first time she'd seen him without a suit, and she tried not to notice that he looked just as good dressed in upscale casual as he did in business formal.

"What?" She forced her eyes back to his blue ones.

"You said you used to like King. What happened to change your mind?"

"Oh, nothing," she said, climbing to her feet, book still in hand. "I just don't have much time to read anymore." She caught herself and glanced down at the book. "That's not true. I guess I don't *make* time to read anymore."

"Don't beat yourself up. Adulthood does that to all of us. Eats up our schedule bit by bit until we don't even realize all of our free time's just . . . gone," he said, coming toward her and reaching for the book, running a finger down the spine the same way she had just moments earlier.

The absent gesture told her all she needed to know. "It's yours."

He smiled ruefully and set the book back on top of the others. "I, too, am a fan. And I, too, can't seem to find a minute to start the damn thing."

"Why is it here instead of your apartment?"

"It's for nights when Janice is out and I stay with Dad. He usually goes to bed early, and I always intend to finally start the book."

"What do you do instead? TV?"

"Yeah. And work, mostly."

She nodded in understanding but said nothing.

Oliver cleared his throat. "Well. Thanks for keeping an eye on him. Normally he's fine while I shower or dress or take a phone call, but he's been restless and irritable all morning."

"Don't talk about me like I'm not here," Walter groused, apparently not nearly as into his television show as he seemed.

"Sure, *now* you pay attention to me," Oliver said good-naturedly to his father as he nodded for Naomi to follow him into the kitchen, out of Walter's hearing.

"Where's Janice?" Naomi asked.

"Her father had a heart attack yesterday. She flew out last night to Birmingham to be with him."

"Is he okay?"

"Still critical," Oliver said, rubbing his neck. "I told her to stay with him as long as she needs, and I'm guessing it'll be at least a week."

The shrill ping of the intercom on the wall near the front door interrupted him. She jumped at the sound, remembering it from childhood. It would buzz whenever someone dialed the Cunninghams' unit number from downstairs.

"How old is that thing? A hundred?"

"Pretty much," he said with a grimace. "It didn't make sense for this place to get updated with the newer option to just buzz tenants' cell phones, given my dad doesn't have a phone, and Janice and I split our time here."

He went to the wall and pushed the Call button. "Hello?"

The reply was every bit as staticky as Naomi remembered as the doorman's voice crackled through. "Hi, Mr. Cunningham, I have Serena Grogan here to see you?"

"Sure, send her up," Oliver replied, before releasing the button.

"Temp caretaker to fill in for Janice," he said by way of explanation to Naomi.

"Oh." She clasped her fingers loosely in front of her.

Oliver pointedly looked at his watch. "Look, Naomi. I appreciate you helping my dad out this morning. Really. But you haven't exactly made a secret of the fact that you don't want anything to do with me, so . . ."

She gave a half smile. "So . . . leave?"

He crossed his arms. "It's been a trying morning. I've got a conference call in a half hour, I have no idea if Serena is going to go on Dad's instant-hate list—"

"He has one of those?"

"God yes. He can't remember much, but once he decides he doesn't like someone, he seems to remember that just fine."

"Really? He's been mostly sweet to me," she said, looking over at the docile-seeming Walter.

"Yeah, well, he likes you. Probably because he doesn't realize the feeling's not mutual." Oliver opened the front door as he said it, a clear dismissal, and Naomi was surprised at the sting of regret.

Still, what could she possibly say? He was giving her exactly what she thought she wanted. He was trying to get the hell out of her life, so why was she still standing here? Naomi managed a stiff nod, then walked past him out into the hallway. She turned back.

"I could help."

Oliver gave her a look. "What?"

"I could help with Walter. I'm still without an office for a couple weeks, so I'm working from home. My schedule's flexible, so if you need someone to stay with him . . ."

Oliver stared at her in obvious surprise.

You and me both, Naomi thought. She had no idea what she was offering. Or why.

Hadn't she just been telling herself that since she wasn't going to get the apology from Walter Cunningham she'd been planning for, it was time to put the whole thing behind her?

And here she was offering to play caretaker?

"Naomi, I can't—"

But before he finished his sentence, the elevator beeped, and a petite blond woman stepped out into the hallway.

She gave a pleasant smile when she saw Oliver and Naomi. "Is this the Cunningham residence?"

Naomi forced a smile back and made a gesturing motion toward the open door.

The woman nodded politely as she and Naomi passed each other, and Naomi listened numbly as Oliver and Serena Grogan made each other's acquaintance.

She couldn't resist a quick glance back over her shoulder, but Oliver had already closed the door, shutting her out.

It was just as she wanted, and yet . . . it wasn't at all.

Chapter Seventeen

Oliver had been fighting a losing battle against an impending headache since three that afternoon, and the now-unmistakable sound of a hard-boiled egg hitting the wallpaper in the kitchen was like a jackhammer on his temple.

He'd set up a makeshift office in his dad's guest room for the day, wanting to stay close and get some work done as Walter and Serena got used to each other.

At least that had been the intention. In reality, he hadn't gotten more than five minutes of uninterrupted time to deal with a single email, and as far as Walter and Serena getting used to each other . . . there'd been little to no progress.

Oliver went to the open door and looked out into the kitchen, watching as Serena calmly and quietly whisked away the plate and water cup that she'd placed in front of Walter for dinner.

"How about some TV, Walter? Your son said you enjoy the History Channel?" she asked, her voice never losing its pleasant hum, even as she went to pick up the egg from the carpet and drop it into the trash.

She paused as she saw Oliver, apparently noting his tension, because she gave him a reassuring smile.

He wasn't reassured. He knew he didn't need to apologize. Knew his father didn't have a grasp on what he was doing, but he felt like apologizing anyway.

His father had been a menace all day. Not just the usual mood swings and unpredictability of dementia, but something different. For whatever reason, he'd decided he didn't like Serena, and his dislike of her seemed to transcend all moods and waves of memories.

To the woman's credit, she didn't seem to mind. No doubt she'd dealt with it before, if not worse. In Oliver's opinion, women like Serena and Janice were saints. Yes, they were paid for their work, but it took a special sort of person to treat Walter with unwavering patience. Walter's former friends didn't do it. His surviving siblings didn't do it. Hell, Oliver wasn't above losing his cool with his father on a particularly rough day.

Janice and Serena though, they never seemed fazed.

Naomi never seemed fazed.

Oliver leaned a shoulder on the doorway, absently watching as Serena coaxed Walter over to the living room, even as his mind was on a different woman altogether.

"Leave me the hell alone," Walter grumbled at her as she tried to put a blanket over his legs.

Oliver entered the room, smiling apologetically at Serena as he went to his father, but Walter persisted in his bad mood.

He shoved at Oliver, "You're in the way." He gave a suspicious look to the kitchen, where Serena had started doing the dishes. "Who's that?"

"That's Serena, Dad. She's going to keep you company for the next couple weeks while I go to work."

"I don't want company."

"It's not up for debate," Oliver said, hearing the tiredness in his own voice.

"Where's Janice?"

"Her father's sick. She's caring for him."

"Thought we paid her to care for *me*. Don't like her." He pointed at Serena accusingly.

"Dad, give her a chance."

"Where's the other one?" Walter demanded.

"The other what?"

"The girl. The one you like with the orange hair."

Oliver froze, a little surprised his father recalled someone he'd met only twice. "Naomi?"

Walter gave him a conspiratorial smile, and Oliver would have warmed to his father's rare attempt to connect as father and son if it hadn't been over the one person Oliver was trying desperately not to think about.

"Where is she?" Walter asked again. "I like her better than that one." He said it loudly, then pointed at Serena again.

There was no way the blond caretaker wasn't overhearing this, and Oliver gave her an apologetic wince across the room, but she smiled and gave a quick wave of her hand as she continued cleaning the counter.

"Naomi's not your caretaker, Dad. She's just our neighbor."

Walter's expression turned mutinous, and defeated, Oliver lifted his hands in resignation. Naomi *had* offered, and Oliver was tired. So tired.

"What about this, Dad? I'll ask if Naomi can help sometimes, if you be nice to Serena the rest of the time."

Walter gave Serena one last dirty look, then a defiant nod.

Oliver exhaled in relief. It was probably a futile argument, since his father more than likely would forget who they all were tomorrow, if not in the next moment, but Oliver was determined to make Walter's lucid moments as bearable as possible, and if that meant Naomi . . .

Oh, who was he kidding. His desire to have Naomi around had very little to do with his father. He was going to figure that woman out if it killed him. And it might. Or *she* might.

Oliver went back into the kitchen to Serena. "Sorry about that."

"Don't apologize. I've been doing this far too long to take anything personally."

"Why do you do it?" he asked curiously. It was overstepping, but Serena was friendly and open in a way that Janice wasn't.

Serena's smile was sad. "My grandmother suffered from dementia. She helped raise me, and when she started to lose her memories, it was . . . rough. I decided pretty early on that I wanted to do whatever I could for those who went through what my grandma did. And for their families."

"You're a better person than me," Oliver said, scrubbing his hands over his face.

"You're doing just fine," Serena said quietly. "Though if I might suggest something . . ."

He looked at her and waited.

"You need a break," Serena said gently. "For his sake as well as your own. Your father needs you to have a clear head on his behalf. I'm scheduled to stay until nine tonight. Why don't you go take an hour or two to yourself?"

He hesitated, thinking of his father's instant, if unfounded, dislike of Serena.

"We'll be fine," she said, reading his thoughts.

"Maybe I'll head home just for a few. I live right downstairs and can be up within seconds if you call."

"Absolutely." He knew she wouldn't call unless it was an emergency.

"About tomorrow's schedule, if you're amenable, I'd like to work out a part-time, as-needed schedule, perhaps in the evenings. But I need to check something first. Can I let you know in a bit?"

"Of course," she said with a smile. Then she nodded toward Walter, who'd started to doze off in his chair. "He seems rather attached to this Naomi person."

"Yeah, he does, doesn't he," Oliver said wearily.

Irrationally so. *Like father, like son.*

"I'll be back in a bit," he said to Serena. "I'll have some answers on your schedule."

She waved him away, and Oliver headed to the second floor of the building.

But not to his own apartment.

Chapter Eighteen

*N*aomi was somehow unsurprised to see Oliver Cunningham outside her peephole. She *was* surprised by the jump in her stomach at the mere sight of him. Like a schoolgirl with a crush.

Suddenly she was glad she'd taken the time to put on makeup and real clothes today, instead of the sweatpants and messy bun she'd been rocking for the past couple of days of working at home.

Naomi opened the door and for a long moment, neither of them said a thing.

"I'll pay you," he said, ending the charged silence.

She blinked. "Excuse me?"

"To watch my father. I'll pay you. He can't stand his new caretaker, and that's too damn bad because I'll need her to stay with him at night, but during the day . . . does your offer still stand?"

She should say no. She should end this thing with the Cunninghams before it got any more complicated.

Instead, she stepped aside, wordlessly inviting him in.

"Have you eaten?" she asked, gesturing at the stove. "I was just making . . . well, *making*'s a strong word. I'm heating up a jar of tomato sauce and boiling water for pasta."

He gave her a surprised look. "Did you just invite me to dinner?"

"Apparently," she muttered, lifting the lid off the boiling water on the stove and adding a generous handful of salt as she'd seen on the Food Network, not the tiny pinch of salt her mom had added on the rare occasions she'd tried to cook.

"I don't have to stay. I was just . . . my dad's decided he likes you."

"That surprises you?" she asked, taking a sip of the red wine she'd poured herself.

"Well, like I said, he doesn't like many people."

"Because of the illness?"

Oliver shrugged. "Because it's *him*."

She watched him for a moment, noticing the shadows under his eyes, the tired set of his shoulders.

"So," he said, shoving his hands into his pockets. "Does your offer to watch my dad during the day still stand? Just until Janice gets back. And seriously, let me pay you."

"I don't need your money."

Her voice was sharp, and he gave her a puzzled look. "I'm aware of that. But I'm also aware I can't take advantage of your time."

She sipped the wine and considered this.

"But there's another part of the deal," he said quietly.

"Aha." She pointed at him in accusation.

He gave a faint smile. "I need you to decide."

She gave him a startled look. "Decide what? What does that mean?"

"It means," he said, coming around the counter to stand beside her, "that you can't be swiping at me one moment and asking me to stay for dinner the next."

"Are you telling me how to behave, Mr. Cunningham?" Naomi meant for her voice to be brisk and businesslike and was appalled to hear it come out a little breathy.

He was so *close*.

Oliver smiled slightly, his eyes never leaving hers. "I'm not sure anyone would dare tell you how to behave. I'm simply warning you."

"Warning me about what?"

His gaze dropped to her mouth before slowly lifting to her eyes once more. "That next time you look at me like you want me to kiss you, I will."

She scoffed, although she was afraid it came off more hot and bothered than anything. "When did I look at you like I wanted you to kiss me?"

"Friday night. Before you got scared and ran away."

Her cheeks flooded with heat, and she wasn't sure if it was anger or embarrassment that he might be right.

She decided on anger. It was safer. "Am I the only woman who's never fallen at your feet? Is that why you keep sniffing around?"

"Sniffing around?" he asked incredulously before giving a quick shake of his head. "Damn, my game is worse than I thought."

"We're not playing a game," she said, taking the opportunity to move away. "Weren't you the one who told me on move-in day that I should try to be neighborly? That's what I'm doing, asking to help you out. Don't read into it."

Oliver closed his eyes and inhaled, looking so exhausted that she had the strangest urge to press her hand to his cheek, to offer . . . comfort. If she were honest, it was a bit of a foreign feeling. She rarely felt warm toward people. That had changed, slightly, with Claire and Audrey. Even more so with him.

Finally he opened his eyes, and he looked more determined than ever as he fixed her with a steady look.

"You have to decide, Naomi. Decide what we're going to be to each other. I can't entrust my father's care to someone so mercurial. So decide how you feel about me. About my father. No more games."

She wanted to argue that she *wasn't* playing games, but . . . he was right. To say that she was inconsistent in her behavior toward him would be an understatement, and that wasn't like her. Naomi had always been an all-in person. She decided how she felt about something and stuck to it.

Which was the tricky thing with the Cunninghams. She *had* decided her feelings: Hate. Resentment. A few revenge fantasies mixed in.

Only they hadn't been what they were supposed to be. Walter hadn't been the cold, heartless patriarch deserving of a scathing set down. And Oliver hadn't been a petulant dirtbag throwing soccer balls at little girls' faces and breaking their glasses.

They'd *changed*, forcing her feelings about them to change, and she was no good at that. A hard admission to make, even to herself, but it was the brutal truth. But maybe she could be better. Maybe she had to be.

"I'm sorry," she said quietly, her gaze on his Adam's apple instead of his eyes because she wasn't *that* brave.

"For?"

"The mixed signals," she said. "I don't blame you for being frustrated."

Oliver nodded in acknowledgment of her apology. "So what's it to be? Barely civil neighbors or . . ."

That *or* was intriguing.

What would happen if she leaned into him right now? If she were to lift onto her toes and brush her lips over his?

Without warning, an image of her mother flashed through Naomi's mind.

She could be civil to Oliver and Walter Cunningham, but she wouldn't *fall* for the man who'd helped set her mother down a path of self-destruction. She wouldn't.

But neither could she continue to let the hate consume her. Perhaps . . .

Naomi lifted her eyes. "Or we could try to be friends."

His head inclined slightly. "Friends."

She nodded. "It makes sense, right? We live next door to each other. Friends and neighbors who lend each other a cup of sugar when the need arises."

Oliver smiled slightly. "You bake?"

"Wine," she amended quickly. "We could lend each other wine."

"Friends," he said slowly. "I can try that. In fact, how about we try that wine thing now?"

"I think that can be arranged," she said, stepping back to retrieve a glass. She poured, and handed him a glass of the zinfandel.

He accepted it with a grin. "You know, I once knew this woman who disliked me so much she'd only serve me drinks in coffee mugs."

"Is that so?" Naomi said, lifting her wooden spoon and stirring the sauce. "She sounds delightfully charming."

"That's one word for her."

"What word would *you* use?" Naomi asked.

He leaned his hip against the counter, watching her stir. "Complicated," he said finally. "I'd say she's the most complicated woman I've ever met."

"A little short on those corner pieces, are you?"

"I am. Getting closer though."

"You're not exactly an easy puzzle yourself," Naomi murmured, dropping a handful of spaghetti into the boiling water, and then adding a bit more for good measure, not sure how much a man like Oliver ate.

Oliver. She was making dinner for Oliver Cunningham.

"You're smiling," he said.

"Hmm? Oh, I guess I am," she said. "I just never imagined that the first meal I'd cook for a man would be for you." He blinked in surprise, and she fixed him with a look. "I don't know why you're so shocked. Do I *look* like the domesticated type?"

Oliver gestured with his wineglass to the stove, and Naomi swore at the boiling water threatening to bubble over as she fumbled for the knob to turn down the heat.

"Very domesticated."

She breathed out a laugh. "I don't suppose you cook?"

"I used to. Not a lot, but in my midtwenties I got it in my head that I could be a pretty hot commodity on the dating market if I knew my way around the kitchen."

"You'd be right," she said. "So what happened?"

"Hmm?" He picked up the spoon and stirred the pasta sauce.

"You said you used to cook. You don't anymore?"

A shadow passed over his face. "My mom got sick, and all my attention went to that. Then she passed. Then my dad got sick . . ." He gave a rueful shrug. "Pity party, I know."

"A justified one," Naomi said, turning to face him. "So did it work?" she asked. "Your grand plan of setting yourself apart on the dating scene by cooking?"

"Eventually. I made a couple of judgment errors early on."

"Such as?"

"Such as shrimp scampi, while delicious, has copious amounts of garlic, which doesn't necessarily make for the most amorous scenario. Also, I spent a hell of a lot of time perfecting a ragu with fettuccine before realizing that it's damn hard to look sexy with noodles hanging from one's mouth."

"Well then, prepare to be thoroughly unseduced," Naomi said, nodding toward the pot of boiling spaghetti.

For a moment Oliver's eyes seemed to heat as they drifted over her, and foolishly Naomi wished she'd made something sexier for dinner. Something fancy and easy to eat, like seared scallops, or a cheese plate, or any sort of pasta that didn't have to be twirled, or . . .

Nope. No. She was not going to start thinking about Oliver and sexy in the same sentence. Okay fine. She wasn't going to *continue* thinking about him that way.

"Plates," she blurted out, pointing at her cupboard. "If you can get plates, this will be ready in just a minute."

Oliver gave her a knowing smirk as he set his wineglass aside. "Doesn't get more friend-zoned than being ordered to set the table."

"What if I added *please*?" Naomi asked. "Then it's a request, not an order."

"True," he said, pulling down two plates. "But still friend-zone."

"Better than enemy-zone, Ollie," she said, dropping his childhood nickname she distinctly remembered him hating.

He went still, his eyes flickering as though with a memory, and for a second she froze, wondering if this would be it. The moment when Oliver reconciled nine-year-old Naomi Fields with twenty-nine-year-old Naomi Powell.

Instead he gave her a vaguely menacing stare. "I'm not answering to that."

"What, Ollie?" she asked innocently. "It suits you."

"Keep it up, and I'll have to think of a nickname for you," he said, setting the plates on the table.

You already have. Carrots.

"Did you ever watch *Anne of Green Gables*?" she blurted, and lifted out a strand of spaghetti to test the doneness.

"Sure, all the time. I used to have the guys over to my dorm room in college, and we'd just watch the hell out of it."

Naomi gave a choked laugh at his sarcasm, even as she fanned her mouth at the too-hot pasta. "So that's a no, then."

"That's a definite no. Never heard of it. Why?"

Naomi set a colander into the sink to drain the pasta. *It's a book, turned into a movie, about a redheaded girl and a little twerp of a boy named Gilbert Blythe, who used to torment her with the nickname Carrots.*

"Nothing. Never mind," she said, mixing the pasta with the sauce and bringing the serving dish to the table.

She looked up in surprise as he pulled out her chair for her. "Pretty manners, Ollie."

"Had to do something to make up for the loss of my cooking skills. Figured I might as well learn how to be a gentleman."

"You really never cook anymore?" she asked as he sat, reaching for the pasta bowl.

"No time," he said, setting the napkin in his lap and taking a sip of wine.

Naomi reached over and dumped pasta on his plate. "To cook, or to date?"

She looked up at him when he didn't reply, and he gave her a crooked smile, sitting back in his chair. "Is that your subtle way of asking if I'm seeing anyone?"

"What*ever* gave you the impression that I'm subtle?"

He laughed. "Good point. But to answer your question, I date about as often as I cook these days, which is . . . well, let's just say it's been a while."

Naomi sprinkled a liberal amount of cheese on her plate and pushed the container toward him. "Intentional? Or just the result of circumstances?"

"The latter. Alzheimer's is sort of a twenty-four-seven situation. Janice already watches Dad nine to five and during any after-hours work functions. I can't ask her to do it for social engagements as well—the woman would never get any time off."

Naomi started to reply, then thought better of it, eating a mouthful of pasta instead. Oliver was giving her a knowing look. "Self-censoring looks physically painful for you. Spit it out."

She set her fork aside and picked up her wine. "All right then. I was going to say that I understand. Really I do. But are you sure that's sustainable?"

He shrugged. "What are my options? He's my dad."

"Yes, and I'm pretty sure he wouldn't want you putting your life on hold for him."

"Really?" Oliver asked, a rare caustic note entering his usually carefully unreadable voice. "I think that's exactly what the bastard would have wanted."

She fiddled with her fork, careful not to give away her agreement that the Walter Cunningham she remembered *was* the sort of selfish bastard who expected others' lives to revolve around him.

"So he and Serena didn't mesh, huh?" she asked.

"Not at all," Oliver said, after swallowing. "It's why I came down here in the first place. For whatever reason, he seems attached to you."

"For whatever reason?" she asked with a smile.

"Yeah, well. He doesn't know you like I do."

Oliver winked as he said it, and it caused a warm churn in her stomach that had nothing to do with the pasta.

"I'm happy to stay with him during the day until Janice gets back, but I'm not accepting your money."

He set his fork aside. "Naomi, I can't ask you to watch him in exchange for nothing."

"I won't be the hired help," she snapped, her own fork clattering noisily to her plate.

"Whoa," he said slowly, leaning back in his chair.

She took a deep breath to calm herself and reached for her glass. "If I do this, I do this as your equal."

Oliver frowned. "Whatever gave you the thought I didn't think of you as an equal?"

Tell him! Just tell him who you are!

And the fact that she couldn't told Naomi the real problem. She was afraid that if she did tell him, if she revealed her past and why she was living in the building in the first place, then she really *wouldn't* be his equal.

He'd stop seeing her as confident Naomi Powell, and start seeing her as the daughter of the whore housekeeper who'd seduced his dad.

"Never mind," she said irritably, picking up her fork again.

"Naomi."

"What."

He waited until she looked at him, then smiled slightly. "Will you please watch my father while I'm at work tomorrow? I promise not to try to insult you with money, but I'm going to insist you let me at least feed you after. Final offer."

She studied him, looking for a catch, but saw only . . . kindness.

"Okay."

His smile grew wider, and he resumed eating. "Good."

After a moment, he said, "Question."

"What?" she asked warily.

"Are you as prickly with female friends as you are with male friends?" He put the slightest emphasis on the last word.

She shrugged. "Hard to say. I don't have a ton of them."

"What about Claire and Audrey?"

"They're friends," she admitted. "But we've only known each other a few months."

"You don't think it'll last?"

She fiddled with her fork, thinking this over. "Honestly? I don't know. On one hand, we clicked. Almost immediately. On the other hand, the circumstances of our friendship are . . . unusual."

"Maybe you clicked *because* of the circumstances. The same man was interested in all three of you. You must have something in common."

"I don't know what," she grumbled. "Claire is kind and responsible. Audrey's sweet and fun."

"And you are . . . ?"

She smiled. "Ambitious and prickly?"

"Driven and guarded," he countered.

"The first one I take as a compliment. The second I can't help. Wouldn't *you* be if you learned that the person you were sleeping with was married?"

"Perhaps. But I also suspect you kept people at a distance long before that."

She pushed her plate away. "The pasta's *really* not good, huh?"

"No," he said, looking like he wanted to press her for an

answer on his last question but decided to let her dodge it. "Got any ice cream?"

"Now you're talking, Ollie," she said, standing and going to the freezer. Then she turned back. "Do you need to get back to Walter?"

He hesitated, and she saw the internal battle raging within. The compulsive need to do his duty by his father. His desire to stay.

"I'll double-check with Serena," he said, pulling his phone out of his pocket and waggling it at her. "Last call to back out of your offer."

Naomi pulled the lid off the Ben & Jerry's carton and looked across her kitchen at the man who'd once made her life utterly miserable. And who also made her feel the most alive she had in years.

"Let's do it," she blurted out before she could rethink the fact that she was willingly entangling herself with a family she'd spent a lifetime resenting.

"Good," he said, turning his attention to his phone. "Oh, one more thing."

"Hmm?" She dug a spoon into the carton and plopped a bite of cookie dough ice cream in her mouth.

"You still dating Dylan with a *Y*?"

The question caught her off guard, and a chunk of chocolate chip lodged in her throat.

"Not sure that's your business."

Oliver stood and shoved his phone back in his pocket. "Maybe not yet."

"What's that supposed to mean?" She asked, as he headed to the front door.

He gave her an enigmatic smile over his shoulder, opening her front door. But he said nothing.

"What's that supposed to mean!" It was a near shout now.

The front door clicked close, and she opened her mouth to tell him he forgot his ice cream.

Damn it. Just as well. If she and Oliver Cunningham were going to continue being in the same orbit, she was going to need the entire carton to herself.

Chapter Nineteen

*W*hoa. You do know it's just the three of us, right?" Audrey asked as she opened her front door to Naomi and took in the copious amount of wine bottles Naomi was holding.

"It was cheaper to buy six," Naomi replied, handing over the bottles and shrugging out of her jacket. "Also, trust me, I need at least half of that to myself."

"Uh-oh. What happened?" Audrey asked, leading Naomi into the kitchen.

"Let's wait until Claire gets here so I only have to explain the nightmare once."

"Here," Claire announced, holding up her arm from where she sat on Audrey's couch.

Naomi craned to look at what she was watching on the TV. "Dang, you really are a baseball nut."

"Yup. But for you, I will turn it off." She reached for the remote, then paused, watching something on the field that had the announcers shouting. "Correction. For you, I will mute."

"If Brayden hadn't jabbed his chopstick into our dumplings, would you have turned it off for us?" Audrey asked.

Claire wrinkled her nose, and Naomi gave Audrey a look and shook her head.

"Damn," Audrey said. "I've been working on that one. Okay, what are we eating?"

"Not Chinese," Claire muttered, joining them in the kitchen and checking the labels on the various bottles Naomi had brought. "Naomi can pick."

"You don't want me to pick. My favorite food used to be Chef Boyardee. The off-brand kind."

"No, pick!" Audrey protested. "Except maybe not Chef Boy-are-whatever you just said."

"You're missing out, but I'll start you off easy. How about pizza?"

"Done," Audrey said, pulling out her phone. "There's a place around the corner that does this classic Neapolitan crust, with homemade smoked mozzarella and—"

"No, not fancy pizza," Naomi interrupted. "Homemade cheese? Are you kidding me?"

"Well, where do you get your pizza?"

"Let's just say it's not the kind of place that has an online ordering system," Naomi said, already dialing a number from the Favorites menu of her phone.

"Hey, Claudio," she said the moment an almost unintelligible rumble of Italian sounded in her ear.

"Naomi! *Mia Bella*. The regular?"

She grinned at the familiar greeting. "The regular times three. I'm about to introduce two friends to the best meal of their life. Grab a pen though, 'kay? I need Jorge to come to my friend's house."

A minute later she set her phone back on the counter. "Done. They should be here in an hour. Or so."

"An *hour*? It's Thursday night. My guys' smoked mozzarella could get made from scratch faster than that!"

Claire handed Audrey a glass of red wine. "Probably not. The mozzarella, yes, that can be done in thirty minutes. The smoked part would take longer."

"Are you making this up?"

"Nope." Claire sipped her own wine. "Brayden and I took a cheese-making class once. Back before I knew he was, you know. Dipping into other fondue pots."

"Nice." Naomi lifted her hand and Claire gave her a high five, while Audrey pouted.

"How is that better than my chopstick one!" she protested.

"Well, for starters, nobody sticks a chopstick into a dumpling. Second of all, the word *dumpling* is just . . . no. Keep working on it."

"Fine," Audrey muttered. "But for real, Naomi, is your pizza coming from Italy?"

"Nope. Belmont."

"Oh God, is someone trying to create some new Manhattan neighborhood where there isn't one again?" Claire asked.

"Nope. Belmont is in the northwest Bronx."

Audrey's eyes bugged out. "You order pizza from the Bronx?"

"And they deliver?" Claire added.

"They do when I pay them an extra fifty bucks, plus extra for the delivery guy."

"An extra fifty bucks for a pizza. It must be amazing."

"Not really," Naomi said. "But when I was in seventh grade, my mom went through a rare patch of being able to keep not only one job, but two. Claudio fed me dinner pretty much every day that year while she worked back-to-back shifts. This is my way of paying him back."

"Well then, I can't wait to try it," Audrey said with an approving nod as they all went into the living room and sat on the couch. "Now, how about you tell us why your wineglass is filled to the brim. Bad day?"

"Not really," Naomi said, swirling her wine. "It's just been . . . weird."

"How so?"

"I'm kind of sort of helping take care of Walter Cunningham."

"Who? *Wait*. Oliver's father? The one who slept with your mom and then threw her out?" Claire asked incredulously.

Naomi made a face. "Sort of?"

"*Why?* What do you mean you're taking care of him?"

"He has Alzheimer's, and as far as the why, I don't really know. It's like one moment I was reminding myself that I moved into the building to show them that the girl they kicked to the streets could buy the entire building they live in and then some. And the next . . . they're not the same. I mean, Walter, obviously not, because of the dementia. But Oliver, too. And before I knew it, I had this weird urge to help an old man who's sick, even knowing he's a jerk. Used to be a jerk. Whatever. And now you think I'm crazy."

"Not crazy," Claire said slowly. "But are you doing it for Walter? Or for his son?"

Naomi's eyes narrowed. "Meaning?"

Claire swirled her wine. "Meaning that we saw the way Oliver Cunningham looks at you like he doesn't know whether he wants to kiss you or shove you against the wall, or shove you against the wall to kiss you . . ."

"Please stop," Audrey said, dabbing her brow dramatically. "I haven't been pushed against the wall *ever*. But seriously. What is going on with you two? You guys looked mighty friendly leaving my party last weekend."

"Did we?" Naomi said sarcastically. "Or did we maybe look that way because you two conspired to set us up."

"Claire's the one who brought him."

"You're the one who made sure Naomi sat next to him," Claire countered.

"And you both all but shoved Dylan in a cab so that Oliver would have to walk me home."

"We didn't want Dylan to be late to the airport," Claire said innocently.

Audrey nodded in solemn agreement. "His job is *very* important. Super demanding. Did he not tell you once or a thousand times?"

Naomi conceded with a laugh. "Okay, I'll grant that Dylan was a little . . ."

"Conceited? Invasive? Full of himself?" Claire said.

"He's a good producer," Naomi pointed out.

"That I'll believe. He certainly was determined to get the dirt on you."

Naomi winced. Dylan *had* been a little obvious in his attempt to get information about her from her friends that night. But he'd called later to apologize, and Naomi could cop to being a little pushy when she wanted something.

"Any regrets on signing the contract for the TV show?"

"Oddly, no. I mean, things are moving fast, but so far I haven't had to do much," Naomi said, taking a sip of her wine. They were right, she *had* given herself a plus-size pour.

It wasn't the most responsible way to deal with the fact that she couldn't stop thinking about Oliver Cunningham, but it was effective.

"Tell ya what," Naomi said, looking back to Audrey to change the subject. "I'll give you the full rundown on Oliver if you fill me in on Clarke."

Audrey blinked in surprise, then laughed. "Clarke? Clarke West? As in . . . Clarke?"

Naomi laughed. "Yes, as in *Clarke*. The Clarke. What's the story there? Gay?"

"Definitely not."

Claire's eyes narrowed. "You've had a straight best guy friend who looks like *that* for twenty years? How does that work?"

"What she said," Naomi said, pointing at Claire. "Wait, no, let me guess. You guys hooked up and had no chemistry but decided to be friends rather than exes. Ooh, or you're secretly in love but aren't ready to admit it to yourself?"

Audrey raised her eyebrows. "Those are my only two options?"

"Pretty much."

"Says who?" Audrey demanded.

Naomi shrugged. "Movies?"

"Every teen TV show ever written," Claire chimed in.

"Well, that's true," Audrey admitted. "But I hate to break it to you ladies, Clarke and I don't fit into either of those categories."

"He's not gay. And not an ex? And you're not secretly in love?" Naomi asked skeptically.

Audrey smiled. "No to all of the above. We really are just friends. When I was in first grade, a mean third-grade girl stole the locket my grandma had given me for my birthday. He made her give it back, then played hopscotch with me until I stopped crying."

"How did you not fall in love then and there?" Claire asked a little dreamily. "That's so romantic."

"I was six, so not so much," Audrey said. "I idolized him, but more in the big brother kind of way, since my actual big brother was much older."

"Okay, but what about after you developed hormones," Naomi asked. "Surely then you realized your best friend was ridiculously cute."

"Yeah, but he's a couple years older, so he got hormones first. By the time I figured out the whole boy-girl thing, he was already a ladies' man, and I was smart enough to recognize a heartbreaker, even if he was my best friend."

"Wait, he was a heartbreaker, at what, twelve?"

Audrey gave Claire a look over their wineglasses. "You've seen him."

"I have. Which is why I can't believe there hasn't been *something*. A drunken fling? Secret crush? Give me something. He's too hot for there not to be a story there."

"No story," Audrey said firmly. "Your turn."

"My turn what?"

"You *know* what. Oliver Cunningham."

"Well, as you ladies now know, Oliver was *not* my childhood hero. Quite the opposite. He makes that bitch who stole your locket sound like a sweetie pie," she said to Audrey. "End of story."

"Um, not end of story. You're neighbors with some seriously delicious animosity. Have you told him who you are yet?"

Naomi shook her head.

"Naomi. You've got to tell him," Claire said.

"What good would that do?"

"Well, the woman he's seriously crushing on wouldn't be lying to him, for starters."

"He's not crushing."

Claire and Audrey exchanged a look.

"He's not! He's just . . . intrigued."

Like she was by him.

"Trust me, I am not Oliver Cunningham's type."

"What's his type?"

"You two," she said, pointing between them.

"Well, obviously you have something in common with us. Brayden certainly liked all three of us," Claire said, her tone just a bit caustic.

"He married you," Naomi retorted. "And he at least let Audrey think he was going to marry her someday. He never made any such promises to me. Brayden saw me for what I am. The real me. Just like Dylan sees me."

"What's that mean? The real you?"

"You know." She waved her hand dismissively. "A little brash. Fun. The one you do tequila shots with on Friday night, not the one you take home to Mom."

"Well, you lucked out there. Brayden's mother was a nightmare," Claire said.

"Still. You know what I mean."

"Actually, not at all," Audrey protested. "Don't talk about yourself like you're . . ."

"Trash?" Naomi said for her.

"Stop it," Claire said sharply. "You want to know who really sees you, it's me and Audrey. And like it or not, it's Oliver, too, if you could see past your childhood grudge to give him a chance."

"Hey!" Naomi said, a little stung. "For the record, we had dinner together."

Audrey clapped. "That is so cute."

"Cuter than Clarke playing hopscotch with you? And it was just dinner."

"What kind of dinner?" Claire demanded.

"Foie gras and caviar, what else? We had *spaghetti*, Claire. What does it matter? I fed him really bad pasta."

"You fed him? Oh my gosh. You *like* him."

"I don't." Naomi was increasingly feeling wildly out of her depth. "Or I don't know if I do. What I do know is that I've had dinner with a guy in the past week, and you haven't. We've already established that Clarke doesn't count," Naomi said, lifting a finger in warning to Audrey, who was about to protest. "I may be confused, but at least I'm *trying*."

"Hmm, I need more wine," Audrey mused, starting to stand.

"You get more wine after you agree to go on a date. *Any* date," Naomi said.

"I haven't met anyone I want to go on a date with," Audrey said primly.

"Me neither," Clare said, more emphatically.

"Well, that's too damn bad," Naomi said. "We agreed to help each other avoid Manhattan's crappy men, not avoid all men."

"Is there such a thing as a man who's not crappy?" Claire tapped her chin.

"Oh, stop. I'm not saying you need to commit to an entree. Just sample the buffet," Naomi said. "It's only going to get harder the longer you wait."

Audrey slumped back against the couch. "I hate that she's right. I swear, every day, I wake up with another bitterness wrinkle."

"A what?"

"Here," Audrey said, pointing to the corner of her eyes. "Bitterness."

"She could be onto something," Naomi said. "My mom fed on bitterness, and she had whopper crow's-feet."

Claire's hand lifted to her face. "So what are you suggesting?"

"Just that we all agree to go on a date. Just one. Painless."

"Says the woman who has two men panting after her."

Naomi didn't dignify that with a response.

"All right," Audrey said after a moment. "I'm in. I'll even let you guys pick the guy, since I confess it was lame of me to bring Clarke to the dinner party when I insisted you guys bring an actual date."

"And I'll let you pick someone for me, too," Claire said. "Since the date I brought was actually for Naomi."

"Whom Naomi didn't want."

"You sure about that?" Audrey waggled her eyebrows. "Who are *you* going on a date with?"

"Dylan. Obviously."

"You sure?"

Naomi opened her mouth, but no words came out.

Damn it. She *wasn't* sure.

Chapter Twenty

*I*s this lip gloss too extra?"

Naomi didn't even glance up from her phone as she replied to her assistant. "Deena, there's not a thing about you that's not extra."

"Which normally I take as a compliment . . ."

"Meant as one." Naomi continued to type on her phone.

"But, I'm worried the sparkle will look too garish on camera."

"Wait, what?" Naomi finally looked up. She and her assistant were sitting at a conference room table at StarZone's Flatiron headquarters while they waited for Dylan and the rest of the team to join them. "You know that we're not actually filming today, or anytime soon, right? They've barely started the script."

"But the casting director will be here, right?" Deena asked, adding an extra coat of gloss that really did seem to have more glitter than a kindergarten art project.

"I want it to be known that the best person to play Deena is, in fact, the *actual* Deena. Not some bimbo poser."

"Noted. But I'm pretty sure the first season is going to be all about my childhood. Pre-Deena."

"Damn." Deena dropped the gloss back in her purse and pulled out a pack of gum. "Wintergreen?"

Naomi shook her head.

Her assistant shoved a stick in her mouth and studied Naomi. "So. This producer guy. Dylan Day. He's hot, right?"

"Don't make me regret inviting you," Naomi muttered, turning her attention back to her phone.

"You need me. I'm going to take notes."

"On what?" Naomi looked pointedly at the lack of notebook, laptop, or tablet.

Deena tapped her temple. "All up here. Big hair, big brain. So is he hot, or what? He looked hot that day in the office, but I only saw his butt. Do you know he dated the actress from that show about the sorority? She was pretty, but like half his age."

Naomi nodded, even as she zoomed in on a picture of Audrey and Clarke on Instagram. *Damn, that woman had good skin, even with those bitterness wrinkles.*

"So are you guys dating?"

Naomi gave in and laughed. "Deena!"

"Don't think I haven't noticed that he's basically the only person who has your direct number."

"Which must mean we've eloped, right?"

"Your sarcasm is extra thick, which means I'm onto something."

"Fine. Okay. We went to one dinner that was half date, half business meeting, and he was my date to a friend's dinner party."

"But he wants to do it again." Deena didn't ask it as a question, and she wasn't wrong. Dylan had made no secret of his interest in seeing her again now that he was back from Dallas, but she'd been dodging, saying she was busy.

Which was true. Her job took up most of her days, and that was before she'd agreed to take on Walter Cunningham. Still, she didn't regret offering to help. Walter had stayed with her all day last Wednesday and most of this morning before Serena had taken over so Naomi could attend this meeting. And as much as Naomi had enjoyed her time with Walter, she'd been even more surprised, and alarmed, to realize that she'd enjoyed the moment Oliver had come home in the evening even more.

And the way it had felt so *right* for the two of them to have dinner—for the second night in a row—was downright terrifying.

"Have you kissed yet?" Deena asked, snapping her gum.

"No! I'm just helping out with his dad for a few days."

Deena's jaw stopped working her gum for a moment. "You know Dylan Day's dad? Damn, woman, you work fast."

She was saved from having to explain—or trying to explain—the mess she'd gotten herself into with her new neighbor and ex-nemesis as the conference room doors opened.

"Sorry for the delay," Dylan said, greeting them with a grin. "You must be Deena."

"In the flesh," Deena said, shaking his hand and giving him an unabashed once-over. "Yep. Hot."

Naomi groaned, but Dylan only laughed and gave Naomi a quick wink.

How was it that a wink from Oliver Cunningham could keep her up all night, but a wink from this guy, who was exactly the type of guy she'd always gravitated toward . . . nothing.

The group took their places around the table, and a tall, wiry woman who introduced herself as Libby, the casting director, got right down to business.

"I've got our little Naomi."

Naomi blinked. "What? Already?"

"Well, we'll still have full casting calls to make sure, but I guarantee you're going to flip over this kid. She's based in LA, but her Bronx accent is spot-on."

Naomi nodded, trying not to get hung up on the irony that she'd spent years trying to get rid of her New York accent, only to have some child star from Hollywood put on that very same accent for entertainment.

No, not just entertainment, Naomi reminded herself. Accuracy. The entire reason for doing this in the first place was so that girls growing up like Naomi did would know there was more than hairstylist and waitress jobs in their future if they wanted it.

"I'm sure she's perfect," Naomi said with a smile. "But when we do open it up for casting, can we be sure to put feelers out in the outer boroughs? It may be a long shot, but I'd love if we could find a girl actually from the Bronx."

"Absolutely. You got it," Dylan said. Naomi thought she might have seen Libby give just the slightest eye-roll, but the other woman nodded and jotted something in her black notebook.

"Naomi, Caleb Davis, head screenwriter," a bald guy to her right said, standing to shake her hand. "I'm delighted to say we've already got some homework for you."

Caleb pushed a fat stack of paper across the table. "The pilot. I'll send you a PDF, too, but I find sometimes the old-fashioned way is best."

"Wow." Naomi blinked down at it.

"Told ya we were moving fast on this," Dylan said.

"Take your time reviewing it," Caleb said. "And by take your time, I mean if you could have any feedback by next Monday, that's my deadline."

Naomi laughed as Deena pulled the script toward her and took a peek at the first few pages. "Got it. Anything I should look out for?"

"Actually, yeah." Caleb shot a quick look at Dylan, who took over.

"The script's good," Dylan said, leaning forward with a smile. "Caleb's a genius, and pulled together a pretty compelling story of your childhood from the dozens of interviews you've done over the years, plus interviews with people who knew you back then—"

"Wait." Naomi held up her hand. *"What?"*

A man from her left wearing the most boring blue suit, white shirt, and blue tie combo on the planet jumped all over her incredulous tone. "It was in the contract. Page twenty-three, section 5C, specifically authorizes us to interview all sources we find relevant."

"Don't know if you could tell, but *lawyer alert*," Dylan whispered loudly, nodding toward Blue Suit.

Everyone chuckled, and Naomi forced a polite smile. "I read the contract. I guess I didn't expect that people who knew me twenty years ago would be considered relevant."

"Well, they're not, really," Caleb admitted. "We rounded up a few former classmates, but while there was no shortage of people who wanted to tell us about how they 'knew you when,' nobody seems to really *know* you."

"I was a shy kid."

It was her standard line, but it wasn't really true. She'd just been a *smart* kid. Smart enough to know that most people would throw you under the bus to save their own ass. She could thank Oliver Cunningham for *that* lesson.

"There is one gap we're hoping you can fill," Caleb said, flipping through a yellow legal pad until he found the note he was looking for. "One of our researchers discovered that you briefly transferred out of the Bronx school district when you attended the third grade in school District Two?"

Naomi went still. She didn't know crap about school zones, but she knew exactly where she'd spent the third grade.

"What does that mean?" Deena asked.

Dylan studied Naomi for a moment, then looked at Deena. "It means Naomi went to third grade in Manhattan."

Deena shook her head. "Nope. They got it wrong."

Dylan looked back at Naomi, and she realized she should have seen this coming.

That they wouldn't be satisfied summarizing her childhood with a series of inspirational anecdotes about how instead of a lemonade stand, she'd sold her own jewelry made out of paper clips and buttons, or how she'd made her own Barbie clothes out of bits of cloth she'd swiped from the mean seamstress who'd lived upstairs. Of course they would want the drama.

And she had to give them credit. They'd gone sniffing and found the jugular of Naomi's childhood in under a week. Might as well admit the bare minimum now to stop them from digging further.

"They're not wrong," she told her assistant quietly.

Deena gave her a startled look. "Really? You grew up in Manhattan?"

Naomi snorted. "Hardly. I lived there for a year. Less than."

"Why? Where?" Caleb already had his pen ready.

"Park Avenue."

Deena's gum stopped smacking for a moment, then resumed a moment later, and she wisely kept from mentioning the calls from 517 Park Avenue and the fact that Naomi had made a last-minute decision to buy that apartment after signing a lease on the Tribeca condo.

Caleb frowned, flipping through his notes. "You live on Park Avenue currently, right?"

"Right." She sat back and crossed her legs, hoping her clipped tone and cool demeanor would signal *nothing to see here, move along.*

"What brought you and your mom to the Upper East Side?"

Naomi swallowed. "My mom was sort of a housekeeper/cook/nanny for a family on Park Ave for a while. We lived with them."

Caleb nodded, jotting something down in his notebook. "Good, this is good stuff. Cinderella stuff. You said you were there for about a year?"

"Yup."

"Why'd you guys leave to head back to the Bronx?"

You and your daughter are trash, and you will always be trash. Get out of my home before I call the authorities.

It was funny that what Naomi remembered most about that awful day was the way Margaret Cunningham never used contractions, chose words like *authorities* instead of *cops*, *police*, or any of the other less flattering terms Naomi was used to hearing, even by age nine.

"The gig had to end sometime, right?" Naomi said, keeping her voice light.

"Sure, I guess," Caleb said, sounding a little deflated. Again, he flipped back through his pages, frowning. "You said she was a housekeeper?"

"Yep."

"You haven't mentioned that before. You said she was a cocktail waitress. A bartender. Manicure gal . . ."

"Oh, they're called nail artists now," Deena chimed in.

Caleb gave her a fleeting smile, then turned back to Naomi, clicking the end of his ballpoint pen. "She have any other housekeeping gigs?"

"No."

The Cunninghams had made sure of that. Naomi didn't remember much about those days after the incident other than the god-awful mildewy smell of the homeless shelters in February, but she remembered watching her mother's face grow angrier and angrier as she was systematically rejected from every house-keeper job she'd applied to, live-in or otherwise.

"All right," Caleb said, tossing his pen down and putting his head between his hands, expression thoughtful. "That's fine. This is still good stuff. If the first six episodes are about Naomi's child-hood, I'm thinking this year in Park Avenue can be an entire epi-sode, at least—"

"No," Naomi interjected.

Caleb frowned. "No?"

"That year is off-limits. You can refer to it, or whatever, but I don't want to show it."

"But it's a huge part of your childhood—"

"I said *no*," Naomi gritted out.

Oliver, is that true? Did you and Naomi see your father with that woman? Angry blue eyes had drilled into Naomi's that day as the lie spilled out of his mouth. *I don't know what she's talking about.*

"Off-limits," she repeated, her voice a little ragged as the memory of Oliver's betrayal ripped through her.

There was a long silence in the room, and some other guy whose name she'd already forgotten spoke up. "Respectfully, Ms. Powell, our aim here is to show the full story—"

"Dude." This time it was Dylan who interrupted. "She said it's off-limits. Drop it."

Naomi's head jerked up in surprise, and she met the pro-ducer's gaze across the table. He gave her a smile and a brief nod, and Naomi made up her mind then and there.

Dylan Day deserved a chance.

Chapter Twenty-One

*D*amn it. It was official. She was broken.

Pre-Brayden, Naomi had loved dating. Specifically, she'd loved getting ready for the date. The primping, the anticipation. The wondering.

But twenty minutes before she was supposed to meet Dylan for their first official date, she couldn't find even a flicker of excitement. She'd thought looking the part would make her feel the part, but nope. Despite wearing Alexander McQueen leather pants that did excellent things for her lower half, an asymmetrical Trina Turk top paired with gold bangles and tiny gold earrings—she felt . . . flat.

Where was the sparkle? The wondering of *what if*. What if he kissed her? *What if* she kissed him? *What if* she owned up to being an independent twenty-first-century woman and slept with him on the first date simply because she wanted to?

She already knew she didn't want to though.

Because when she'd pulled out her best black-bra-and-pantie set, she hadn't been thinking about Dylan. When she'd carefully lined her eyes with a bit of black liner and gray shadow that she knew made her blue eyes pop, she hadn't been thinking about Dylan. And now, as she stood in front of her shoe rack, debating between red patent Manolo Blahniks and strappy black Jimmy Choos, she wasn't thinking about Dylan.

"Damn you," she muttered at a man who wasn't even present. A man who, despite her friends' assurances, Naomi wasn't even sure was *interested*.

She hadn't seen Oliver all day, which shouldn't have been a big deal except for the fact that she'd gotten sort of used to him. She'd gotten accustomed to listening for the sound of his key in the door. Gotten accustomed to their bickering over whether or not ordering pizza counted as proper fulfillment of his end of the bargain to feed her. Gotten accustomed to sitting with a glass of wine, watching him cook when she inevitably won the argument that pizza did *not* count.

And she'd deny to her dying day that she pushed for the home-cooked meal over takeout because it tended to extend their time together.

But today was Saturday, which meant she was off Walter duty, and since her role as his caretaker was apparently the only use he had for her . . .

"Enough," Naomi snapped, disgusted with herself. She grabbed the red stilettos. Good enough.

No, better than that. Perfect. They were exactly the shoes that the good girls Oliver Cunningham liked to date wouldn't wear.

Next, she dug through her makeup bag for a matching shade of lipstick, one eye on the clock as she did so. Plenty of time.

She and Dylan were meeting at the cocktail bar. Her idea. Naomi had never bought into that whole gentlemanly, escort-the-little-lady-to-and-from-the-date practice. If the date was a dud, the transportation time to and from her apartment to the date location only extended the agony. And if the date was a good one—really good—they'd eventually end up at his place. Never hers—that was just asking for a clinger.

Plus, look what had happened last time Dylan had walked her home. She'd run into Oliver and his date, and had been haunted for days.

Her phone buzzed, and Naomi rolled her eyes at the incoming text.

Audrey

Pic. Now.

Naomi

That feels a little bit like 'what are you wearing,' creeper.

Audrey

It's EXACTLY that. I NEED to know your outfit.

Naomi obliged, going to the full-length mirror in the bedroom and snapping a photo she sent off to Audrey.

A moment later, her phone buzzed again.

Audrey

Had to include C on this. Couldn't be alone in my jealousy that you can pull off those pants.

Naomi

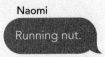 Does it help to know I can barely breathe, and definitely can't bend down?

Claire

It does a little. Very little.

Audrey

Still hate you. What are we talking, Pilates fanatic?

Naomi

Running nut.

Audrey

Hate you more.

Claire

A runner? Friendship officially canceled.

Naomi

Nope. Neither of you get to cancel until we ALL go through this.

Naomi bit her lip and hesitated only a moment before sending the question she really wanted to ask.

Naomi

Did I make a mistake picking Dylan?

Their replies were immediate.

Audrey

Yup.

Claire

Definitely.

She rolled her eyes, sorry she'd asked.

Naomi

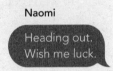

Heading out.
Wish me luck.

Claire

Did you have to wear
Spanx to pull up those
pants?

Audrey

Did you tell Oliver?

Naomi shook her head as she dropped her cell into her purse without replying.

There was no room for anything other than her tiniest thong beneath these pants, and as for telling Oliver she was going on a date? No. Just no.

With one last look at the mirror, Naomi swiped a finger across her front teeth to remove any stray lipstick smudges and stepped into the hallway.

She was just pulling her door shut when the door next to hers opened.

Oliver's door.

No! she pleaded silently. *No, no, no . . .*

"Hey, neighbor."

Damn it.

She turned toward Oliver as he stepped into the hallway, trash bag in hand.

"You wear glasses?" she blurted out.

He crossed both arms and leaned against the door as he pulled it shut, managing to look incredibly sexy even with a trash bag dangling from his right hand.

"If we're going to be discussing appearances, Ms. Powell, *yours* is the one worth mentioning."

His appraisal was slow, deliberately so, and she felt it, from the black bra he couldn't see all the way down to the four-inch red heels that he could.

"But to answer your question," he said when she felt too tongue-tied to reply, "yes, I wear glasses."

"Since when?"

He gave a crooked smile. "You've known me for all of a month. Surely I'm allowed to have a few secrets."

Oliver hadn't worn glasses as a kid. She knew because she had, and he'd called her four eyes, when she wasn't Carrots. And she'd be lying if she said that that long-ago name-calling hadn't had a little something to do with her decision to get LASIK three years ago.

Belatedly she realized that the glasses weren't the most important question. "Where's Walter?"

Oliver jerked his chin in an upward direction. "His place. We had a rough day, so I asked Serena to come by and stay with him for the night. He and I both needed a break."

Naomi nodded because she understood. Overall she hadn't minded watching Walter, but when he was frustrating, he was *really* frustrating. She imagined it would be even harder for a family member to deal with the volatile ups and downs.

"Ah, gotcha," she said, tucking her YSL clutch further into her armpit and juggling her keys lightly in her hand. "Well, have a good night."

"Naomi," he said as she turned away.

She sighed and turned back. "Yeah?"

Oliver pushed away from the door, slowly ambling toward her, his eyes piercing behind the lenses of his rimless glasses. No suit today, but he may as well have been wearing one. His slacks were perfectly tailored, with an immaculate seam running down the front as though they'd come straight from the tailor or dry cleaner, his white button-down starched to perfection . . .

She swallowed, only her mouth seemed to have gone dry, causing the motion to be almost painfully audible in the otherwise silent hallway.

He stopped a few paces from her. His expression never changed from easygoing, but his eyes blazed down at her. "Where are you off to?"

"Out."

His gaze dropped to her red mouth, then back to her eyes. "Girls' night?"

"None of your business," she said tartly.

His jaw tensed. "So it's a date."

"I didn't say that."

"No, but if it was a girls' night, you would have said *that*."

"Fine," Naomi said, giving in. "I'm going on a date. Okay?"

The way his eyes narrowed slightly said *not okay*. But then he lifted his shoulders in a casual shrug. "Cool. Have fun."

Naomi had started to open her mouth to tell him that she could date whomever she wanted, when she wanted, but then his actual words sank in and her mouth snapped shut.

"Oh. Thanks."

He grinned. "Sure."

And then he walked past her, whistling on his way to the garbage chute. *Whistling!*

So much for her worrying about telling him—or thinking that he'd care.

Naomi took a deep breath to gather her thoughts before she pivoted on her heel and headed toward the stairs.

Oliver was just coming out of the trash room as she reached the stairwell, and he gave her a perfunctory, neighborly smile as they passed. She returned the smile with gritted teeth, not entirely sure why she was mad at him, but her temper simmered all the same as she reached for the door to the stairs.

"Oh, hey, Naomi," he said, snapping his fingers as though just remembering something.

She turned, startled because he was *right there*. "What's up?"

"Just this," he said.

Then his hand slid beneath her hair, cupping the back of her neck, as his mouth came down on hers.

Her eyes widened in surprise at the unexpected kiss, then fluttered closed because it was also a really *good* kiss. Firm, yet teasing, full of possession and promise and . . .

Then it was over. *Way* too fast.

Dazed, it took Naomi a full fifteen seconds to open her eyes after he pulled away, another ten to remember her own name. "What—what was that?"

Instead of answering, he reached out and gently brushed the pad of his thumb beneath her lower lip. "Your lipstick's smeared."

"Whose fault is that?" she muttered, her voice a little shaky.

His hand dropped from her face and he shoved both hands into his pockets, rocking backward on his heels. "Sorry."

"Are you?"

"Not even a little bit."

She searched frantically for some witty retort, but instead she found her gaze locked on his mouth. Wanting a repeat. A long repeat.

Finally she lifted her gaze back to his. "Want to explain what just happened?"

"Nah." He continued to rock on his heels looking boyish and painfully appealing.

"But—"

"Naomi." He stopped rocking and gave her a look that heated her to her very core. "Figure it out."

With that, he turned and walked back to his apartment, resuming his whistling and looking as though he had no idea that he'd managed to turn Naomi Powell's world upside down with one simple, unforgettable kiss.

Chapter Twenty-Two

*O*liver picked up his glasses and pencil for the tenth time in an hour, only to toss them back onto his standing desk. Also for the tenth time in an hour.

It was no use. It didn't matter how badly he wanted to land the Gabe Green project, he wouldn't be able to draw so much as a single straight line until he could get a certain red-haired temptress out of his mind.

Not an easy task, considering he now had the memory of her taste and feel to contend with.

Kissing her on Saturday had been . . . a mistake.

No, not a mistake, because he'd do it again in a heartbeat.

It had been a misstep—what he should have done was kissed her and not stopped.

He should have backed her up against the wall, wrapped her legs around his waist, and told her to forget the date. To forget the other guy. To be his.

Instead he'd let her walk away, hoping like hell that his gamble would pay off, that she'd realize that if she was ready to start dating again after Brayden, that the right guy was right here . . .

Oliver dug the heels of his hands into his eyes as he realized his train of thought. *Was* he the right guy? For anyone? There was a reason his fiancée had bailed on him years earlier.

He barely had time to take a shower in between work and Walter obligations, much less make it to the gym. Much less squeeze in a date. Much less have a girlfriend.

Especially a girlfriend like Naomi, who wasn't exactly the easy, docile, low-maintenance type. The woman was fire and energy, and at the top of her game. He'd done his homework. Her company, that she'd so modestly dismissed as a "start-up," was valued at close to a *billion*.

A billion! And yet the woman had zero trace of snobbery. If anything, her dislike of him seemed to be because of his perceived snobbery. Oliver had never been quite so aware of the stigma of being born with money, which he could understand if it was from someone who had none, but Naomi Powell was loaded.

From what he could tell, her life had been one long string of interviews and photo shoots and 30-under-30 features. She was frequently photographed at the newest restaurants, seen dancing at the hottest clubs, often with some beefed-up arm candy by her side.

Oliver didn't fit into that picture. Old Oliver maybe could have swung it. He'd never been one for late nights and clubbing, but he hadn't been stodgy, either. He liked to go out, have a few drinks, maybe one too many. He liked the satisfaction of wowing a woman with reservations at some swanky place. Hell, he didn't even mind the occasional black-tie affair necessitating a penguin suit and small talk.

But that wasn't his life now. It couldn't be. He was lucky if he got one night off a week, and those were usually spent catching up on work, trying to maintain the few friendships he still had left, or just getting some damned peace and quiet.

Oliver didn't know if Naomi had even heard of the concept of peace and quiet.

Though, perhaps that wasn't fair. This past week and a half she had offered to watch his father, and she'd seemed oddly content to relax in his apartment . . .

Until she'd gotten bored, apparently. Until she'd gone on a date.

"I know that face. You're chewing on a problem."

Oliver turned toward the open door of his office to see one of his best contractors and longtime friends stroll through the door.

"Hey, man," Oliver said with a genuine smile as he went to give Scott Turner a one-armed man hug. "Where the hell've you been?"

"Seattle. Just got back last Thursday," Scott said, helping himself to one of the coffee pods Oliver's assistant kept on an end table before popping it into the machine on the far side of the room.

"Right," Oliver said, dropping into the chair at the small table he kept in his office. He liked to stand as he worked, so his actual desk was tall and facing the window. The table was reserved for client meetings, or in this case, catching up with friends. "How'd it go? Worth turning down my project?"

"Your project was a swanky hotel. You know that's not my thing."

"And weird museums are?"

"Pretty much," Scott said, picking up his coffee mug and joining Oliver at the table. "Though, joke was on me. The project was cool on paper, but the client was a diva."

"Hovered?"

Scott grunted in confirmation, and Oliver gave a single nod of understanding.

He and Scott Turner had met at Columbia, both setting out to get their masters in architecture. Scott had dropped out after the first year, realizing his passion was building, not design. He'd started his own construction firm, and though he kept it small, he was known as a perfectionist and had his choice of projects.

Oliver always recommended Turner Construction for his projects, knowing that Scott got Oliver's designs in a way the bigger companies didn't always see. But Scott was picky. If one of Oliver's projects didn't suit his mood, he went for something else.

Seattle, in this case.

"How was it, besides the douche client?" Oliver asked.

"Good. As rainy as they say, but my wardrobe certainly fit in better there."

Oliver believed it. Though Scott had a loft apartment on the west side, he was no Manhattan yuppie. Come to think of it, Oliver couldn't remember the last time he'd seen his friend wear anything besides jeans and a T-shirt. Even now, in late October, Scott had layered a short-sleeve navy tee over a long-sleeve white T-shirt. There were no signs of the usual aviator glasses, but Oliver was betting they were tucked into the bomber jacket Scott had set over the back of the chair.

"So what's next?" Oliver asked.

"TBD," Scott said, taking a sip of the coffee and studying him. "I need a palate cleanser. Something . . . simple. Basic. You ever miss your earliest projects? Back before we knew how to do fancy and just sort of threw our backs into regular stuff?"

"No," Oliver admitted. "But considering the first thing I ever saw you sketch was a log cabin, I think I know what you mean."

"Yeah, well." Scott rolled his shoulders in impatient irritation. "I want something like that. I want to gut something small, then take my time getting the details right."

He nodded in the direction of Oliver's desk. "What're you workin' on?"

Oliver tipped his chair back, leaning over nearly to the point of tipping over, to grab his sketch pad before dropping it on the table in front of Scott.

Scott picked it up, rubbed a palm absently over his chronic five o'clock shadow, which was really a twenty-four-hour shadow in Scott's case. "Good old cock and balls. Nice."

His friend tossed the pad aside—it really was a cock and balls Oliver had doodled on the pad in utter, uninspired boredom—and studied him. "Blocked?"

"No. I'm thinking a building of exactly that design would be perfect next to the High Line. Thoughts?"

"Plenty of people would get a kick out of it," Scott said, propping a booted foot on his opposite knee. "I also think you're avoiding my question. How's Walter?"

"Good," Oliver said. "I mean he's not, but . . . no change."

"Did the Tribeca fancies pick your design for that mixed-use monstrosity downtown?"

"Yeah," Oliver said distractedly, pulling his pencil from behind his ear and fiddling with it.

"All right, so it's not family. Not work. Woman."

Oliver's gaze flicked up and met Scott's before moving away again.

"Nailed it," Scott said, not bothering to hide the gloat. "Who is she? You haven't taken up with that bitch Bridget again, have you?"

"Tell me how you really feel," Oliver grumbled.

"I have. Many times. Any woman who'd walk away within a

month of your dad's diagnosis isn't worth a second more of your thoughts."

Oliver nearly reminded Scott that he, too, had been engaged. At the same time as Oliver. The two couples had been nearly inseparable at the time, though neither had made it to the altar. As much as Bridget bailing on Oliver had hurt, it had nothing on what Scott had gone through when Meredith cheated on him.

"To her credit, Bridget did stick around through my mom's illness," Oliver said. "It wouldn't have been fair to ask her to deal with another round."

"Why not? *You* have to deal with it."

"Can we not?" Oliver said tiredly, rubbing his forehead. "This isn't about Bridget. I haven't even talked to her."

"Ah. Someone new. Good. It's been too long."

"Yeah, since you're a real relationships guy," Oliver said sarcastically. "You know, other than Meredith, I've never even met a woman you were seeing? Random chicks you take home from bars don't count."

"Good thing we're not talkin' about my love life, then," Scott said, taking another sip of his coffee. "Talk to old Scotty. Who's the girl who's got you drawing *this*?" He flicked the notepad.

"New neighbor."

Scott's eyebrows lifted in surprise. "Tell me she's under sixty."

Oliver laughed. "She's around our age. No idea why she moved into a building where the mean age is about seventy-four though."

"You ever ask her?"

"I—" Oliver's mouth dropped open. Had he? Maybe during the interview process. But as a person? Friend to friend? Interested man to woman?

"Truth be told, I don't know much about her beyond what I've found on Wikipedia."

"Hell, that sounds like trouble."

"Not what you think. She's a businesswoman, started some jewelry empire. Maxcessory?"

Scott shook his head. "Never heard of it."

Shocker.

"Anyway, Naomi's my neighbor, and she's . . ."

"Hot?"

"Hot. Frustrating. A complete pain in my ass."

"Sounds like a real dream come true. Any good qualities beyond the hot?"

"She's good with Dad."

Scott nodded in understanding. A woman being good with his father may not be the sexiest foundation for any relationship, but ever since Bridget had coldly left him when he'd needed her most, Oliver had promised himself he'd never get involved with a woman who couldn't handle Walter—who didn't understand that he and his father were a package deal.

"Okay, so she's hot," Scott said, holding out a thumb. "She likes Walter, and that's no easy task . . ." He held out his pointer finger. "She's built her own empire, so she's not in it for the money," he said, ticking off another point.

"So true," Oliver muttered.

"So what's the problem?"

"What do you mean?"

Scott shrugged. "Seems to me like a pretty clear-cut situation. You're attracted to your new neighbor, and she hasn't gone running off because of your family situation. Neither of those reasons explains why I'm getting major depressed vibes coming off you right now."

"All right," Oliver said, deciding to lay it all out there. "How about the fact that from the very second she saw me—literally, the very first second—she decided not to like me."

Scott made a considering face, waggling his hand. "To be honest, dude, I didn't like you much the first time I saw you, either."

Oliver glared at his friend. "What?"

"You're sort of . . ." Scott narrowed his brown eyes and studied Oliver. "Starchy."

"Excuse me?"

"You know. Like your mom used to make you dress for the dinner table, and like you don't own shirts without collars, and you have a cuff link collection that dates back four generations."

"I do not have a cuff link collection."

Though his mom *had* made him change for dinner growing up. And his amount of non-collared shirts wasn't exactly numerous.

"Question," Scott said, setting his mug aside and steepling his fingers. "You work for yourself, right?"

"Yes," Oliver said impatiently. "You know that."

"So you're the boss."

"Point?"

"You don't have to wear a suit." Scott looked pointedly at Oliver's pinstripe suit. "Nobody's making you."

"Correct," Oliver said, smoothing a hand over this gray tie, "I'd just prefer not to look like a . . ."

Scott made a *continue* gesture with his hand. "Lumberjack? Bohemian? Vagabond? Construction worker?"

"I'm not walking into that trap," Oliver muttered.

"Look, man, I got over it. Saw that you weren't actually a prig, you just dressed like one. But it took me a while. People like you don't generally associate with people like me, and I wasn't exactly prepared for you to be decent."

"What the hell do you mean, 'people like you'?" Oliver asked, genuinely puzzled.

"Where am I from?" Scott asked.

"Ah . . ." Oliver racked his brain, was a little embarrassed to realize he had no idea.

"Exactly. Never told you. Why? Because you were born and raised and *still* live on Park Avenue. Me? A shitty little town in New Hampshire you've never heard of, in a two-bedroom house I shared with my dad and three brothers. Two of my brothers still live there. Hell, I probably would, too, had I not decided to elbow my way the hell out, but it doesn't mean I'm not braced every damn day for someone to see right through me."

Oliver stared at his friend. It was a monotone, dispassionate delivery, but his words were . . . telling. It was more than Scott had ever told him. But before he could think of what to say, Scott was pulling his phone out of his pocket.

"Let's test this out. What's this girl's name?"

Oliver told him, and Scott typed it into his phone. "Here we go. 'Naomi Powell, best known' blah, blah, blah. Ah. 'Born and raised in the Bronx, Powell has cited her poor upbringing as a major motivator . . .'"

Scott looked at Oliver over the phone. "You haven't read this?"

"No, I have," Oliver said, shifting in his chair. "So it's a rags-to-riches story."

Scott shook his head and put his phone away, his point made. "Sure, but I bet you anything there's a part of her that still sees herself in the rags, and meanwhile you're . . ."

"Starchy," Oliver said, realizing what his friend was getting at.

Scott spread his hands to the side. "My work here is done."

Oliver laughed. "Like hell it is. You've merely insulted me and given me literally zero advice."

"You know when I first realized you weren't a complete ass-wag?" Scott asked, leaning forward slightly.

"Can't wait to hear."

"Study group, just shortly before I quit. Remember, it was at your place, and there was supposed to be that cute blond girl with the great rack, but she got sick last minute and never showed, so it was just the two of us?"

Oliver shrugged. "Vaguely?"

"Well, I was dreading the hell out of it, fully expecting you to serve cucumber sandwiches off china plates."

"And?"

"And you answered the door holding an egg roll, wearing Nike joggers and an undershirt with soy sauce down the front."

"Jesus," Oliver said with a laugh.

"That was when I knew we could be friends. When I knew you were real. When I knew there was a man beneath the priss," Scott said, standing and picking up his mug.

"I think it's going to take a little more than spilled soy sauce to win over Naomi."

"All right, so evolve your methods," Scott said matter-of-factly. "But you want a chance, Cunningham, you've got to show this woman that there's a man beneath those pinstripes."

"I feel like this conversation just turned weird."

"Says the man doodling penises."

Oliver picked up the sketch pad, then flipped it around. "Maybe I can just show her this?"

Scott gave him a boyish grin. "If you take my advice, I'd say you've got a pretty decent chance of showing her the real thing."

Aaaand sold.

Chapter Twenty-Three

*W*alter, I swear to God, I'm not going to handle it well if you throw that egg at me," Naomi said, lifting a finger in warning.

The older man gave her a dirty look but to her surprise—and relief—opted to take a bite out of the egg rather than hurl it at her, as he had the past two. She'd dodged them just in time, but he'd thrown them with enough force to send the makings of egg salad crumbling all over the carpet.

"Okay, I'm going to clean this up," she said, pointing at the eggs. "And you are going to say sorry."

He chewed, glaring at her mutinously. "Who are you? Where's Margaret? Get the hell out of my house."

Naomi inhaled and made a mental note to ask if Janice was Catholic, because if so, Naomi was seriously going to nominate her for sainthood for dealing with this every damn day.

"My name is Naomi. I'm taking care of you while Janice is taking care of her father."

"Janice," he said slowly, squinting as he did when he was trying to put pieces together.

"Yep. You remember her?" Naomi asked, taking the trash can from under the sink and carrying it around with her as she began picking up bits of egg.

"Sure, I remember Janice. Mannish."

"Walter!" Naomi said, giving him a glare. "Be nice."

She'd never met Janice, so she had no idea if Walter was remembering her or someone else, but she wasn't in the mood to listen to one of his jackass rampages.

"I like 'em curvy," he muttered.

"Yeah? Margaret was a real hourglass, huh?" she asked, gingerly picking up a piece of egg white.

He snorted. "Margaret? She was a beanpole."

Naomi slowly stood up. "So, when you said you like 'em curvy, you meant women *other* than your wife?"

Women like my mother?

He took another sip of water and said nothing.

"Walter?"

"Hmm?"

Naomi opened her mouth to push him, then closed her eyes in self-loathing. Was she seriously doing this? Using a man's confusion to get answers for her own sake.

No. She was better than that. Better than him.

She noticed his eyes had a vacant, sleepy look, and she sighed, setting the trash aside.

"Come on, let's get you ready for bed."

He nodded, and she was grateful it wouldn't be one of those battles to get him to change into pajamas.

She walked with him to his bedroom, and as usual, refused to look at the bed, knowing full well what had happened there between him and her mother decades earlier.

Naomi pulled out flannel pants and a T-shirt, handing them

both to him. "Here you go. Let me know if you need help with the buttons."

"Where's Oliver?" His blue eyes were cloudy and a little scared.

"He'll be home soon, okay?" she said, giving his hand a reassuring squeeze, relieved when his fear seemed to recede slightly. "You can wait up for him if you want."

He nodded, but when Naomi knocked and came in a few minutes later to check on him, he was already in bed, covers tucked up to his chin, his gray hair spread out in tufts against the white pillowcase.

Naomi smiled a little as she turned off the nightstand lamp, acknowledging that her feelings about this man were complicated.

To say nothing of her feelings for his son.

She was just squirting some carpet cleaner on a stubborn yolk stain when Oliver came in the front door. He immediately winced when he saw her on her hands and knees. "One of those?"

"One of those," she said, using her forearm to brush an errant hair out of her face.

"Sexy gloves though," he said.

She held up her hands, covered in yellow rubber. "You like these, baby?"

"Stop. Don't tease," he said, dropping his briefcase by the front door.

For a moment they just looked at each other, a silent standoff to see if either would mention the kiss from a couple of nights before.

Instead he looked away, back down at her hands. "But seriously though, take those off. I'll finish cleaning."

"All good," she said, standing and peeling off the gloves. She tilted her head, taking in the white plastic bag in his hand. "Take-out?"

"Chinese. Too much of it, probably, given that Dad's already asleep." He looked at the closed bedroom door. "How bad was he?"

"Lashed out more than usual," she said, putting the carpet cleaner and gloves under the sink with the cleaning supplies. "Threw eggs, yelled at the TV, barked at some strangers in the park, made some saucy comments about liking his women curvy."

Oliver gave her a sharp look. "He didn't . . . he's never . . . made a move?"

"Hmm?" Naomi was in the process of trying to untie the knot on the Chinese food bag, and it took a moment for his words to sink in. Her head snapped up when it did. "Oh. No. No." She swallowed. "Why, has he . . . with Janice?"

"Not with Janice," Oliver said quietly. "But he wasn't . . . he wasn't loyal to my mom. Sometimes he would have affairs right under her nose."

Naomi had gone very still. It was the perfect opening. *Tell him. Tell him who you are. Who your mother was.*

And she was going to, she *really* meant to, but his eyes were so shadowed, he looked so utterly exhausted. And for the first time, Naomi realized that she wasn't the only one impacted by Walter Cunningham's actions. His son had paid the price as well.

"Do you want to talk about it?" she asked softly.

He stared for a long moment at the bag before giving a quick shake of his head. "No. Not right now. I want a beer and I want an egg roll and . . ."

He broke off, then smiled, then outright laughed.

She lifted her eyebrows. "Got an inside joke with yourself there, Cunningham?"

"An inside joke, though not with myself." Then he looked up, his eyes a little lighter than before. "Actually, you cool if I leave you for just five minutes? I'll be right back. I just need to grab something from my place."

"Sure, no problem," she said, tearing open the knot when she grew impatient with trying to untie it. "Just don't expect me to wait before diving in. I'm starving."

"Help yourself. Be right back."

True to his word, Oliver was back in five minutes, and Naomi did a double take around a mouthful of chow mein. "Are you wearing . . . *sweats?*"

He grabbed a plate and began loading food onto it. "You sound surprised. What did you think I wore in my downtime?"

"Elbow patches?"

He gave her a look.

"Okay, no," she said, taking a sip of water. "But I did imagine you had some sort of monogrammed robe."

Again with that crooked smile that was almost painfully appealing. Combined with the tight black T-shirt, the low-slung gray sweatpants that did wonders for his, um . . .

He grinned wider now, taking a bite of egg roll. "Ms. Powell. Are you checking me out?"

"Your fault," she said, pointing her chopsticks at him. "You kissed me the other night."

"I did," he said casually, dropping into the chair next to her. "Why?"

He chewed his egg roll and swallowed, then helped himself to her water glass. "You figure it out yet?"

"No!" she said, pushing her plate aside. "You kiss me right before I'm supposed to go on a date. I ask you what happened. You tell me to figure it out, and I spend the entire date with another guy thinking about it, and— Why are you smiling?"

He just grinned wider and took another bite of egg roll. "You *did* figure it out. You just didn't realize you did."

"No," she said, stabbing her chopsticks in his direction. "No more cryptic talk. Explain."

"You said you spent your entire date with another guy thinking about me," he said, digging into a carton of sweet-and-sour shrimp.

"Yes, and— Wait. *That* was your plan? That is so . . . so . . . you sabotaged me. And Dylan!"

Oliver winced. "So it was him."

"You already knew I was dating him."

"*Was* past tense, or *was* past participle?"

She paused chewing. "Huh?"

"Are you still dating him?" His voice was somehow both patient and demanding. And far too compelling.

"I don't know," she replied.

"Are you going out with him again?"

"I don't know!"

He continued to watch her, then tossed his chopsticks aside. "I want a beer. You want a beer?"

She stared after him aghast as he went to the fridge and popped the caps off two bottles before bringing both back to the table. Naomi sat back in her chair and studied him as she took a sip of her beer. This version of Oliver was . . . unnerving. The suit Oliver, she could handle. Sort of. Or at least she was working on it. Because suit Oliver was easy to remember as a Cunningham.

But this Oliver, with his bottle of beer, his tired-looking T-shirt that fit entirely too well . . . He unceremoniously wiped his mouth with one of the flimsy paper napkins that came with the takeout, and Naomi bit back a groan.

"You're doing it on purpose."

"What?"

She looked away. "Nothing."

His beer bottle froze halfway to his mouth as he studied her, then he let out a disbelieving laugh. "I don't believe it. Son of a bitch was right."

"Who was right?"

"Never mind," he said, setting his beer aside and turning to face her. "Why Dylan?"

"Why Dylan what?"

He gave her a look that said *you know what*.

She hesitated, wary of the intensity in his expression. "Because he's . . ."

She almost said *easy*, then remembered that's exactly what Oliver had accused her of the night of the dinner party. Dating Dylan didn't present a risk. Damn it. Had he been right the entire time?

"Allow me to be clearer," Oliver said in a low voice, reaching out and grabbing the leg of her chair and dragging it, and her, closer.

"Why"—his hand slipped behind her neck as it had the night of their kiss—"if you were ready to date again after Brayden, why was it him?"

"As opposed to?" Naomi meant it to be a sassy little quip to keep the upper hand, but she was losing the battle.

Especially when his thumb stroked slowly along the sensitive skin on her neck. How could he possibly know how much she liked that? How a hand slipping beneath her hair to the sensitive skin of her neck always made her a little weak in the knees? He'd done it first at the dinner party, and again with the kiss, and now crowded around his father's kitchen table, the same kitchen table where . . .

Naomi reared back. *That* kitchen table. The very one where she'd watched through a crack in the guest bedroom door as the three Cunninghams had sat with their perfect posture in their "dinner outfits" eating things like duck confit and asparagus with beurre blanc, while she'd wolfed down a cold burrito from Taco Bell her mom had bought her hours earlier.

"Talk to me," Oliver said, his grip staying firm even as she tried to wiggle away. "Talk to me about what just happened right there, Naomi. Why do you keep fighting this?"

His voice was soft yet commanding, his touch on the back of her neck gentle but determined.

"This will never work," she said. "We're so different."

"Only according to the skeletons in your closet."

What?

"Hey, you don't know—"

"No," he said, shaking his head. "I don't know, because you don't tell me what's going on in your head, but here's what I do know, Naomi. We've got something here. You want to bring your baggage on in, fine, we'll deal with it. Because it's time for you to start admitting that we could be damn good together if you just give it a chance."

She sat perfectly still, wanting to believe him, to trust him . . .

Oliver studied her expression for a long moment before slowly releasing her.

He picked up his chopsticks. "How's work?"

She blinked at the abrupt change in subject and mood, telling herself that she wasn't disappointed, and yet feeling the absence of his touch acutely. "What?"

He opened up a carton of fried rice and dumped some onto his plate. "Work. Maxcessory. How's it going? How's working from home?"

"Ah—"

He looked up and smiled. "What, you thought I just wanted you for sex? I definitely want that. But I also like to know the women I'm sleeping with. So tell me."

She took a deep breath and moved her chair closer back to its original position as she, too, picked up her chopsticks again. "Well. Let's just say I'm not exactly the paragon of productivity when it comes to working from home."

"Because of Dad?" he asked, glancing over. "You know I can get a full-time caretaker anytime."

"No, not that. I mean yeah, he demands quite a bit of my time, but a lot of my non-Walter time has been focused on something else."

"Your handsome neighbor?"

"Maybe," she muttered irritably.

He grinned, then picked up his plate. "I'm going to reheat this. You want me to heat yours first?"

She shook her head. "I'm done, actually."

They both stood and moved toward the counter, him to put his plate in the microwave, her to rinse hers. Well. This was sexy.

Was she the only one still thinking about Saturday's kiss?

The microwave beeped, and Oliver punched open the door, but instead of taking out the plate, turned back to her.

"Screw it," he muttered, taking a step toward her.

She instinctively stepped back, even as her heart pounded.

"Wait. *Wait.* You don't even like me," Naomi said quickly.

He smiled. "Wrong. *You* don't like *me.* I've never said a damn thing about not liking you."

Her breath quickened at the intense look on his face. "You *shouldn't* like me."

"Call me crazy," he murmured as he eased toward her,

moving slowly as though not wanting to startle her. "But I've always been a sucker for beautiful women who play hard to get."

She gave a nervous laugh as she stepped backward. "Trust me, that's not what's going on here."

"No?" His hands slowly lifted, resting on either side of the counter as he leaned toward her, almost touching but not quite.

"I can't breathe when you do that," she whispered.

"When I do what?" His lips drifted over her jaw, a feather-light almost-kiss.

"When you look at me like that," she said, her voice husky as his lips moved down her neck. "When you touch me."

"I'll back off if you want," he said against her skin, his mouth coming back up to hover just over her lips. "Say the word and we can go back to antagonistic neighbors who set off fireworks every time we're in the same room."

She wanted to. She wanted to tell him that this would never work, that they were all wrong in ways he didn't even know. That he would hate her if he knew who she really was, that she was the housekeeper's daughter he'd so despised . . .

And there lay the crux of her issue. She'd started this driven by her loathing of the Cunninghams, but she was increasingly coming face-to-face with a more alarming reality:

That her anger was really fear. That she'd been clinging to her hatred of everything Oliver represented not because of old grudges, not even because of her promise to her mother, but because she was terrified that she would never be good enough. That at any minute, the life she'd so carefully built could come crashing down, taking it all away. And if she let Oliver in and then lost him . . .

He seemed to register her indecision, and though his gaze flickered with frustration, he started to pull away.

It was *that*. The fact that this man could not only read her but seemed to care about what she wanted.

Naomi's hand reached out, fisted in the front of his T-shirt, and Oliver froze. Their gazes locked and held for a second. She pulled him forward at the same time he leaned in, their mouths colliding in a kiss that was somehow both sweet and frantic, a battle of wills that neither could lose.

Oliver's palm spread wide against her back, her fingers slowly releasing his shirt so her arms could wind their way around his neck.

If the kiss on Saturday had been the promise, this was the delivery. The sort of kiss that ruined a girl for all other kisses in the future.

His other hand found her hip, his fingers digging into the soft flesh there, tilting her toward him so they both gasped.

His mouth moved once more down her neck, and Naomi's head fell back. Something clattered to the ground as he lifted her onto the counter, but neither paused in their restless exploration of the other's taste and touch.

Naomi's legs wrapped around his waist, his hand finding her butt, pulling her close . . .

"Who's there?"

They both froze.

Slowly Oliver pulled back, his gaze locking on hers for a moment before closing his eyes in resignation. He cleared his throat. "Hey, Dad. It's me."

"Ollie? What the hell you doing out there, boy?"

Naomi smiled a little at the childhood nickname, and Oliver's forehead came down to rest on her shoulder with the slightest laugh. "Nothing. You need something?"

"Where's your mom?"

Oliver stiffened under her arms, and Naomi's heart went out to him. She wondered if it would ever get better. If it would ever not hurt to have his father lost in time, forcing his son to relive the fact that both of his parents were essentially lost to him, over and over . . .

Knowing the moment had passed, Naomi's legs slowly dropped from around his waist, though she surprised herself by giving in to the urge to brush her hand against his hair in comfort.

He caught her hand just before it slipped away, holding her gaze as he pressed a quick kiss to her palm.

Then he helped her down as Walter shuffled into the kitchen, and she sent up a silent thank-you for all their sakes that he hadn't been in one of his pants-off moods.

"Who are you?" he asked, blue eyes sleepy, hair wild.

"Hi, Walter," she said, adjusting the hem of her shirt and refusing to feel embarrassed.

"Dad, this is Naomi. You know her."

The confusion in Walter's gaze faded slightly, replaced by something a little . . . meaner. "Sleeping with the help, eh, son?"

Naomi flinched, and Oliver tensed beside her. Walter either didn't notice or didn't care about their reaction. He let out a chuckle as he went to the fridge. "Don't worry about it. I won't tell your mother. Our little secret."

Naomi swallowed against the sudden bitterness in her mouth at the memory of another little secret these two men had kept, also involving "the help." The roles had been reversed, but the damage was the same.

No, not the same, she silently amended. She was not her mother.

And she would not let either of these men treat her the way Danica had always let men treat her.

Oliver grabbed her wrist as she turned away. "Naomi."

She shook her head. "Take care of your dad."

She pulled her wrist gently from his grip but turned back once more before leaving. "I'll be here tomorrow morning to watch him, but after that . . . you need to find another caretaker until Janice gets back."

He searched her face and frowned, before giving a single nod in confirmation.

He let her go.

Chapter Twenty-Four

*T*hree days following her ill-fated make-out session with Oliver, Naomi finally had something to smile about.

She and Deena had just finished the first tour of the new office, and it was absolute perfection.

Truth be told, she'd been prepared to make the new office earn a place in her heart, but she'd been smitten within seconds. Naomi thought she'd given the design team an impossible task—make the space feel open while still ensuring everyone had privacy to focus.

She knew "open floor plans" were all the rage, and she was all for collaboration, but she also respected that not everybody worked well staring at the person across from them or listening to their neighbor chirping in their ear. The design team she'd brought in had been worth every penny. Each floor was centered around a communal area with conference tables, couches, and multi-person desks, while the perimeter of each floor housed "micro-offices"—individual spaces for employees to close the door and work in silence or take a phone call, but with glass walls ensuring that even the center workspace was lit by natural light.

Naomi's own office was a bit smaller than her old one, per her request, but it didn't feel it. The glass desk and white cabinets felt fresh and fun, as did the pop of coral accents to match Maxcessory's distinctive logo.

Over the past few weeks, Naomi had deliberately pulled back from her usual 110 percent. Partially to see how her team handled it, partially to address the stress of Brayden's death, and then Walter coming into her life.

But now she was more ready than ever to get back to it. Move-in day for the new office was Monday, which couldn't come soon enough. She needed something to distract her, needed distance—literal distance—from Oliver Cunningham.

Naomi was humming a Spice Girls song that had been going through her head ever since it came on her Throwback Thursday running playlist that morning, but she stopped dead in her tracks as she got to her floor in the apartment building.

There were flowers sitting at her door. Not a lavish bouquet, but small and elegant with white roses and little sprigs of green.

"Hello there, my pretties," she said, crouching down. She poked gingerly amid the buds, looking for a card. Not finding one, she picked up the cardboard box covering the base.

"Birthday?"

Naomi's head whipped around to see Oliver coming up the steps. She hadn't seen him since Tuesday afternoon when he'd gotten home from work and told her coolly that Janice would be back on Wednesday, and she was off the hook from Walter duty.

Then, as now, he was back to wearing his usual suits. All

signs of casual, teasing Oliver were long gone, and she told herself it was better this way, even as a little sliver of her heart wondered what she was missing out on. What they were missing out on.

"No," she said by way of response, standing with the flowers in hand. "I don't actually know what they're for."

She didn't mention that for one idiotic moment she'd thought—hoped—they might be from him. But his expression said otherwise.

"Perhaps they're from last weekend's date," he said casually, coming to lean on the wall beside her door. "Or this upcoming weekend's date?"

There was a clear question in his voice, which she ignored. "I don't know who they're from," she said honestly. "I can't find a card anywhere."

He frowned slightly and reached out to search within the blooms. "You're right. Maybe in the box?"

"Probably." She started to juggle the flowers in one arm to get at her keys in her purse, but nearly dropped the bouquet. She shoved it at Oliver. "Here, hold these?"

"Every man's dream, to hold flowers for a woman."

"They're probably from Claire or Audrey."

"Girlfriends send each other flowers?"

"Sometimes. If they need cheering up," she said, finding the keys at the bottom of the bag. "Say, like if her love life was feeling really complicated?"

"Hey," he said, his voice sharp enough to have her looking up. "You're the one who walked out, Naomi."

"Because your dad caught us and called me the help," she snapped.

"He's sick! He doesn't know what he's saying!"

"Yeah, well, I got the impression he was pretty lucid at that moment."

Oliver's eyes turned angry. "What's that supposed to mean?"

"It means that I think the Walter we saw that night was the real Walter."

He looked away, telling her that she was right. Not that she needed the confirmation. She already *knew* the real Walter, and it wasn't the petulant man-child who adorably liked hard-boiled eggs and the History Channel.

"You know what?" she said tiredly, shoving her key into the lock. "I don't even mind what your dad said. Whether it was because of the illness or just because he's a jackass. But I do mind that you didn't say a word in my defense. The *help*?"

He dragged a hand over his face, looking as exhausted as she felt. "What would it have mattered? He'd have forgotten in thirty seconds anyway."

"Yeah, but I would have remembered, Oliver. *I* would have remembered."

She reached out to take the flowers, but he held them away from her. Naomi gave him a look. "Really?"

"I was engaged," he said out of nowhere. "Did you know that?"

Her hands dropped slowly, and she adjusted her purse on her shoulder. "I did not."

Oliver gave a jerky nod. "A few years ago. We put off the wedding planning when my mom got sick. We talked about trying to do it faster, so Mom could be there, but my mom refused. Said she'd rather miss our wedding than die knowing we'd rushed it. So we waited. Bridget held my hand through the funeral. Waited the appropriate amount of time before diving into wedding planning. Then Dad started showing symptoms . . ."

Naomi swallowed, not at all liking where this was going. And not liking this fiancée one bit.

"We took turns caring for him, and I thought, okay, this sucks, but we're in it together. But the worse he got, the more reluctant she became to set a date or even discuss wedding details. By the time we got his diagnosis and it became clear this wasn't a short-term problem, she was just sort of . . . done. Said she loved me, but that this wasn't what she'd signed up for, that it was just too much."

Oliver shrugged as though it wasn't a big deal, but the way he wouldn't meet her eyes told her it was. Of course it was. What sort of person agrees to marry someone and then bails when the going gets tough?

"Why are you telling me this?" she asked softly.

This time he did meet her eyes. "I told myself then that if and when I got involved with someone again, it had to be someone who understood that Walter and I were a package deal. Someone who wouldn't bail when things got difficult."

Well . . . crap.

"And I bailed," she said softly.

He lifted a shoulder. "I don't blame you. But he's not going to be better, Naomi. That stuff he said to you on Monday? Not even close to the worst I've heard him say. Not about you, just . . . in general. He wasn't a nice man before, and now that he's confused, he's . . . difficult. I *am* sorry for what he said, but I also can't help it. He can't help it. I understand completely if you want no part of it—you barely know us, but . . . I can't—"

"Be with someone who can't handle your dad?"

He nodded jerkily. "But I am grateful for what you've done for Dad these last couple weeks. And for me. It's been a long time since I've had someone to come home to who didn't throw hard-boiled eggs at me. Someone to just talk about my day with . . ."

He broke off and gave a quick shake of his head. "Anyway. Here are your flowers." He handed them back. He nodded, then turned back toward his own apartment.

Naomi chewed her lip, weighing the wisdom of what she was about to do.

"Hey, Oliver."

He paused just before entering his apartment.

"Do you want to come in? If you don't have to relieve Janice quite yet? I could make us a drink. Coffee? Tea?"

He narrowed his eyes slightly, clearly trying to figure her out.

"I liked talking to someone about my day, too," she admitted, surprised at how vulnerable the admission made her feel. And how true it was.

He hesitated. "I don't know if—"

"As friends," she said quickly. "I understand you're not looking for . . . more. At least not with me. But you still need friends, right?"

He studied her a long moment, then gave her a smile that melted her insides. "Yeah. Okay. Let me change clothes real quick, and I'll be right there."

Naomi nodded, then went into her apartment, setting the flowers on the counter, resuming her humming of the Spice Girls song as she gently pulled the arrangement out of the cardboard delivery box.

Her pausing hummed when the box fell away to reveal the base of the bouquet. Not a vase, as she'd thought.

A mug.

As expected, the card had slipped to the bottom of the box, and though she already knew who the flowers were from, the message had her smiling all the same.

It's no Dom Pérignon, but this is a nice use for a
mug, too.

—Ollie

The flowers were so much better than expensive champagne.

Chapter Twenty-Five

I can't believe I let you talk me into this," Claire said, staring into the full-length mirror in her bedroom, glaring at her reflection. "I thought my blind-date days were behind me."

"I can't believe I'm sitting on the bed where you did it with my ex-boyfriend," Naomi said, giving a little bounce on the light blue duvet.

Claire gave her a look in the mirror. "Seriously?"

"Oh, come on," Naomi said. "How can we not joke about it? He wasn't even good, was he?"

"Naomi!"

"What! He wasn't! Unless it was just me . . ."

Claire reached out and grabbed a mascara wand off the dresser, stepping closer to the mirror to add another coat, before muttering, "It wasn't just you."

"Yes! Knew it," Naomi said, flopping back on the bed. "Come to think of it, I don't know why I stuck with him so long. He just *seemed* like the right kind of guy, you know? Nice. Pulled out chairs. Educated. Polite."

"Yes, I'm aware. I married him," Claire said, applying the mascara lightly along her bottom lashes.

"Right."

Claire turned toward Naomi. "If I do this, will you tell me what's going on with Oliver? I'm between TV shows, I need a couple to 'ship, and I've decided you guys are it."

"Well, sorry, babe, you'll have to find someone else. There's nothing to tell."

"But he kissed you. Twice."

"Yes, and we agreed that it was better if we were just friends."

Claire lifted her eyebrows.

"Okay fine . . . I freaked out after his dad called me 'the help,' and I had this moment of horror that we were turning into our parents, and I was going to end up on the streets like my mom . . ."

"Whoa, honey," Claire said, coming to the bed and sitting beside her. "What?"

"I know." Naomi pressed her fingers to her temples. "It was a real B-list movie moment, let me tell you. I took a step back, figuring I'd get my act together. But in the meantime, he realized he didn't want someone like his fiancée—"

"Oliver's *engaged*?"

"*Ex*-fiancée. She ditched him when she learned just how rough things were going to get with Walter, and now he's, like, protecting himself, and his dad probably. And I get it, because Alzheimer's is the worst, and—"

"Okay, slow down," Claire said, pressing a hand to Naomi's knee. "Let's just back up a minute. What do you want?"

"I don't know," Naomi said on a sigh, pulling her legs up onto the bed and resting her elbows on her denim-clad knees. "I don't know anymore."

"Well, what did you want at the start of all this?"

"Don't you have a date to go on?" Naomi asked grumpily.

"I've got time for this," Claire said, glancing at the watch Naomi had given her a few weeks earlier. "Why did you move into the building?"

"Because I promised my mom I'd make the Cunninghams face what they did to us."

"And have you?"

Naomi wrinkled her nose. "No."

"Why not?"

"Because Walter isn't well enough to understand any of that. And Oliver . . ."

"And Oliver?" Claire nudged patiently when Naomi broke off.

"He's not the same," Naomi said, fiddling with an errant string on Claire's duvet. "He's not like I remember."

"Of course not," Claire said, in a zero-BS tone. "He was ten, Naomi. Most little boys are awful at ten. Girls, too. And no disrespect to your mother, but I don't know that it worked in your best interest to be poisoning your ears about the Cunninghams all these years. Yes, his dad did an awful thing. Oliver, too. But it was twenty years ago. Maybe it's time to let it go, even if your mom never could. Like you said, you're not going to get what you want from Walter. And ask yourself what you're going to get out of it if you continue to hold it over Oliver's head."

"So you don't think I should tell him?"

"Oh, no. You should *definitely* tell him," Claire said.

Naomi wrinkled her nose. "I had a feeling you were going to say that."

"Because I'm very wise."

"You are, but you're also going to be late," Naomi said, reaching out and twisting Claire's watch toward her so she could see the time.

"What are we thinking for lipstick? Neutral? Bright?"

Claire shrugged indifferently. "You picked the guy. What do you think?"

Naomi tapped her fingers against her cheek as she thought it over. Her contribution to their trio's dating pact was a perfectly nice broker she'd gone out with a time or two, and had zero chemistry with. He'd lost his wife several years ago in a car accident, so Naomi figured he'd be respectful of Claire's need to take it slow.

"I still can't believe I'm going out on a date this soon after losing my husband. People will think the worst of me."

"People don't have to know. And besides, your husband was a cheating snake. Regardless of what happened to him, he doesn't deserve your loyalty," Naomi said, climbing off the bed. She was about to go into Claire's bathroom to assess the lipstick options.

Claire studied her hands, not looking up as she spoke. "Naomi. Do you think . . . do you think . . . am I silly?"

Naomi turned back. "You're a lot of things, Claire, but not silly."

"I don't mean like . . . fluff. I mean silly for thinking that I get a redo. A second chance."

"At marriage?" Naomi asked.

Claire hesitated, then nodded.

"Of course not. I don't believe in soul mates. Or at least, I believe we each have lots of soul mates. You'll find someone so much better for you than Brayden."

Claire twisted her bracelet and didn't meet Naomi's eyes.

"What else?" Naomi nudged.

"What if I don't want it?"

"Don't want . . ."

"Any of it. Love. Relationships. Hell, I'm not even sure I miss sex. What if I'm thirty-four years old and done with that part of my life?"

"If you want to be, then you can be," Naomi said, going to her friend and squeezing her hand. "But until you decide . . . maybe keep your options open?"

Claire lifted her head, gave a tentative smile. "Okay. I'll try, if . . . you tell Oliver Cunningham who you really are."

"Pass."

"Fine. But you at least have to stop seeing Dylan, Naomi. Oliver deserves better."

Naomi frowned. "What are you talking about? I haven't seen him since that tepid date, and all of the TV stuff's been handled over email."

"But I saw him at your place. The other day when I texted, I was right by your building, asking if you were around and wanted to grab a cup of coffee. You said you were at your new office building, which sounds amazing by the way—"

"Yeah, yeah." Naomi rolled her finger to move the conversation along. "About Dylan . . ."

"Right! Well, I'm pretty sure it was him. He was talking to an older guy. I thought at first maybe it was Oliver's dad, but then my head exploded at the thought of one of your boyfriends chatting up the other boyfriend's dad . . ."

Claire chirped on, oblivious to the slightly queasy feeling that had overtaken Naomi.

"Are you sure it was him?" she interrupted. "Dylan?"

"Well, now that you mentioned it, I sort of waved, and he didn't wave back but just walked away. So maybe it wasn't him."

Or maybe he didn't want anyone to know he was there.

Naomi reached for her phone. "Give me one sec, 'kay?"

With one arm wrapped around her stomach, the other holding her phone to her ear, Naomi wandered into Claire's guest
room as she waited for Dylan to pick up. She made it only about
a foot into the room, it was so full of stuff. Naomi flinched when
she realized it was Brayden's stuff, heaped carelessly across the
bed, thrown angrily into boxes.

She flinched again when a man who reminded her far too
much of Brayden picked up the phone. "Naomi! Hi! I've got to
say, I was pretty sure you'd decided to brush me off," he said with
a little laugh.

"Is that why you were at my apartment building?"

She didn't bother asking if. Her gut told her that he had been
there—and that it had been Walter he'd been talking to.

"Ah—" His nervous laughter gave him away. "I stopped by
when I was in the neighborhood."

Naomi rolled her eyes. "And just decided to chat up my
neighbors?"

"Is that a crime?" His voice was defensive. A bit like a petulant teen who'd gotten caught smoking. Or in this case, gotten
caught snooping.

She inhaled a long breath and then let it out slowly. "You figured it out."

Dylan gave an irritated sigh. "That you currently live in the
same building where your mom worked as a housekeeper? Yeah,
our researchers figured that out about five minutes after that
meeting with you and your *Jersey Shore* assistant."

His tone was snide, and she closed her eyes, wondering how
she could have been so blind. Still, she clung to hope . . .

"But you told them to back off. At that meeting . . ."

"Because I didn't want your filtered version of what happened. I wanted what actually happened. Look, I know it sucks, but good TV happens in the messy stuff. Plus, you signed the contract."

"Yeah?" she asked sweetly to mask the anger that was building at his betrayal. "And did you find what you were looking for?"

"No," he admitted after a beat. "I couldn't get into the building, and the only person who came out was this crackpot old man who didn't know a person from a lamppost . . ."

Naomi's gaze went white with rage.

"How do I get a new producer?" she asked, interrupting his petty rambling.

"What?"

"A new producer for *Max*. How do I get one?"

He gave an incredulous laugh. "You can't be serious. What sort of self-righteous—"

"I don't work or associate with people who stab me in the back. I'll have my lawyer take care of it." She hung up before he could say another word.

She closed her eyes and set a fist to her forehead, making a conscious effort to slow her breathing despite the sheer anger rolling through her.

"Everything okay?" Claire asked softly from the doorway.

Naomi dropped her hand and opened her eyes. "Actually? Yeah."

Claire frowned. "You sounded upset. And pissed."

"Oh, I am. But I also just had an epiphany."

"Ooh, I love those! What kind?"

Naomi smiled. "The kind where you realize your story has a twist ending. And you had the wrong villain all along."

Chapter Twenty-Six

Oliver was sitting on his couch, whisky in hand, college football on in the background, hunched over his coffee table as he searched for the puzzle piece that had been eluding him the entire quarter.

Normally he searched with ruthless determination for a rogue piece, refusing to quit until he found it. Instead, he flopped back into the couch cushions.

It was no use. He'd been trying to convince himself that he was enjoying having a night to himself. Trying to remember that he used to relish nights exactly like this one, with a drink, a puzzle, the game . . .

But what he really wanted was to be cozied up with the redhead next door.

Preferably naked.

His phone buzzed, and he picked it up, wincing when he saw it was a text from Janice saying that although Walter had finally gone down for bed, he'd been more difficult than usual.

Oliver told her to let him know if Walter got up again and

wouldn't settle, though he sent up a quick prayer that it wouldn't come to that. He'd been on Walter duty last night, and it had been more exhausting than usual. Lately nothing seemed to please his dad, and he let his displeasure be known through increasingly violent means. Throwing, kicking, shoving . . .

Oliver pulled up the reminders on his phone, made a note to give Walter's doctor a call on Monday to discuss the recent behavioral changes.

The game went to commercial, and Oliver was standing up for a whisky refill when there was a knock at the door. Not Walter or Janice. He knew both Walter's pounds and Janice's brisk taps.

This was more . . . tentative.

He opened the door and blinked, wondering if he'd conjured her up. "Naomi?"

She was wearing jeans and a tight-fitting black T-shirt, her hair pulled back into a ponytail, looking very much . . . well, girl next door. Literally.

"Come in," he said, hoping his voice didn't betray just how happy he was to see her. The last thing he wanted to do was scare her off when he was finally close to breaking through her walls.

She stepped inside and looked around. "You know, this is the first time I've been in here?"

"Is it? That can't be."

She nodded. "You've been in my place, but the rest of the time we're always in Walter's."

"Ah. Well . . . eat your heart out."

"It's very . . ."

"Bachelor pad?"

"Well, it looks like you just moved in," she said, looking at the bare walls, the minimal furniture.

He rubbed a hand over his neck, trying to see it through her eyes. It was depressingly barren. What was even more depressing was that he'd never really noticed. It was a place to eat and sleep in between work and Walter duties.

"I guess decorating's not really my forte."

She nodded in acknowledgment, wandering around. She paused when she looked down at the coffee table, at the puzzle, then shot him a bemused look. "Really?"

"Told you I liked puzzles."

"I thought you were joking," she said, bending over to get a better look at the London scene. Or at least, what would be the London scene. He hadn't even finished the border pieces of this one yet.

"How do you even know where to start?" she asked, picking up a piece, running a finger around the edge as she studied it.

He watched her for a moment, wondering what sort of childhood had resulted in someone never doing a puzzle.

"Well," he said slowly, coming around to stand beside her. "It's like I said a while ago: you start with the corner pieces."

She smiled and looked up at him. "I remember. You thought you'd found one of mine."

"I know I did."

"What'd you figure out?"

He held her gaze. "That you don't trust people. And that you definitely don't trust men."

"Yeah, well." She dropped the piece back to the coffee table. "That applies to most of the women of Manhattan."

"Because of Brayden?"

She shrugged lightly. "Because of a lot of things. In my experience, men generally aren't . . . nice."

"I am."

She looked up at him again. "Yeah," she said slowly, as though surprised. "You are."

His gaze dropped to her lips.

Just friends, he reminded himself. He'd meant what he'd told her the other day. He didn't think he could survive another Bridget. Couldn't handle another woman who couldn't handle Dad. Couldn't risk falling for her only to watch her walk away.

She bent to the table again, this time to pick up his cup. She sniffed the contents. "High West?"

The woman knew his favorite whisky by scent?

It was too damn late. He was already falling for her. Falling for every one of her moods, and there were many. Falling for her strength and her vulnerabilities, falling for the fact that she was kind even when she didn't want to be . . .

"Why are you looking at me like that?" she said with a nervous laugh. "You can get back to your football game. I can read or maybe figure out how to do this nerdy puzzle thing . . ."

Oliver slid a hand behind her head, tilting her face up to his.

"Wait," she said a little breathlessly, placing her hands against his chest when he bent his head toward hers. "I just came over to hang out. I thought we weren't doing this."

"I don't know what the hell we're doing," he said, his voice a little lower than usual. "Do you?"

Wordlessly she shook her head, and the hands against his chest moved slightly, going from pressing in resistance to tugging slightly at his shirt until . . .

His lips brushed over hers, teasing, testing, wanting.

Her lips softened beneath his, bringing him in, drowning him in her spicy-sweet cinnamon taste, seducing him with every sexy move against his mouth.

He meant to take it slow—to sate them both with a kiss to

take the edge off, but his willpower began to fade the second he got his hands on her.

Oliver wanted this—wanted her—in a way that went beyond physical need.

Since the day he'd met her, she'd gotten under his skin, pissed him off, confused the hell out of him, and he was damn grateful for it. Naomi Powell had brought him back to life, made him realize that he hadn't died with his mom, or with his father's diagnosis; he'd just been living that way.

He was thirty years old. He was a man.

And right now, he was a man who needed a woman—*this* woman.

Her hands slipped under his shirt, her nails digging into his back as he kissed her neck. "You like this," he murmured against the hollow of her throat.

In response she arched into him further, pressing soft feminine curves into everything that was hard and masculine.

"Tell me to stop," Oliver said, even as his palm found the fullness of her breast. "Remind me . . ."

He lost his train of thought as Naomi stepped back slightly and, holding his gaze, reached down and pulled the hem of her shirt up and over her head so she stood before him all white skin and plain black bra.

Oliver's tongue stuck to the roof of his mouth. She was beautiful. Stunning. But that wasn't what undid him. It was the soft vulnerability in her eyes, the quiet warmth that told him this was more than just about the physical for her, too.

He stayed still too long, because her cheeks began to flush and she started to reach for her discarded shirt.

Oliver's hand shot out to her waist. "Don't."

Slowly, deliberately, he bent his head, bringing his mouth

once more to hers as he tugged her closer. Naomi sighed against his lips as his hand glided up her slim back. Her breath caught when his fingers unhooked her bra. She cried out when his hands found her bare flesh.

He was lost. Utterly and entirely gone for this woman.

Oliver bent slightly, scooping her into his arms, the old-fashioned gesture feeling exactly like the right one with this thoroughly modern woman.

He carried her to the bedroom and set her on the bed. He saw something flicker in her eyes, something almost familiar that told him he was missing something crucial.

Then Naomi reached for him, warm and willing, feeling very much like his future.

Chapter Twenty-Seven

*N*aomi woke up slowly, registering first that the window had moved. She was lying on her right side, as she usually did, but the window wasn't where it was supposed to be. She was looking at a bare wall.

And the pillow was different, too. It was warm, and . . . moving.

She froze as Oliver shifted beneath her.

Oliver.

She'd slept with Oliver Cunningham.

Naomi squeezed her eyes shut, bracing for the wave of self-loathing, bracing for the onslaught of guilt. *What would her mother think?*

But . . . nothing came.

For the first time in a long time, Naomi's primary thoughts weren't of the past, but of the present. Present Oliver. And Present Oliver, or at least, Last Night Oliver had been . . .

Perfect.

She tilted her head up slightly, wanting to run a finger along the scruff on that sharp jawline but not wanting to wake him up. She liked him with a little bit of facial hair. Liked him without it, too. Liked him in sweats, liked him in suits. Just . . . *liked* him.

He spoke without opening his eyes. "Why are you watching me?"

She laughed. "That obvious?"

Oliver glanced down, blue eyes soft and a little sleepy. "Morning."

"Morning," she said softly.

His arm came more fully around her, and she burrowed closer. She'd never been much of a cuddler, but for some reason she couldn't seem to get close enough. Maybe because she knew this was likely to be short-lived, because once he found out who she was . . . that she'd been lying.

Claire was right. She had to tell him.

"Hey," she said softly, dragging her finger in lazy patterns on his chest. "So—"

Oliver groaned just slightly. "Naomi, something you should know about me—I'm no good for talking before coffee."

A reprieve.

She didn't know if she was relieved or disappointed.

"Noted," she said, lifting up slightly so he could slide out of bed. "Never stand between a caffeine addict and his coffee."

"You don't drink it."

"No, I do," she said, flopping back down on the pillow. "As long as it's like, half coffee, half sweet creamer stuff."

He winced as he pulled sweatpants out of a dresser drawer. "I'm going to pretend I didn't hear that. Where's your key?"

"Hmm?"

"Your apartment key. I don't think I even have milk, but if

you have the makings to bastardize coffee in your place, I can go grab it."

"Back pocket of my jeans," she said, sitting up and pulling the sheet under her armpits. "Which are . . ."

Oliver picked them up from the doorway, where they'd been dropped. Flung? Hmm.

"I'll go," she said as he held up the key.

"You'll stay. I find I'm really liking the looks of you in my bed."

"Good, because I'm pretty damn happy to be here."

Naomi flopped back on the pillows as he disappeared.

Several minutes later, he reappeared with two steaming mugs and her trusty Coffee-mate tucked under his arm.

"Okay, I added some," he said, setting one of the mugs on the nightstand and handing her the other. "I was assuming you didn't literally mean half-and-half, but . . ."

"No, I meant it," she said, waggling her fingers for the bottle of vanilla creamer.

"I don't think I can watch this," he muttered, handing her the bottle and pulling a spoon out of his pocket.

She added a generous dollop more and stirred. "You know it's right when it's mostly white with just a little hint of brown."

He stared at her, horrified. "I think I want to break up."

Naomi popped the spoon in her mouth, sucked it clean.

Oliver blinked. "Or not."

"Break up. Seems to me in order to break up, we'd first have to be . . . together?" she asked, taking a sip of the perfectly sweetened coffee.

Oliver sat on the edge of the bed. "Seems like it."

Are we? she wanted to ask.

She didn't. Because she couldn't, in good conscience, ask him to think of her like a girlfriend when he didn't even know her. Didn't know their history.

Damn it, she'd done that thing.

That thing where you wait too long to tell someone something important, and what would have been merely an awkward conversation now felt monumental.

"Oliver—"

"Naomi." His voice was steady. Calm. Because he was steady and calm. He was a rock. For his mother when she was sick, for his father now. He was *that* guy. The one people could count on. The one who stuck around when shit got difficult.

She studied him, trying to remember the monstrous little boy he'd been and . . . couldn't. Adult Oliver had replaced all memories of crappy, brat Oliver. The boy she'd hated had become a man she—

"Do you want to go to brunch?" she blurted out. "There's this great little place in the Village with the most amazing French toast and eggs Benedict. It's impossible to get into without reservations, but one of my employees is dating the owner, so I could probably get us a spot at the bar . . ."

Even as she babbled, she saw the light go out of his eyes, watched as he shut down.

"You don't like brunch?"

Never before had she seen someone dim so much at the mention of French toast.

"No, I do." He rubbed a hand over his hair, looking suddenly exhausted. "It's just—it's not really a luxury I've been able to indulge in the past couple years."

Ah. "Walter."

He looked at her, eyes tired. Apologetic. "Janice does brunch and church with her sister's family every Sunday. I'm on Walter duty. If I know in advance, I can sometimes make it work, but—"

"No, of course," Naomi interrupted, holding up her hand. "I should have realized . . . I know you're usually with him on weekends. And evenings."

"Rethinking that together thing?" he asked, his eyes bleak as he looked at her.

Yes, but not for the reason you think.

"Maybe you're right," Naomi said quietly. "This whole thing is complicated. It's happened fast. If we could just slow down for a second—"

"Naomi. I get it," he said. "It's like I told you the other day, I don't hold it against anyone who wants no part of this, but this is also my life. You're young, gorgeous, successful. You deserve the brunches and the fancy happy hours and the late-night dinners. But that's never going to be with me. Not anytime soon."

She nodded because it was easier to let him think that was the reason she was walking away than the real reason.

Naomi took another sip of coffee before handing him the mug. "I'll get dressed."

He stayed still for a minute, looking at her with undisguised regret before he stood and took both mugs into the kitchen. Naomi got out of the bed, finding her underwear and jeans, then wincing when she realized her bra and shirt were still in the living room.

Deciding that borrowing a T-shirt without asking was decidedly less embarrassing than leaving the bedroom topless, she helped herself to a Columbia University shirt she found in a drawer.

Oliver did a double take when she came out of the bedroom wearing it but said nothing as she picked up her bra and shirt as calmly as possible, wrapping the bra inside the shirt in case she ran into any other neighbors on the way back to her apartment.

"So." She turned and faced him. "Um."

He smiled. "You don't have to."

"You don't even know what I was going to say."

"I just meant you don't have to say anything," he said, setting his mug aside and coming toward her. "I'm not boyfriend material. Not right now."

He stopped, setting a hand to her cheek. "No regrets about last night. Promise me."

"I promise," she whispered, turning her cheek into his hand and closing her eyes, relishing his scent. His warmth.

He kissed her softly, before stepping back. "See you around, Naomi."

She swallowed, a little puzzled to realize there was a lump in her throat. "See you."

Naomi left his apartment and walked woodenly down the hall. Blindly, she climbed into the shower, hoping the warm water would wash away the sense that this was all wrong. That she was being an idiot.

And that maybe he was, too, for not having the courage to ask someone to stick with him. To tell him he was worth the sacrifices that came with his situation.

When she realized she was being an idiot, Naomi hurriedly shut off the water. She dried her hair in record time, tugged on yoga pants, and pulled on Oliver's college T-shirt once more.

Two minutes later, she was out the door, five minutes after that, she was at the grocery store, then back to her apartment to pick up the bottle of cheap champagne she kept in the fridge.

It was just before ten when she knocked on Walter's door with the toe of her sneaker, since her arms were full of grocery bags and a bouquet of confetti roses she'd bought on a whim.

Oliver opened the door, his expression nonplussed. "Naomi? What are you doing here?" Automatically he reached out to take one of the bags. "What's all this stuff?"

"Eggs. Hash browns. Bacon. Some sort of cinnamon bread that looked too delicious to pass up. Orange juice and bubbly, because what's a brunch without mimosas," she said, pushing past the stunned man.

She went on her toes and kissed his cheek. "You couldn't go to brunch, so I brought brunch to you. And Walter. Good morning, Walter," she said, turning and seeing him in his favorite easy chair by the TV.

He glanced over, lifted his hand in greeting. "Naomi."

She smiled at Oliver. "See? Off to a good start. Okay, how are your scrambled eggs skills? Mine are mediocre, but I'm really good with bacon—"

Oliver hauled her toward him, cutting off her bacon bragging with a searing kiss.

It was long and hard, and loaded with emotion. They were both breathing hard when he pulled back, resting his forehead on hers. "Thank you."

She brushed her mouth over his softly. "You're welcome. Now feed me?"

He grinned in response, off-loading the rest of the bags as she went to search for a vase for the flowers. "Walter, how do you like your bacon? You a crispy kind of guy?"

"Sausage. You got any sausage?"

"Work with me here, Walter," she said, giving the man an exasperated look.

He looked over and smiled, and Naomi was surprised to feel herself smile back.

This wasn't even remotely close to how Naomi had envisioned her relationship with the Cunningham men.

And she couldn't remember the last time she'd been so . . . *happy*.

Chapter Twenty-Eight

*Y*es, I know it's last minute. Yes, I understand—nope, absolutely understand your agency prefers twenty-four hours' notice . . . yep, and I appreciate you making an exception. Yes, six o'clock tonight would be perfect."

Oliver spent another minute groveling on the phone with the caretaking agency before making another phone call, this time to one of his favorite restaurants that he hadn't been to in . . . way too long.

Sure, Monday nights weren't the most popular date nights, but he wanted to surprise Naomi. To show her that he could meet her halfway, to find a way to make them work.

The woman had gone above and beyond. First with brunch yesterday, not even batting an eye when it had devolved into an expected tantrum from Walter. Then this afternoon when Oliver had gotten hung up with a client at the same time Janice had a sudden, severe tooth pain, Naomi had casually offered to stay with Walter so Janice could get to the dentist.

Just like that, as if it were no big deal. As if they were partners in this, even though he had no right to ask it of her so soon in the relationship.

Oliver knew he was dangerously close to falling in love with the woman, and the only thing holding him back was the nagging sense that *she* was holding back.

That was what tonight was for. Just the two of them. Nice wine. Fancy clothes. No hard-boiled eggs. Not even puzzles.

To give them a chance, he needed to get them beyond the walls of 517 Park Avenue, to show her—to show himself—that they could make it in the real world.

After making dinner reservations, he made one more call, this time to Naomi. She didn't pick up, which wasn't all that surprising, considering his dad frequently demanded all of someone's attention.

He nearly sent her a text, letting her know that he'd gotten alternate care for the evening, since Janice—on pain pills following an emergency root canal—would likely be ill-equipped to deal with Walter.

He decided instead to surprise her, stopping on his way home to get her flowers. She'd insisted on leaving the roses from yesterday at his place to "brighten it up," and he wanted something for her place—a congratulations on the new office.

Oliver selected a bouquet of pink roses at a corner shop, then headed home, taking the stairs two at a time up to the fifth floor.

Pre-Naomi, Oliver had always stopped by his own place to catch his breath, change his clothes, switch gears from architect to patient's son.

Post-Naomi, getting to his father's place and seeing her there was the highlight of his day. Week.

The woman was becoming the highlight of his life.

Oliver pulled out his keys, then skidded to a halt when he saw the door of his father's apartment was open.

His heart pounded as he slowly walked toward the door, pushing it open with a combination of urgency and dread.

Nothing.

"Naomi? Dad?"

No response. The only sound he heard was the History Channel on full volume.

Oliver broke out in a cold sweat. They could have gone for a walk, but there was no way Naomi would have left the door unlocked, much less open.

"Dad!" he called, more urgent now, going to the bedroom. Empty.

Absently, he reached for the remote to turn off the TV, the silence only ratcheting up his sense that something was very wrong.

A cell phone buzzed against a hard surface and he scanned the room until he saw Naomi's phone on the kitchen counter, distinctive in its coral case.

Oliver went for it, reaching for it, when he came up short.

His heart stopped.

"Naomi," he said on a rush.

She lay crumpled on the floor of the kitchen, a small pool of blood beneath her head.

"Naomi!" She didn't move.

He crouched beside her, running a hand over her side, even as his first aid training reminded him not to move her.

Oliver softly touched her cheek, but she didn't stir. He pulled out his phone and dialed 911 with a shaky hand.

"Yes, I need an ambulance at 517 Park Avenue. There's a woman unconscious."

He barely recognized his own voice as he answered the operator's questions.

No, he didn't know what happened.

Yes, there was blood.

Was she breathing?

Oliver swallowed. He hadn't checked, because it hadn't occurred to him—he wouldn't let it be true.

With a shaky hand, he put his fingers to Naomi's wrist. Found a pulse. To calm his heart, he put his hand beneath her nose, felt her breath.

"Yes. She's breathing."

"Okay, an ambulance's on the way. Can you stay on the line, help me tell them where to go when they get there?"

He started to say, yes, of course, when he remembered. Walter. Walter was missing.

And suddenly Oliver was faced with the worst decision of his life: stay with the bloodied, unconscious body of the woman he loved, or try to find his lost, ill father.

Chapter Twenty-Nine

*N*aomi's first words upon opening her eyes were ones she'd learned in the Bronx housing projects, and most definitely not fit for church.

But damn her head hurt.

She lifted her hand to the pain, only to freeze when she noted the tubes sticking out of the back of her hand.

"What the . . ."

She felt a wave of panicked nausea and closed her eyes again, both to try to ward off the pain and to remember.

She was in a hospital, clearly.

But why?

It came back. Slowly. Blearily. Walter. He'd been in one of his moods. She'd asked him to turn the TV down, he's shouted . . . Well, let's just say she wasn't the only one with a foul mouth.

He'd demanded whisky, she'd said no, knowing alcohol would only inflame his current state, and he'd . . .

Hit her. Shoved her?

She couldn't remember the details. She only knew the fear of seeing his much larger frame coming at her, eyes unfocused and furious, remembered hearing the crack of her own head against the cabinets . . .

Naomi felt a soft touch against her hand and turned her head slightly, opening her eyes to see a concerned-looking Deena.

Deena's eyes went wide. "The nurse was right! You did call out!"

"Rather spicy, too," came a male voice to her left. Naomi slowly rotated her neck, and looked over to a portly man in scrubs adjusting something with her IV.

"How you feeling?" he asked.

She tried to speak, but her mouth felt dry. She swallowed and tried again. "Like you better be increasing the morphine in that thing."

He smiled. "Any dizziness? Nausea?"

She considered, then shook her head. The nausea she'd felt when she'd first opened her eyes had passed, and she wasn't seeing doubles of anyone. "Just the headache."

"I'll send the doctor right in to look you over. I gave your friend there some ice chips if you need any."

Deena shook a paper cup, but Naomi shook her head no. She didn't want ice. She wanted answers.

"What happened?"

"We were hoping you could tell us," Deena said with a smile.

"Who's we?" She scanned the room, but it was only Deena.

"Oh, you know, only everyone from the office. They've all been clamoring for a visit, but they'll have to get in line."

"In line behind . . . ?" Naomi asked, her heart desperate for one name, and one name alone.

"Me. Those fancy girls who were sleeping with your ex."

"Claire and Audrey are here?" Naomi asked, feeling a little guilty that her heart sank that Deena hadn't mentioned Oliver.

Deena nodded. "They'll be back any minute. It was their turn for a Starbucks run, and I hope they got my order right. What's the point of a Frappuccino if there's no extra whip?"

"Deena," Naomi asked softly. "Have you seen a guy here? A—"

She was interrupted by a knock on the door as a woman in aqua scrubs walked in without waiting for a response. "Hi, Naomi, I'm Dr. Estrada. Rumor has it you got quite the bump on the noggin."

Yay, one of *those* doctors.

Deena squeezed her hand in reassurance and then backed out of the room so Naomi could speak with the doctor in private.

Dr. Estrada checked something on the IV, jotted something on her clipboard, and then pulled a small flashlight out of her pocket.

Several annoying minutes later, after having the light shone in her eyes and being instructed to follow the finger and do basic math and describe her pain level on a scale of one to ten, the doctor announced that she wasn't showing any signs of a concussion, but that they wanted to do a CT scan to be sure.

"When can I leave?" Naomi asked.

Dr. Estrada gave an impersonal smile as she scribbled on her clipboard. "Depends what that CT scan says. I'll have someone in shortly. You need anything?"

An escape route. Oliver. Answers.

"No, I'm good."

Dr. Estrada nodded and left. There was another knock, and Naomi resisted the urge to tell whoever it was to go away so she could think for a minute, but her protest died when she saw who it was.

"Oliver."

She smiled, but he didn't smile back. In fact, he looked . . . different. Not just because of the jeans and sweater in lieu of the usual suit, but he looked . . . cold. Removed.

"Oliver, I'm so sorry," she said, trying to sit up. "Walter—is he?"

Oliver gently pushed her back to the pillows, though it was an impersonal, don't-do-that sort of touch, not a lingering touch of a loved one.

"He's fine. I found him at the Central Park dog park."

"Oh, good," she said, a little confused by the anger in his tone. "He does love that place."

Oliver didn't nod in acknowledgment. Didn't smile. It was like dealing with a robot.

"Do you remember what happened?" he asked, crossing his arms.

Naomi hesitated. How did you tell someone that you were in a hospital bed because their sick father had gotten violent?

"Not exactly. He got mad, and pushed—hit? I'm not sure."

Oliver sighed and his arms dropped. "I figured it was something like that. Walter couldn't tell us anything, but—I apologize."

"You *apologize*," she said, mimicking his frosty tone. "It wasn't your fault. It wasn't even Walter's fault, he didn't know—"

"No, it was his fault," Oliver interrupted. "And mine, I suppose, for not recognizing sooner that someone of his size, in his condition, needed more than home care."

"What do you mean?" She searched his face, trying to read him.

He swallowed, the motion so awkward and strained that she heard it.

"I dropped him off at a facility this morning."

"Oliver," she said, reaching for his hand.

He didn't reach back. "It's up near Westchester. A little further than some of the places in the city, but it's nicer. More outdoor space. He didn't—" He swallowed again. "He didn't seem to hate it."

"You didn't have to do that just because of this—it was a one-time thing—"

"No, it was a *first*-time thing," he said quietly. "I've known for a while it would come to this. Sooner than I thought, but . . . it's better this way."

"No, it's not. You're obviously upset, you—"

"I came here as soon as I found my dad," Oliver interrupted. "And my neighbor Ruth was with you the entire time up until then."

"Oh. Okay. Thank you—"

"They couldn't get ahold of your emergency contact. I was the first one here, before your assistant or your friends. They asked if I knew how to get in touch with her."

"With who?" she asked, her head pounding harder, knowing she was missing something but too disoriented to figure out what.

"The name on your emergency contact. Your mother."

"Oh," Naomi said, wincing. "I guess I never updated . . ."

She went still, her hand falling away from where it had been exploring the bandage on the side of her head.

Her mother. Oliver had heard her mother's name . . .

"Danica Fields," he said, his voice cold. "I knew that I knew it as soon as I heard it, but it took me a while to place it. Took a while for the memories of my mother spitting that name like it was an epithet to come screaming back."

Naomi closed her eyes. "Oliver."

"I had no idea you were that Naomi, but you knew I was that Oliver, didn't you? *Carrots?*"

His use of her childhood nickname might have made her smile in other circumstances, but not now. Now she was merely the Carrots to his Ollie, and he hated her every bit as much now as he had back then.

The trouble was, she didn't hate him back. Not anymore.

"I was going to tell you," she said, still not opening her eyes.

"When?" His voice cracked just the slightest bit, and he cleared his throat. "When?"

"I tried, a bunch of times, but . . ."

"But nothing. How could you just—how could you not—"

She opened her eyes, just as he shut his, and the tired pain on his face ripped at her.

"Is that why you moved into the building?" he asked, meeting her gaze coolly once again. "Was it some sort of, what, revenge plan? Is that why you hated me on the spot?"

"Yes," she whispered. "I mean, I didn't want to hurt you or your father, I just wanted . . . closure."

"On something that happened twenty years ago? When I was a kid? When we *both* were? Grow up, Naomi."

"Hey," she snapped, feeling apologetic, but also not prepared to take all the blame. "Those twenty years passed a little bit differently for you and me. Do you know that we had nowhere to go after you lied to cover for your dad? I slept on the street with my backpack as my pillow. From there, it was a homeless shelter, and then on to a disgusting motel. And then a lot more disgusting motels, and even more disgusting apartments—"

"That's not my—"

"Not your problem?" she guessed. "Not your problem that my mother went off the rails after she got tossed out by your parents?

They blacklisted her. And when she couldn't get another house-keeping job, she just gave up, Oliver. So no, maybe it wasn't your problem, but it sure as hell was your *fault*. Your mom never would have let my mom keep her job, but maybe we could have at least gotten her final paycheck. Maybe we could have had time to find someone to stay with had your dad not thrown her and me under the bus."

Oliver's gaze flickered with regret, and he stared at her for a long moment. "You're right."

She opened her mouth, primed for another fight, but his simple words caught her off guard, and instead she gave an awk-ward nod that made her head hurt even worse.

He stepped closer. "Naomi. I didn't know. Really I didn't, and I can't tell you how sorry I am. I'm not proud of how I handled that back then. And I know it doesn't make it better, but though it wasn't the last time my dad cheated on my mom, it was the last time I covered for him. I was a shitty little kid, but I got better."

"I know," she whispered.

"Christ," he said, dragging a hand over his face and looking at her. "Naomi Fields. I haven't thought about you in . . . Where are your glasses? Your hair's darker. You're not so . . ."

"Feisty?"

He gave a reluctant smile. "No, you're still definitely that. I was going to say frustrating, but you're still that, too."

His smile disappeared as he held her gaze. "What you did was pretty messed up. I can understand wanting some closure over what happened. Maybe even some sort of reckoning. But to wiggle your way into our lives—you must have been thrilled to see what happened to us. My mom dead. My dad, hardly aware of who he was. Me, falling head over heels for you. Was that the plan, Naomi?"

"No, it wasn't like that!" she protested, trying to sit up again, batting away his hand as it tried to keep her still. "Yes, I moved into the building because a part of me wanted you to have to live side by side with the help's daughter, with the daughter of the woman your father cheated with. But I didn't know . . . I didn't know your father's condition. I didn't know you had . . . changed."

"And yet when you did find out, you didn't exactly rush to come clean. Instead you let us—me— Damn it, Naomi, we *cared* about you. I mean, yeah, Walter's form of caring is complicated, but you let me bring you into our lives. Hell, I left my father with someone who hates him."

"I don't— Okay, I did," she admitted. "A lot. But I don't hate him now, Oliver, I swear to you. I want him to be okay. I want you to be happy—"

"You'll get your wish on the first one. Walter will be fine. Probably better now that he'll have round-the-clock care better than I can give him. And as for me being happy . . . I'll get there, too. Eventually. But not with you, Naomi."

She croaked out a little sound of dismay as her eyes watered. "Oliver."

He nodded at the bandage on her head. "I'll take care of the hospital bills. It's my fault you're here. And I'm glad you're okay, but Naomi . . ." His gaze came back to hers, cold and hard. "We're done."

"No!" she said, getting a concerned look from a nurse in the hallway.

He started to turn away, then turned back. "For what it's worth, I really am sorry about back then. I'm not proud of myself. Or of my parents. And if I could change it, I would."

"I know you would. Oliver—"

"But," he continued tersely, interrupting her, "I've found another one of your corner pieces, Naomi. The one that shows you're dishonest and maybe a little revenge-hungry."

No longer able to hold them back, her tears spilled down her cheeks. "Maybe. But I have other pieces, too."

He shrugged. "You're no longer a puzzle I'm interested in solving."

And then he was gone.

Chapter Thirty

*T*urn that off," Walter groused at her from his bed.

"All right," Naomi said easily, even though he'd asked her to turn on the television just a few moments before.

"What would you like to do?"

"Where the hell is Margaret? Probably off shopping again." He tugged at his sweatshirt, then looked down as though surprised to see it.

"I'm not hungry," he barked, even though she hadn't said a word.

"Okay, no problem," she said.

He gave her a suspicious look for a long moment, then he reached for the book on his nightstand and held it out to her.

His eyes met hers in a silent request, and she smiled. "Sure. Let's read."

She sat in the chair beside him, opening the enormous biography on Benjamin Franklin to the bookmarked spot. She hadn't been reading this to him, so it must have been Oliver.

Her stomach twisted a little at the thought. She hadn't

spoken to him since that day in the hospital. She hadn't even seen him, which was no easy task, considering they were still neighbors, as far as she knew.

Not that they would be for long. The first thing Naomi had done after getting out of the hospital was to make arrangements to move into the place in Tribeca. And fabulous though she knew the condo was, at this point, she'd have been just as happy to be back in one of the various gross Belmont motel rooms of her childhood. Anywhere but at 517 Park.

She'd moved in for all the wrong reasons, and it was as she'd known all those years ago—she didn't belong there. Not then and not now, though the reasons were different.

Then, because people like Margaret and Walter Cunningham were unlikely to ever think of people like Danica and Naomi Fields as anything but beneath them.

Now, because Naomi knew people weren't above other people. In character, maybe, but not in status. And her character the past few weeks had been sorely lacking.

Still, even though Oliver had ignored her texts, calls, and the letter she'd slipped under his door, she was holding on to the slight hope that he didn't hate her entirely.

Last weekend she'd shown up at the only Alzheimer's care home in Westchester with the large outdoor space he'd mentioned and asked to see Walter Cunningham. Only stupidly, she hadn't thought it through to realize that *of course* they wouldn't allow a random, unplanned visitor access to their patients.

After much sweet-talking and stubbornness, she'd managed to convince them to call Walter's next of kin and request permission for her to see him.

Even as she knew full well Oliver would be the point of contact. And that her chances of him giving her the go-ahead were slim.

But he'd surprised her. He'd given Naomi permission to visit whenever she wanted, so long as the visits were supervised by a staff member. That had stung, but she got it. And it was better than nothing.

She'd meant to just come the one time. To make peace or whatever, but this was her third time out to see him, and she found she enjoyed her time here. Sure, the man was the reason she had a small bald patch on her head where they'd had to shave her hair to stitch up the head wound, but a tiny part of her thought maybe she deserved that for keeping the truth from Oliver and Walter.

Like maybe they were even now in some weird, warped way. Or maybe perhaps it wasn't about being even at all.

It was about forgiveness. And understanding. Maybe it was about choosing kindness, regardless of what had come before.

"Not that one," he snapped as she began to read. "Your book."

"My book?"

"The one you read before."

Naomi smiled at the fact that he remembered her last visit, though she was a little surprised. She wasn't much of a reader save for her Stephen King fetish, and since she could practically *feel* the observation caretaker's judgment when she'd suggested *It*, she'd pulled up the only other book on the Kindle app of her phone—a childhood favorite that she never got sick of.

"You like *Anne of Green Gables*, huh?" she asked, finding the chapter they'd ended on last time.

He shrugged and looked out the window, but he didn't ask her to stop when she began to read.

Naomi lost track of how long she read, consumed with the story of a redheaded orphan and her coming of age on Prince Edward Island.

Eventually she glanced up and saw that Walter had fallen asleep, looking peaceful and content as a ray of sunshine fell across his face.

Naomi set her phone aside, pulled a blanket off the foot of the bed, and draped it over his knees.

"I'll see you next week, okay, Walter?" she said quietly to the sleeping man.

Without realizing she was doing it, she smoothed an errant flyaway on his gray hair and waited for the instant self-loathing, the guilt that she was betraying her mother.

It never came.

She swallowed, a lump in her throat at the bittersweet realization that she finally had her peace.

And at how much it had cost her.

Naomi picked up her purse, turning to tell the facility's employee that she was off babysitting duty.

She froze. It wasn't the petite blond woman who'd escorted her to Walter's room standing in the doorway.

It was Oliver.

He was wearing a blue shirt that made his eyes look even lighter than usual, and his feet were crossed at the ankles as he leaned with one shoulder against the doorjamb.

"Hi," she said nervously. "I didn't—how long have you been here?"

He shrugged. "A while."

"I'm sorry. I didn't mean to cut in on your time with him. You could have kicked me out."

"And missed story time?" he said with a slight smile.

She looked down, feeling embarrassed. "Ah, yeah. It's an old favorite. He seems to like it. Well, at least until he fell asleep."

Oliver nodded but said nothing else.

She forced a smile. "Well. It's good to see you. And thank

you, truly, for letting me see him. I would have understood if you'd said no."

Still, he said nothing, his expression watchful.

Naomi forced yet another smile and walked toward the door. He straightened, making way for her to pass, careful not to touch her.

"Take care, Oliver," she said, keeping her voice light.

"You, too."

He let her get halfway down the hall before calling her back. "Hey, Naomi?"

She turned back.

He jerked his chin at her purse. "That book you were reading. The girl—Anne. Her nickname was Carrots. Sounds familiar."

She laughed. "You were listening quite a while. And yeah, it was only her nickname in the mind of Gilbert, who was sort of her tormentor."

"Ah. Whatever happened to them?"

"To who?"

"Anne and Gilbert."

"They eventually became friends," she said, choosing her words carefully. She was a little at a loss as to why they were discussing the fictional characters of Anne Shirley and Gilbert Blythe when they had major unresolved issues between them.

Oliver studied her a moment, then nodded and stepped into his father's room without another word.

"Um, okay," Naomi muttered to herself.

Still, she was a little proud of herself as she left the building. At least she hadn't broken down and told him how much she missed him.

Her heart might belong to Oliver. But her pride was still her own.

Chapter Thirty-One

I just want to point out that we've been friends for fewer than six months, but I have helped you move twice. Surely there should be an award for that."

Claire paused in the process of unwinding packing material from a serving dish and gave Audrey an incredulous look. "You realize that *help* is a strong word in your case, right?"

"Hey, I'm doing stuff," Audrey said, lifting her wine mug from where she sat perched on Naomi's new kitchen counter. "I told those cute boys where to put the dresser."

"You're a real lifesaver, dear," Naomi said, patting her friend's knee.

"Right? I do love this place though. I mean, the other place was okay, too, but I did think it was sort of an odd choice for you. It smelled like mothballs in the hall."

"A little bit," Naomi agreed, ripping open another box marked KITCHEN and pulling out her pasta pot.

"This is much more you," Audrey said, hopping off the counter and spinning in a circle.

"How much wine have you had?" Claire muttered.

"Enough." Audrey went to the window overlooking the Hudson River. "You know, I hardly ever come to the west side?"

"*No*," Claire said, sounding scandalized. "We are shocked. Just shocked, aren't we, Naomi?"

Naomi only smiled, relishing the sound of her friends' good-natured bickering because it meant that she didn't have to deal with her own thoughts.

Not that she didn't love her new apartment. Audrey was exactly right. It *was* more her. A brand-new high-rise on the west side of Manhattan, in a trendy neighborhood, Naomi's new apartment was perhaps the opposite of 517 Park Avenue, with its impeccable pedigree and old-money vibes.

Naomi may be new money. She may not be of the fur coat and Scotch set. She may drink cheap wine out of cheap glasses and fail to appreciate "good coffee," whatever that meant, because it was all good with enough sugar . . .

But she was successful. She was financially secure, and then some. She was happy.

Well. Mostly happy.

She was sort of happy.

She was getting there, damn it.

She missed Oliver.

As she unwrapped a skillet, she noticed Claire checking her watch. For the fifth time in less than twenty minutes.

"Claire."

"Hmm?"

"Got somewhere to be?"

"No! No, not at all, actually."

"Well, maybe you would, if you'd given Naomi's blind-date setup a chance."

"I already told you, he was nice, I had a good time. And I have no intention of going out with him or anyone else for at least a year," Claire said.

"Why a year?"

"I've decided it's the proper amount of time for a widow to mourn before getting back on the dating horse."

"It kills me to say so, but you've been right all along," Naomi said glumly. "I should have waited a year. Maybe then I'd have been smart enough not to get involved with Oliver . . ."

Damn it! How long would that last? The agonizing drop in her stomach every time she so much as thought of his name.

Claire checked her watch again, and Naomi tossed the box cutter on the counter and crossed her arms. "Spill. What are we counting down to?"

Right on cue, Naomi's doorbell rang, and Claire gave her an innocent smile. "Don't know who that could be."

"Me neither, since I haven't added anyone to my authorized guest list, and the doorman didn't call to announce a visitor."

"Well." Claire picked imaginary lint off the sleeve of her sweater dress. "Hypothetically, a friend of yours could have mentioned to the doorman that you were expecting a visitor and to send him on up—"

Him . . .

Naomi went still. "Claire."

Her friend was already moving toward the door, and even before she opened it, Naomi knew who was on the other side.

"Oliver, hi," Claire said.

"Well, well," Audrey said, with a knowing glance at Naomi. "Isn't this an interesting episode of déjà vu."

Even more so when Oliver entered the apartment carrying . . .

"Dom Pérignon!" Audrey announced excitedly, already reaching for the bottle of champagne. "At least we'll get to enjoy it this time . . ." She caught Claire's look. "Or, you know . . . not."

"I've heard it's excellent when served in a coffee mug," Oliver said in a low voice.

Slowly Naomi forced herself to look at him, mentally cursing Claire for not telling her to change into something other than ratty sweatpants and Oliver's Columbia shirt, which she'd "forgotten" to return.

His eyes dropped to the tee, then rose back up to hers. "Nice shirt."

She put her hand to her stomach to calm the butterflies, ended up fisting the shirt, looking very much a flustered, awkward teen and not the cool, composed woman she'd imagined being the next time she saw him.

"You lied to me," Oliver said quietly.

Claire was busily dragging Audrey toward the door, though they both gave an alarmed glance at that.

Naomi tried to wave them on with her eyes. Whatever Oliver needed to say to her had to come out. The sooner they did this, whatever it was, the sooner she could come to grips with the fact that she'd ruined things with them.

Audrey was clearly reluctant to leave, but she handed Oliver the champagne bottle as she passed him, along with a whisper that sounded suspiciously like, "She's more fragile than she looks."

Naomi wanted to deny it. To insist she wasn't the fragile type, especially over a man, but it was hard to deny that she was incredibly close to shattering.

Oliver inclined his head slightly, taking the champagne bottle, but he didn't give her friends another look as they scooted out the front door, pausing only long enough to make twin gestures to Naomi of "call me."

Then the door was shut, and it was just Naomi and Oliver and a big, empty apartment.

He looked around. "Nice place."

"Yeah."

He looked back at her. "Sudden move."

She refused to apologize. She would have told him she was moving if he'd bothered to be around. Or respond to any of her dozen messages.

"I don't know that I belonged there."

"No?" He asked it casually, looking down at the bottle as he did. "I don't know if I do, either."

Naomi frowned in confusion. "But you're from there. You've always lived there."

He said nothing, just stared at the label before holding the bottle up slightly.

Naomi answered just as silently, pulling two mugs off the counter that hadn't found a shelf yet, and held them both out while he popped the cork.

Oliver filled both cups, set the bottle on a stack of boxes, and lifted his mug. "To your new home."

She clinked her mug against his and took a sip, holding his gaze all the while.

Then she went for it. "What are you doing here, Oliver?"

"You lied," he said again.

She closed her eyes. "Look, I can only apologize so much. I should have told you who I was—"

"You said that Gilbert Blythe and Anne Shirley became friends."

Naomi blinked rapidly, trying to follow. "Um, what?"

"The other week, you read my dad *Anne of Green Gables*. The boy called Anne *Carrots*, much as I called you Carrots."

"Right?"

"Well, I read it."

Naomi gave a startled laugh. "You read *Anne of Green Gables*?"

"Whole series," he said, taking a sip of the champagne. "You lied."

"About—"

"Gilbert and Anne. They weren't friends."

"Well." She fidgeted with her mug. "They were, they just . . ."

"They were a hell of a lot more than that."

"Yeah. Okay," she relented. "Gilbert called Anne Carrots because he was in love with her all along, that was the only way to get her attention. But surely you're not comparing that story to . . . us. You didn't call me Carrots because you were in love with me at ten."

"Oh God no," Oliver said, setting his mug beside the bottle on the boxes. "I hated you."

She smiled at the emphatic tone.

"But I think I'm in love with you now."

Naomi's smile dropped, even as her heart soared. "What?"

He took the mug from her hand, set that aside as well. "I'm going to need a little time to confirm for certain. Preferably naked time. But I'm pretty damn sure. Actually, no, scratch that. I'm sure. Seems I can't stop thinking about you. Even my dad can't stop talking about you, and *that's* something."

"Oliver—"

"Why'd you go to see him?" he asked, stepping closer.

Naomi swallowed. "I don't know. I just . . . well, I guess I missed him a little. I don't have family, and he needs someone, and I think I need someone, too."

"Any chance you need two people?" Oliver asked, his hand

slipping beneath her hair to cup her neck in that way she loved. "One as a difficult, trying father figure, the other as . . . a lover?"

"Don't say it if you don't mean it," she whispered, her hands coming up to grip the lapel of his suit. "I can't lose you twice."

"Oh, I mean it," he growled, brushing his lips against hers. "*Carrots.*"

Naomi smiled against his lips. "You really thinking about moving?"

"Eventually," he said, his hands coming up to her face to kiss her more deeply. "I need a fresh start."

"I've got a proposal that might sound a little crazy."

"I'm listening," Oliver said, still kissing her as he slowly backed her up, maneuvering around boxes, until her hips hit the kitchen counter.

"Keep your place," she said, her hands sliding up his chest, her arms going around his neck. "But spend some time here. A lot of time here. And maybe when you're ready to move, you'll want a roommate?"

"Would this roommate have red hair, blue eyes, and a bit of a temper? Maybe prone to holding a grudge?"

She smiled against his lips. "Perhaps."

"Did you just ask me to maybe, someday, move in with you?"

"I guess I did. Romantic, right?"

"You know what would be more romantic?" he asked, lifting her so she sat on the counter.

She tried to kiss him again, but he caught her chin between his thumb and forefinger. "If you told me how you felt about me."

"Ah," she said, lightly setting her hands on his shoulders and brushing her lips against his temple before moving her mouth near his ear and whispering, "I love you, Oliver."

His arms tightened around her, pulling her closer. "I love you, too, Naomi."

Later, much later, a naked, panting Oliver kissed the side of her head where it rested on his shoulder as they lay on her hardwood floor.

"Woman, we have *got* to stop wasting nice champagne."

"Who said anything about wasting," she said, wiggling away to retrieve their mugs. She handed one to him as he pulled himself to a sitting position against her counter.

Naomi sat in front of him, her back resting against his chest. "Warm champagne and boxes," she said, sipping her sparkling wine and tilting her head back to look at him. "Is it all you ever wanted?"

Oliver smiled down at her, running a finger over her cheek. "All I ever wanted and more."

*O*kay, so it's big enough for the two of you," Audrey said, gesturing with her cracker at Naomi's apartment. "But what happens when you have babies?"

Naomi choked on her wine. *"What?"*

"Easy," Oliver told Audrey, setting a hand on Naomi's back and giving it a slight pat. "I haven't even managed to coax her into a ring shop yet."

"Because it's too soon!" Naomi insisted. "A cautious woman does not get engaged to a man she's known for a year—and has been dating less than that. At least this one doesn't."

"No? What about a man she's known for twenty years?" He waggled his eyebrows.

"Doesn't count. Anything prepuberty is off-limits."

"I agree with Naomi," Clarke said as he refilled wineglasses. "All of the good stuff starts when hormones kick in."

"Don't your loins get tired?" Audrey asked.

Clarke shrugged. "Not really. Claire, love, more wine?"

"I shouldn't."

"You should," he said, topping off the wine. "We're celebrating these two smitten kids moving in together."

Naomi looked at Oliver and grinned. "Told you my plan would work."

"It was actually my plan, Carrots. And besides, we didn't technically move into your place. We moved into your building. But a bigger unit."

"I'm jealous," Claire said wistfully. "My place is so tired."

"Oh, but your plans for it are so perfect!" Audrey said. "How's the hunt for a contractor coming along?"

"Not," Claire said glumly, pulling a piece of salami off a platter and nibbling the edge. "Everyone's either out of my budget or has their own stupid ideas on how to modernize the place in a way I don't want. I want it classic, but better. How's that so hard to understand?"

"Actually," Oliver said thoughtfully, pointing his glass at her. "I may have someone. One of my contractor guys mostly does high-end commercial stuff, but he's been looking for a change. Something simple."

"I can't imagine a tired brownstone's what he had in mind."

Oliver shrugged. "I'll ask him."

"Clarke." Audrey was scolding. "You can't just turn on someone else's TV without asking."

"Oliver, can I watch the Yankees game without asking?"

"Ooh, *yes*," Claire said, going to the couch and plopping down.

Clarke began flipping through the channels when Audrey snatched the remote out of his hand. "You do remember why we're here, right?"

He gave a mock sigh and reached for some popcorn. "All right. Fine." He glanced back at Naomi. "For the record, this is the *only* thing I'd sacrifice the game for."

"We don't have to watch it," Naomi said, biting her lip and resting a hip on the arm of the couch. "The viewing party was Oliver's idea, but—"

Claire pulled her down on the couch. "Shut up. We're watching this."

Naomi groaned and squeezed her eyes shut. "I don't think I can. Do you know they started the show when I, well, TV me was a baby."

"I bet you were cute!" Audrey protested.

"I was *orange*."

Oliver leaned over the back of the couch and kissed her head. "No, Carrots. You were perfect."

Then he joined them on the couch, and together they waited for the premiere of *Max: The Naomi Powell Story*.

A story that Dylan Day had had no part in, thank you very much.

Once Dylan had made an inglorious departure from the project, the show wasn't nearly as excruciating as she'd been expecting. Sure, the network pushed for the juicy details, but her new producer respected her decision to leave her history with Oliver and the Cunninghams out of it. And actually, the show was good, she admitted, a little sheepishly. Really good. She was allowed to tell her story, show little girls that they could make it with hard work and determination. Tell them that she'd be there to help open doors for them.

Oliver found her hand and squeezed as Claire's arm linked with hers, and Naomi smiled.

Because no matter how good the show was?

Her real life was better.

Acknowledgments

Turning a story idea into a published book takes a village.

To my village, you know who you are. As always, I am so grateful.